THE CRUELEST TRUTH

L. RENÉE RICHARD

Cover Design by: Designs By Charly
https://www.designsbycharlyy.com/

Interior Formatting by: Designs By Charly
https://www.designsbycharlyy.com/

Editing Services: Havoc Archives
https://www.thehavocarchives.com/

ALSO BY L. RENEE RICHARD

STAND-ALONE
Waves of You

SERIES
Black Wave (Book 1)
Twisted Tides (Book 2)
The Complete Forged Heart Series

ANTHOLOGY
The Lovesick Anthology

NOVELLA
Heart-Shaped Box

DEAR READER,

Thank you so much for choosing to read this book. It might be my favorite one I've written so far because I love the characters, and I hope you enjoy getting to know them as much as I did writing them. Please note that this story contains sensitive themes that may be triggering for some readers. For a detailed content list, please visit my website at L. Renee Richard. If you decide to continue, I hope you enjoy what is truly the heart of the story—healing, love, and, above all, forgiveness.

L. Renee Richard

PLAYLIST

Morgan Wallen- Lose Somebody
Metallica- Master of Puppets
Bloody Valentine- Drive It All Over Me
Chappell Roan- Pink Pony Club
Kendrick Lamar- Not Like Us
Taylor Swift- Red
Killers- When We Were Young
Send Me On My Way- Rusted Roots
I Don't Want To Wait- David Guetta and One Republic
Oasis- Don't Look Back in Anger
Pink–Just Give Me a Reason
Keane- Somewhere Only We Go
Taylor Swift–Love Story

Listen on Spotify

https://open.spotify.com/playlist/06QL8BP1X3ddzQxnv7Z5J0

PROLOGUE

I sit outside the house, watching moments pass by in cinematic fashion through the curtains, just like I've always done. I feel like an outsider looking in because that's all I'll ever be. Now that college is over, they'll be thrilled to have their precious daughter back home, and it pisses me off more than I can fathom.

"What makes her so special?" I scoff. My father never cared to know me, and my mother, the homewrecker, bounced from man to man as long as someone was there to take care of her. But me? I never asked for any of this shit. I watched men come and go through her bedroom door while I sat alone, hungry—not for food, but for affection. I just wanted someone to love me.

I've never spoken about it, staying silent because I didn't want to upset anyone or hurt their feelings. But what about my feelings? Does anyone even care?

I feel like I'm already dead inside, and it's no wonder why I can't seem to love someone back. I mean, how can I when it's something I've never truly known? I pretended to give it once, but I can't even do that anymore. I'm drowning in my self-pity, fixated on the feeling of being discarded like the trash left on the curb, waiting for someone to pick me up.

That's when I formulated this plan and decided what I had to do. I all but hit rock bottom, and now, all I can do is come up from here. For me to be able to move on, I have to confront him once and for all. I was told that I needed closure, and for that, I need to understand what made me so unlovable. So, with a deep breath in and the positive affirmations my therapist tried to teach me many times over, I channel enough strength to do it.

"You are enough. You are worthy of love. You cannot change other people. You can only decide to change yourself. Confront your fears. Love yourself." I repeat these words while breathing deeply. I choose my own family, and for once, I am going to feel better—to *be* better—even though that, too, fell apart.

I open the car door and walk across the street. It's still daylight, but evening is fast approaching, and I know he's inside. His car is parked out front, but I intend not to let it go this time. I have to do this because it's been long enough.

I march up the steps, determined for him to hear me out. I ring the doorbell and wait, but no one answers. I look over once again at the car in the driveway and turn back to the door. I'd know his vehicle anywhere. I'm just about to ring the doorbell again when it opens, except it isn't him.

A woman stands in the open doorway and scrutinizes me before speaking. "Can I help you?" she asks, brows furrowed.

My mouth opens, but no words come out. I stand there shocked, unable to answer because I don't know what to say. I had this scenario play out in my head. The way that I would confront him about not answering my calls or refusing to see me when I showed up at his work. But she wasn't something that I had planned for. I try to recite my well-rehearsed speech, but again, nothing comes out. I must look insane, and a part of me almost believes that to be true. I'm like a baby bird—opening my mouth, waiting for a tidbit of nourishment that isn't coming as I struggle to find my words. She tilts her head to the side and stares at me intently. Her eyes widen, and that's when I know she pieces it all together. "No," she says, backing away. I move forward, but she puts her hand out to stop me. "It's you. You're the one who has been calling and stopping by his work." Her lip trembles, and she points her finger at me. "You've been following us, too!" She shouts a little too loudly for my liking, and I look around because I'm afraid that the neighbors are going to hear. I only came here to force him to see me, but I didn't want *this*. I guess I didn't think it through all the way. I mean, what are the chances? I'm freaking the fuck out on the inside. But this woman...she is freaking *all the way* the fuck out, and really loud, too.

"I'm sorry," I tell her, because I am. I fight the urge to curl into myself, like I have done after every encounter where he turned me away. I know it will hurt her, but I'm hurt, too, and none of this is my fault. It's all his fault. He's the liar.

She starts to cry. Her hand goes to her mouth, and when I think she isn't going to say anything else, she asks, "How old are you?" I tilt my head, wondering why it matters, because *he* doesn't care how old I am, but instead of putting further thought into it, I answer her.

"I'll be twenty-four soon." She shakes her head. Her sobs grow louder in intensity. I want to reach for her. To comfort her because I know how it feels, but there was also no one there to offer me any comfort. The only person who did gave up on me a long time ago, but not because it was entirely their fault. I pushed everyone away, including the only one who gave me a chance to prove myself time and time again. The pieces of my shattered heart are hanging on by a single thread.

She steps back, her beautiful manicured finger in the air, pointing at me like I'm a disease she doesn't want to catch.

"Leave my family alone!" she screams at me before shutting the door in my face. I lean into the door, my head making an audible *thunk* against it while my hands rest limp at my side. With my head resting against the ornate wooden door, I raise them to help my tired body push away from it, standing there in front of his house, defeated yet again.

A neighbor next door stares at me as she walks up her driveway across the street. My cheeks flush with embarrassment. I don't think she heard, but I can't be sure. I pull the hoodie over my head to hide the tears that fall again at yet another dismissal. As I turn around to walk away, I hear a loud crash coming from inside, causing me to promptly pick up my pace and jog back to the car in a hurry. I want to escape from whatever that noise is, the person responsible for it, and the screams accompanying it. "Oh, God," I cry. More pain that I caused in someone else's life.

"I'm sorry. I'm sorry. I'm so, so sorry." I gasp aloud as I open my car door and jump into the driver's seat. I fall into the seat, throwing my hands around my body in a hug while rocking myself back and forth. It's a losing battle as I attempt to calm the fleeting thoughts swirling around in my head. All the toxicity I tried to banish before I walked up those steps now comes crashing back to the forefront of my mind.

You are unlovable. No one wants you. Your father. Your mother. How can anyone love you? They all race through my mind, making me want to pull my hair out by the roots or vomit the contents of my stomach. God knows my already thin frame can't handle more loss of any kind.

I don't know what I was expecting, but it wasn't this. I try to stop it, still hearing the voice screaming at me as I hang my head in shame. I don't know how long I stay like that, but I hear a car door slam that wakes me from my depressive thoughts. When I look up through my tear-streaked eyes, I see them getting into the car together. Rage consumes me. I will not let this go. I deserve to know. To understand why.

I decide to follow them, only because I want to get the answers I came here for. I come up behind them at a stoplight and see her face in the rearview mirror staring at me. She hits her husband's shoulder, and he flinches like that small woman is inflicting pain. But I know he's just a coward. She continues yelling at her husband, and he then turns around to look my way. I reach out my hand to signal him to stop, letting him know that I just want to talk, but instead, he speeds up.

"What the fuck!" I blurt out. Unable to stop myself, I follow him a little more closely. Except this time, I'm pissed. I don't want to lose him or miss this chance because I might not get another one. Besides, I just want to clear the air so he can help me understand why.

"God, why won't he talk to me?" I throw my hands in the air, laughing hysterically. That's all I've ever wanted, for him to acknowledge me. My molar almost cracks at the grinding I'm doing, breathing loudly through my nostrils.

He runs a red light, forcing me to run the red light, too, so that I won't lose him. "This ends now." I smack my hand against the dash, emphasising each word. "No more hiding and being a dirty little secret!" I scream to no one.

It's affected me so much in my relationships, and I won't let him treat me this way any longer, so I continue my pursuit. He turns a corner, tires screeching, and I follow, hot on his tail. I see his wife looking back. Can she see the determination in my eyes? Her eyes widen in what I can only contemplate as fear. The car swerves a little. I honk at him, and he speeds up, so I do the same. Tit for tat. He takes another corner—

"No. No. No," I pant.

He loses control, and his car turns sideways. I watch it all in perfect clarity, unable to stop it.

I don't have time to react as I hit them at full force. The impact and the acceleration behind my car sends us into a guardrail. I hear the impact before I feel it—the crunch of metal, glass breaking. I feel fuzzy, and as I try to lift my head, my vision swims, fighting the urge to vomit. I sense a trickle of something hot traveling down my lip—metallic copper lands on my tongue. My face is hot from the airbags' impact as dust coats the car's interior, clouding my vision, and a hissing noise follows. Is it coming from the car, me, or both? I need to stay alert, but as I blink my eyes a few times, trying to keep them open, my head just feels so damn heavy.

"I'm so tired," I say, but there is no one there to hear me. There never is. So I give in and place my head on the little chalky pillow inflated in front of me. It feels warm, comforting me in what I can only imagine a warm embrace would be like. I hear shouting, and someone running over, crunching glass. "I think I am going to rest my eyes for a minute," I think aloud, talking to the hands that try to grab at me, pulling me away, as the darkness reaches out to welcome me home.

THE CRUELEST TRUTH

And then there's nothing.

CHAPTER
ONE

NADIA

I pick up the call right before it goes to voicemail. "I'm on my way," I shout into the phone. I wave goodbye, blowing air kisses to Eliza and Zachary as I grab my bag. "Just a second, Mom." I pull my phone away briefly from my ear. "Bye, my littles," I sing-song as I continue to wave my goodbyes to the most well behaved kids I have ever had the privilege of babysitting. Their mother, Molly, mouths a very grateful, *Thank you.*

I wink. "I'll see you next time." My voice rises as I wrestle the door closed behind me, not allowing any further chance for conversation. I can't. There's no time.

Molly barely arrived home from work in time for me to make it to my birthday dinner this evening with my parents. Twisting the knob once again to ensure it is locked behind me, I check my watch before hurriedly walking away from the apartment.

Now that I'm out of the chaos, I take a deep breath, replacing the phone against my ear. "Okay, Mom. Sorry. Are you there?" I listen on the other end of the line and hear what I think is a sniffle. *Wait, what?* My eyes widen, and my lips part as my mind catches up to this unfamiliar sound. "Mom? Are you...crying?" I stop mid-stride in the hallway, trying to determine whether or not she is, something I think I've seen her do maybe once, while I continue listening for the tiniest sounds to confirm it. When I don't hear anything on the line, I briefly move the phone away from my ear to check the screen, wondering if the call has accidentally dropped. I frown, seeing that the call is still connected.

I repeat myself, stopping when I hear a sign of life coming from her side. Then she finally answers. "N-no. I mean, I'm just sad that my daughter is entering a new phase of life. Twenty-one years young." She sniffles. "Where did the time go?"

Bullshit. That's my first response, but then I remember we don't lie to each other. It's my mom. We are always honest with each other. My shoulders sag in relief, and I feel the anxiety lifting. I have never known my mother to cry. She is more of a "if I am crying, you better run because I will take you out" kind of woman—her words, not mine, and I love her for it. She never cries tears out of sadness, or at least none I have ever witnessed, except when my grandmother passed away, following her husband into the grave a decade later.

She takes another breath, and this time, I can tell she is trying to hold back her sobs, and I am pretty sure that it is *not* because of my birthday. I've never seen her like this. Frankly, I am kind of scared. I have nothing to compare this to except a gut feeling telling me not to let this conversation go.

"Are you sure, Mom?" My heart begins racing, and my breathing feels shallow. "Please..." I plead, begging her to tell me, no matter how cruel this truth could be on my birthday. I need to know she is okay. I bite my lip, wondering what could have upset my mom so thoroughly that she is lying to me about her crying on the phone. We don't have secrets. We are not that type of family.

If my mom cannot be honest with me right now, then I am

concerned more for her mental health and her need to keep whatever is bothering her from me. My mind begins to run through scenarios. Maybe it is because it's my birthday, and she doesn't want to ruin it with terrible news. Perhaps she will tell me later. Or maybe she is waiting for the right time.

Rapid-fire questions shoot through my mind without any resolution. I force myself to continue the trek to the car. Mindlessly placing one foot in front of the other, the sounds echo in the dimly lit corridor. I reach the elevator button and press the down arrow, illuminating the circular button that will take me to the parking garage.

"Don't worry about me, honey." Her voice sounds strained. I can visualize her trying to smile through the tears. This has the absolute opposite effect. It makes me worry all the more. "I will see you at the restaurant." I hear her swallow. "I am just waiting on your fa-ther, and then we will leave shortly." I hear the mention of my father and her inflection of that one word, which takes up two syllables to force out in an interrupted breath, and real worry overtakes me.

Is it something with my dad? The elevator door dings, and I stand there immobile. Is he okay? "Mom," I say, but my voice is a little shaky this time, matching hers. The elevator doors close, but my feet are planted firmly on the floor, fixed on this pivotal moment and this call I silently pray not to end. Or at least not to end without me finding out what is wrong.

She ignores my pleas and continues. "Just give the hostess your name, and she will take you to our table." Her voice is firm and resolute. I hear her take another breath before she replies, "I love you, Nadia. Remember that." She promptly hangs up, not allowing any further questions, and I am left bewildered, wondering what the hell just happened. My mouth is dry. I lick my lips, pocketing my phone as I hit the button again. The elevator doors open, and this time, I step through.

My eyes shift back and forth with each scenario that comes to mind, like a slideshow, as I conjure up reasons for her behavior. A deep sense of foreboding settles deep in the pit of my stomach, and it drops along with the cab's descent toward the parking garage. My intuition tells me to call my mom back and demand that this dinner be called off, to find out what happened, and get to the bottom of this. However, my brain tells me that I'll see them in a few minutes, so waiting should be okay.

I hear my shoes tap on the concrete slab as I quickly approach the car, hitting the key fob. The chirping sound reverberates in the concrete garage as I open the car door and slump into the leather bucket seat. It feels cool against my leg, causing goose bumps along my flesh as a shiver sweeps through me. Or maybe the unsettling feeling in my heart makes me feel that something isn't quite right. Shaking it off, I hit the button to illuminate the seat warmer setting despite the warm weather outside. I start the car and place it in reverse, and as I exit the parking garage, my mind remains preoccupied with our recent conversation as I navigate through the streets on autopilot. Stopping at all the red traffic lights and keeping pace with the steady flow of traffic at this time of day, an ominous sense of trepidation fills me as I continue to ponder what could be happening.

It came across as so much more than what she led me to believe. Is it just my mom being sad about me getting older? Images fly through my head of coming home from college to visit. Since I've been in college, I've only seen her this sad, and that was when I left for college in my first year. She hugged me, telling me I'd understand when I become a mother and my own child leaves to know how hard it can be on a parent. My dad told me they were going to do more things together as a couple since Mom wasn't coping well with the empty nest situation, but she did seem happy when I saw them over winter break that year. Her mood had improved, and they both seemed happy. So no, that can't be the reason then.

Whatever it is, we will talk about it later. I calm my breathing and realize I'm just working myself up. I have to trust that my mom will let me know what happened when the time is right. I audibly sigh, releasing the negative energy and breathing in positive thoughts in an attempt to change the somber mood to a more favorable one in preparation for seeing my parents.

After finishing up another school year, I took a little trip with one of my best friends, Savannah, so I haven't had the chance to spend time with them yet. I only just dropped my stuff off at an empty house before going to one of my regular nanny jobs when I am home on breaks from school, but this will be the first time I have seen them since the holidays.

After tonight, we are off to spend the summer at our lake house. It has been in our family for years, passed on from my grandparents on my mother's side. I relax, thinking about all my beautiful memories with my parents, and I wish we could leave tomorrow instead of next week.

I look forward to spending time with them every year, and this is no exception.

As I pull into the restaurant, I know that this year will be more memorable than all the others because it will be one of the last times I can spend with my family and best friend before I graduate from college and join the workforce. But for now, I'm glad not to have to grow up just yet.

CHAPTER
TWO

NADIA

As I enter the packed restaurant, my mood officially turns one-eighty. I practically skip to the hostess station, stopping abruptly and placing my hands at the podium, where a young woman greets me with a genuine smile and kind eyes. "Hi. I am here for a reservation under the name Kennedy." I feel like I'm shouting at her because of all the noise.

She looks at her computer screen and then glances up—a mischievous twinkle lights up her eyes. "You don't say," she replies in a teasing voice. I would think she is about to prank me from the look on her face if I didn't know better. I tilt my head assessingly. Her smile widens; her poker face is shit. "Of course, Nadia. Please follow me, and I will take you to your table."

I follow her and wonder how she knows my first name. It's odd, but I shake it off, following her to the back of the restaurant, where the doors are closed. Maybe we went to high school together? I am about to ask when she raps her knuckles on the door, holding onto the sliding door handle.

"It's just right through here," she says, looking back at me. With a flourish of her hand, she encourages me to enter. I push forward, side-eyeing her. "After you, my dear."

I lift a singular eyebrow at her theatrics. She winks at me, but I don't have time to question her as she slides the rustic-looking barn door across the track. I attempt to step through but halt mid-stride. My hand goes to my heart in an attempt to stop its erratic beating as I am greeted with a loud echo of voices erupting in unison, causing me to stagger back in shock.

"Surprise!" I look up, glancing around at the familiar faces in the room. I'm taking in the scene before me when my best friend approaches me.

"Happy birthday, Nadia," she says as she envelops me in a hug. My smile couldn't be any more expansive, but it drops just a bit as I scan the room, searching for my parents and coming up empty.

"Savannah? Where are my parents?"

She seems confused, too, looking behind me. "They're not with you?" She turns her attention back to me. I hear others questioning the same thing when a sinking feeling lodges in my stomach.

"No." I shake my head. "Mom called, and she said they were running late, but shouldn't they have been here by now?" I gulp. "Right?"

Savannah shrugs. "I'm not sure," she offers. "Maybe your dad had to work late? That's common for him."

I nod. She isn't wrong. If my parents had any disagreements, it was because of his schedule. *"He's working late again,"* my mom would reply whenever I asked about him during our weekly calls. My head tilts from side to side, pondering her question. "Yeah. My mom did say that she was waiting for my dad." I bite my lower lip, trying not to jump to conclusions.

"See?" She sends a smack to my arm with the back of her hand. "That's probably it." Her smile widens as she laces her arm through mine, marching me into the familiar sea of faces.

"Maybe," I reply, not sounding as convincing as I'd like. My eyes shift around through the crowd of people, angling my head and glancing around again as if my parents are going to magically appear by my Aunt Nora. I'm taken into the crowd as everyone present walks up to me for welcome-home hugs and warm birthday wishes. I begin to lose track of time, but the door starts to slide open, and I stop talking, turning abruptly from a family friend, muttering my apologies, to walk over and finally greet my parents. But as the hostess steps through, two police officers are behind her instead.

She must see the confusion on my face, and I recognize the look on hers. I step away. "Nadia," she says, grabbing my arm and halting my retreat. I shake my head, my eyes widen in shock, and my skin feels clammy. "There are some officers here asking for you." I look from her to the officers. Her hand is constricting, and my forearm begins to feel numb. "Nadia," she repeats, more forcefully this time. The hostess shakes my arm, but I don't hear what she says. Her words are muffled, as if I am underwater, drowned with the imminent news.

Savannah walks over and places her arm around me. "Breathe, Nadia. Take a deep breath in." I do. "Now another. Good, slow your breathing." The spots begin to lessen before my eyes, and my vision clears a little more. "You got this." She looks away from me and back to the officers. "What is going on?" I continue taking deep breaths and clear the haze-like fog invading my senses. She looks behind her.

The officers walk over and stand there, watching me. "Are you Nadia Kennedy?" the tall, younger man questions. He watches me warily, and I nod once. I look briefly at the other middle-aged officer at his side before returning my focus to him. "I am," I say, struggling to get the words out. He looks over at his partner but doesn't look back at me, immediately setting off my nerves.

The older officer steps toward me, lowering his gaze. "I'm sorry to have to tell you this," but I cut him off.

"No," I say softly as Savannah squeezes me tightly.

But he continues to speak, needing to get the words out. "Your parents were involved in an accident on the way over here."

Savannah gasps, and I shake my head fervently, not wanting to hear what they have to say because I know it will forever change me. My hand goes to my mouth, stifling the cry that threatens to escape. "Are they—"

"They were pronounced dead at the scene." I can't breathe. "They didn't make it." This time, my knees buckle with the weight of his words, and I fall to the floor, cradling my face. A wail erupts from the depths of my soul, and a searing cry leaves my lips.

"No! No!" Guests start coming out of the reserved room, and other patrons dining at the restaurant turn to see what is happening. Savannah drops to the ground with me, holding me tightly as I break apart in front of everyone.

"Oh my God, Nadia." These are the last words I hear as I mentally and physically shut down. I don't know how I get home. I vaguely remember Savannah pushing two pills into my mouth as I chased them down with a glass of water. But that's it.

I wake up sometime in the middle of the night, groggy. I see a glass of water on the side of the nightstand as I swing my feet over the side and pick up the glass, draining the entire contents. My head feels heavy, as does my heart, but I stand up and walk out of the bedroom into the living room, where I find my best friend curled up on the couch.

She sits up immediately when I walk past her. "Nadia," she calls out, but I don't stop. I stride past her and open the door to my parents' room. "Nadia," she calls out again, her footsteps quick behind me. I take in the scene before me. The bed is made—

The scent of my mom's perfume suddenly hits me. The fragrance is overwhelming. My eyes water as I follow the strong floral tones toward the bathroom, where the elaborate vanity mirror once stood. The glass is shattered, and large shards surround the counter and floor. A perfume bottle is also broken on the floor, the presumed cause of the mirror's destruction. No doubt, it was catapulted into the reflection of my mother, who once stood here in this exact spot. Its potent scent hangs in the air like a perpetual, dismal cloud in the wake of all the destruction. The glass immobilizes me from taking another step. I look at the now-broken bottle my father bought her last year. My mother always wore this scent. It was my father's favorite; he bought it for her every year on Valentine's Day.

Savannah follows me around, looking at everything I already see, and I wonder if she sees it, too. The scene plays out before me: my parents fight, and my mom is upset with my dad before they leave. I stop to turn around to look at her. Her eyes are sweeping, taking in the devastation that surrounds us in equal measure. Her breathing is labored as she tries to regain control of her feelings.

"Leave it," she says through gritted teeth, steering me away from the shattered glass and out of the room. I hear the door click behind her. She clears her throat. "I'm going to stay and go with you tomorrow to the morgue, and then I will help you make the necessary arrangements for your parents, okay?" I look at her and nod. I can't speak. I think I'm in shock, but I don't know because I've never encountered something like this. I can only presume that's what this is. I don't know how I feel. I only sense a numbness, like I am floating and no longer part of my body. I wonder if this could be some sort of cruel joke, but I know it's not, and I can't help but wonder what happened.

As if reading my mind, Savannah blurts out, "We will get answers tomorrow." I nod and continue into the kitchen to grab another glass of water. She scrutinizes me as I wander back to my bedroom, but doesn't try to stop me this time. "Try to get some sleep. Please, Nadia." Her voice cracks when she voices my name. I fall onto my bed in a heap, but sleep never comes.

CHAPTER
THREE

NADIA

ONE WEEK LATER...

I open the car door and step out of the vehicle into the bright sunlight. Its penetrating rays directly contrast the grey cloud that emanates pervasively around me. A gentle caress strokes my cheek as the breeze blows my hair back in the open-air expanse of the small town's woodsy cemetery. I reach in to retrieve the flowers that I had placed on the passenger front seat, shutting the door and pocketing my keys. I open the little wrought iron gate, and the creaking sound is eerie in the way only a cemetery can bring about. I notice lambs beneath willow trees set into elongated and rounded panels on the gate. The scrollwork is accentuated with roses, and the willow trees are bent over as if they are mourning, too. The gravel crunches under my feet on the path to where my parents now reside. A necropolis of ornate headstones surrounds them now, and nothing more.

Before I step onto the grass, I glance at their burial plots—a stark contrast to the others surrounding their own without headstones. After only a week, the gravesite is plain, lacking the vast array of flowers placed on top after the dual caskets were lowered into the ground and the earth was replaced with discarded, fragmented soil. The wilted flowers were also undoubtedly removed by the facility's maintenance crew.

I walk up to the disrupted earth, noticing the soil settling and how the surface runs off around the site, presumably from the excess rain this week.

Why does it always seem to rain at or after funerals? Are they my parents' remorseful tears, plunging from the heavens as a sign of their sorrow for leaving me all alone on this earth? For dying so young, without a proper plan in place to counsel me on how to navigate this life? All that is left is a legal trust. Although I'm no longer a child, they were all I had in this world.

I have no one left—no grandparents, siblings, or even a boyfriend. The burden of their burial and estate falls on me and me alone. I guess I am better off than most. The house, the lake house, cars, and retirement accounts they never got the opportunity to use all passed to me.

"I'd give it all up in a heartbeat just to have them back with me again. I don't have that opportunity though, do I?" I say, verbalizing every thought, hanging my head as I stand before their graves. The mound of solid earth that hides their new resting spot for all eternity. "I don't know what I'm supposed to do without you guys." A sob erupts from my mouth as I fall onto the grass. I roll into a ball, grabbing my knees.

No one can hear me, and I don't have anyone left who cares about me. Maybe Savannah and some of my parents' friends. But family? No. My dad was estranged from his, and my mom was an only child like me. I roll onto my back, my vision blurry from the tears that pool in my eyes. The clouds pass by in the clear blue skies above, and on any other day, I would enjoy the perfect weather, but not today. A storm rages in my heart, threatening to burst with anger and sadness. Most of all, those feelings combat each other because I know I never got to say goodbye. I never got to hear my mom's voice one last time, and for her to tell me what caused her such sadness during our previous conversation. I thought I could just ask her the next time I saw her. But that chance never came, and now everything remains a mystery. The broken mirror and perfume bottle, her signature scent, are forever tainted by the destruction I walked into in their shared bathroom. I'll never know the absolute truth.

I stand, pick up the fresh flowers I brought to their grave site, and place them on the mound near the top. When asked what I wanted to have etched onto their headstone, words escaped me. A forever reminder of the day they left the world and, most importantly, when they left me. They left me utterly alone. When the ground settles, I will return and have a proper headstone placed as a memorial of their life. Until then, I'll continue with my summer plans, minus my parents, and go to the lake house one last time this summer.

I'm walking back to my car when I hear my phone ringing. Opening the door quickly, I reach over to the front passenger seat. "Shit," I mutter as I reach into my tote and pull out my phone from the side pocket in a hurry before they hang up, and almost drop it in the process. "Hello?" I say as I start the car engine, and the phone automatically switches to Bluetooth as I place it down.

"Hello, Ms. Kennedy?" I glance down at the wireless charger that cradles my phone. Hm. It's the police department. I sit there and place the car back in park.

"Yes. This is Nadia Kennedy speaking." I reply hesitantly while waiting for the person on the other end to speak. Silently pleading up at the sky above not to receive any more earth-shattering news, I also remain hopeful about receiving some closure. Maybe they will have something else to report as to what caused my parents' deaths and about the person involved in causing the accident.

"This is Officer Stanley." Without pause, he gets straight to the point. "Do you think you can come down to the station?" His deep, baritone voice lacks any emotion. "I have some information that

I'd like to share with you." I gulp the bile down, which threatens to erupt from my churning stomach. "Ms. Kennedy?" he asks, and I nod even though I know he can't see me.

"Yes," I manage to say, clearing my throat and looking in the direction I just walked from mere moments ago. "Yes, I can come now."

"Great," he replies. "See you soon." Disconnecting from the call, I continue to look over at my parents' grave, hoping that this will provide some insight into what happened, who was responsible for their untimely death, and my undoing. Without thinking, I dial the only person I have left who loves me—her name, my SOS.

By the time I arrive at the police station, I am a nervous ball of energy. I called Savannah, and without hesitation, she promised to meet me here to provide some level of emotional stability that I currently lack. I walk through the police station door, and Savannah is already there waiting for me. When she sees me approach, she stops biting her nails and rushes over to wrap me up in a tight embrace.

"You beat me here," I say rhetorically, but the meaning is clear, and I feel relief. She's silent, but her presence is more than words could ever convey. She nods, letting me go, pivoting over to walk toward the desk, where a female officer sits with her eyes locked on the computer screen in front of her.

Savannah stares at me. "Of course!" she exclaims, throwing her hands up. Like she can't believe I said that. "I will always come when you need me. That's a promise, Nadia." I want to tell her that she shouldn't make promises she can't keep, much like my parents, who have said similar phrases to me over the years. But because they didn't keep theirs either, I hope that today I can gain some insight into why that was the case. Regardless of my roller coaster of emotions, I keep myself in check.

So instead, I smile at my best friend, taking her hand in mine and squeezing it reassuringly. I drop it when we are standing before the counter, and the officer ignores us.

"Can I help you?" she eventually asks without looking up.

"Yes. I'm here to see Officer Stanley. He called and wanted me to come down to the station." Without further question, she picks up the phone.

"Mitch," she says informally, "I have a woman here who says you called her about wanting her to come to the station." She removes the phone from her ear, places her hand over the receiver, finally looks my way, and spares a glance at Savannah. "What's your name, Miss?" she asks as her fingers fly over the keyboard. The noise grates on my every nerve, and I want to scream at her to fucking stop.

"Nadia Kennedy." I watch her return the phone to her ear and relay my name to Officer Stanley. Whatever she hears on the other line causes her to stop typing. Her eyes shoot back to mine, and I wonder what he told her.

"I'll send her in," she says and hangs up, hitting a button under the desk. I hear a loud click as she motions at us to proceed with her hand. "Go through that door, and he will meet you as you walk down the hall."

I nod. "Thank you." She smiles at me, sympathy shining in her eyes. I don't smile back. I don't need her second thoughts about compassion. Savannah takes my hand, and we walk through the door. It abruptly shuts, locking us in on the other side with finality.

Just as she said, Officer Stanley is heard before I see him. His shoes make a percussive, *thunk* sound on the polished tile floor. "Thank you for coming so quickly, Ms. Kennedy." He looks over to Savannah, and I begin the introduction I know he is waiting for.

"This is my best friend, Savannah. She is here to support me and is coming in with me." He lifts a brow quizzically. I understand the implication of what he silently asks. "I'm okay with her hearing whatever you tell me."

He nods once. "Okay. Then follow me, ladies." We turn the

corner of the monochromatic landscape of the police station, enveloped in varying tones of grey. He holds a door open for us and motions toward a sitting area with a small couch directly opposite his desk, along with a couple of upholstered, straight-backed chairs. All that is lacking is just a tray of Prozac pills to help aid in the depression that this place evokes. We take our seats, and rather than proceeding to his desk to sit, he plucks a folder from the desktop and drops himself down onto one of the armchairs next to us. His position on the seat comes across as intimate. My spine stiffens at his actions. His body mechanics quickly place me at unease, and I know that whatever he tells me will be bad.

I gulp loudly, and Savannah reaches for my hand, clutching it in support. Officer Stanley clears his throat. "We did some investigating after you told us something had upset your mom." He pauses, opens the chart, and slides his hand inside, holding its place but not yet disclosing what is inside the dossier. "We did find out something that could have been the reason as to why your parents were fighting." He withdraws a single sheet of paper and places it before me. "Your father was having an affair."

I gasp, my hand flying to my mouth. I shake my head. "No, that's not possible. My parents loved each other. He would never do that."

Savannah bristles beside me. "So much for subtlety," she mumbles angrily under her breath.

Officer Stanley pretends not to hear her and continues his verbal diarrhea without acknowledging my outburst. "Your mom had gone to his office, and the staff heard her threatening to file for divorce and calling him names regarding his bouts of infidelity." After hearing such shocking news, I bite my bottom lip to stifle any sound that threatens to erupt from all my emotions. A metallic taste coats my mouth as I release it, welcoming the pain that reminds me how fluid this life is.

I don't see how this can get any worse, but I know I will be proven wrong before he opens his mouth. The look on his face tells me everything. He points to the picture he placed on the table of a girl around my age, maybe slightly older. Her features look familiar, but I can't place them. I stare a bit closer, looking over her face once again. Then I see it, and Savannah must jump to the same conclusion as me, gasping. The full lips and the dimpled chin are uniquely similar to my father's. Those facial features that are unquestionably my father's genes. Officer Stanley sees the recognition on my face as he continues explaining his discoveries.

"She tried to contact your father—her biological father—but found your mother at the house instead. She didn't have to tell your mom anything for her to know the truth. It's as plain as day on her face—your father's face." And just like that, a cacophony of chaos erupts inside me, and emptiness replaces any love I had in my heart. The betrayal is too great.

CHAPTER
FOUR

NADIA

"We tried for years to have a child. I found myself so depressed, Nadia. Year after year of not being able to conceive, and then I felt your father pull away. It's like my world was falling apart. I can't say that I blamed him for staying away. I was miserable, and he didn't know what to do to help me. Hell, I didn't know how to help myself. I noticed your father took on longer hours at the office. I pulled away both physically and emotionally. You know, I thought I had a stomach bug." Her fingers reached up to ghost over her lips. A smile forms around the outline of her hand. "And when I found out I was pregnant..." She trails off, her smile widening with joy. "I called you my miracle baby." She giggles. "Your dad and I became closer than ever after that. Because you fixed us. You are our whole world, Nadia." She places her pearl necklace around my neck. The one that belonged to *her mother once, when she was sixteen. "Now it's yours. Happy birthday, my love."*

I blink, and the memory is gone. This news shakes me to my core and rocks my world so off its axis that I don't know what to believe anymore. How could two people who were so in love and shared that same love with me cause each other so much pain? How could my dad do this to my mom as she was drowning in her sadness? Maybe he felt so helpless that he found solace in another woman. Although my mom isn't totally innocent of this, anything she could have done was negated by my father's indiscretions, which are unforgivable to me. No condom? The worst. How could he do this to Mom? To us?

I can't hear anything else Officer Stanley has to say. I stand up. "Enough." I hold my hand up, halting him from telling me anything else. "I don't want to know anything else," I tell him. Pleading. My voice breaks as I say, "My parents are dead, and there isn't anything I can do to bring them back. There's no point in knowing because the outcome won't change."

He nods. "Don't you at least want to know her name?" I tilt my head, pondering this question. Things might have been different if she hadn't told my parents this information on my birthday. We might have already been at the lake house, enjoying our summer. If she hadn't tried to pursue my parents in a car chase, they might still be alive. My anger morphs into something viable. "It's also important for you to know that—"

My humor is caustic as I laugh, cutting him off and causing Savannah to look at me like I'm a stranger. I barely recognize the voice that leaves my lips. "It's bad enough that I know her face," I spit out. "It's something that will haunt my dreams, knowing that my dad had no respect for my mom and that he had her, and then she killed them." My words are vitriol. "I don't want to know her." Hanging my head as the rage tries to consume me, I feel Savannah grab onto my arm. "I wish it was her who died instead." I don't contemplate my following words, but I'm a runaway train on a collision course set on causing the most destruction. I can't stop myself. "So, no. I really don't." My tone is seething. Anger rushes in, and my teeth grind hard enough that I may have cracked a molar. I lift my head, making eye contact as I stand from the chair, Savannah rising with me. "I hope she rots in that jail cell." My strides are in quick succession, taking me to the door as my last parting words ring out. "She deserves to be all alone, and I hope she suffers the same pain that she causes me every day."

My rapid heartbeat thumps in my head. The swooshing sound in my ears is all I can hear. The artificial light of the police station is a live, breathing force around me, enveloping me in a constricting embrace. A tightness forms around my wrist, which is the only thing holding me to this spot, grounding me from getting lost in the anger I feel. Savannah ushers me out of the police station, never letting go of my wrist until we get outside. Once we get to the parking lot, she places her arm around my waist, guides me to her car, and places me in the passenger seat. As she drives me home, I keep replaying the words over and over in my mind.

Your dad had an affair. That's why your mom was so upset. Your parents argued. The young woman, his other biological daughter and product of his infidelity, tried to speed up and drive after your father. Your mother was crying, and your father was frantic, trying to outrun his past indiscretions as he was already late to your surprise birthday dinner. He had been drinking. When he took a corner too fast, her car came crashing into your parents' car, causing them to lose control and veer off the side of the hill. Their car tumbled over and over, finally landing on its hood. The young woman was alive after her car was found wrapped around a guardrail, but your parents were dead.

I need to get out of here. I need to escape to the only place that has ever brought me peace—the lake house.

I'm packing up the car Savannah had dropped off at the house sometime during the day. We rushed out and left my car at the police station. I should've waited until morning to do this, but I can't spend another day in this house, knowing my parents will never stroll through our front door again. So I choose the most logical option. Run.

We were supposed to be together at the lake house this week, and I still intend to go. I *have* to go. I have an indescribable, nagging feeling that tells me I should be there. The truth is, I don't know who I am anymore. Staying here isn't helping, so I will go to the lake and spend this summer mending the pieces of my shattered heart. I know Savannah will be pissed that I am leaving without telling her, but she's my best friend. She'll forgive me, and most importantly, she'll understand why I left. She'll know where I am.

"See, it's not a problem that I leave now," I say, trying to convince myself as I stand in the foyer, looking at the back of the house where the kitchen is. I envision my mom cooking dinner and remember when my dad would sit at the granite island with a glass of whiskey. My mom drinks her wine as they laugh with each other, talking about the day's events while she makes our dinner. It was a frequent scene in our home, but no longer.

I blink, and the vision is gone. There is no laughter and no more smiles. It's just an empty house that holds too many painful memories. Everything seems tainted, and the house that was a home is now dormant. Their lies are splattered along the walls, festering among the wallpaper in the hallway where our family pictures depict a different portrait of the past.

With a sad smile, I turn the light off and lock the door behind me, punching the alarm code onto the illuminated keypad. I hear it arm itself as I walk away toward my car and leave those memories behind.

I drive out of the circular driveway, glancing back in the rearview mirror, expecting to see my mom waving, and I instinctively wave back, bidding her farewell. As I pull onto the two-lane county road, I immediately feel some of the tension release from my shoulders, making my way to the place where I have always felt the most at peace. A place of solitude that contains so many wonderful memories. No broken glass and smashed perfume bottles defiling the house.

This will be a chance for healing and for me to move past all the lies that have been concealed. I know my parents loved me. I believe that wholeheartedly, but my father's betrayal cut deep. What he did to my mother was just so wrong, but I also don't know what occurred in their marriage. I always thought they were happy, but I'll never truly know. The young woman mimicking my dad's features looked similar in age to me, but her haunted-looking eyes held years far beyond her presumed age.

I'll never know if we would have moved past this as a family. What I do know is that I will try to hold onto the happy memories and keep them safe for eternity, because life is fleeting and can be taken away at a moment's notice.

Nightfall approaches as the setting sun dips through the hills and vast greenery before me. The sky is streaked with hues of yellow, orange, and red, earthy tones that saturate the rosy landscape. I continue to drive until the roads become windier and the tree growth thickens. New Hampshire is beautiful in the winter, but it is devastatingly beautiful during the summer and fall. Summer is the best time of the year, because after the winter snow cleans the earth, the blooms ignite the terrain in luscious colors. Forsythia and burning bushes line granite stone walls along the route there, reminiscent of a time when the bush wasn't considered invasive. Sometimes, the prettiest ones are the most dangerous.

I slow down before reaching the road sign that indicates a sharp corner ahead. I could navigate these roads in any condition, driving with the familiarity of two decades of repetitive travel behind my belt. The scenic landscape boasts lush foliage amidst moss-covered stone boundary rock walls, marking property lines along the rural stretch of pavement.

I let down the window, allowing the cool air from the nearby lake to permeate the car's interior. My hair blows around, tickling my cheek. The gentle tug of the strands causes a feeling that prickles at my scalp like a lover's caress. I revel in this feeling, never wanting it to end. It's a momentary reprieve from the shit storm that is my life.

I put both windows down all the way, greedy for more of these sensations as I turn up the radio volume. Morgan Wallen's "Love

Somebody" plays on my music app as I sing along to the lyrics. I tap my hand on the steering wheel, feeling empty like the song describes, wishing I had some whiskey. I stick my hand out the window, letting the wind hit it, embracing the feeling of life smashing against my palm.

I breathe in the distinguishable resinous smells of assorted woodsy pine trees, which are crisp, unlike the city's. I inhale deeply, looking around at the sights as if seeing them for the first time. Maybe I am seeing the world through different glasses—ones not so rose-tinted but with a deeper appreciation for the things I once took for granted. I always drove this path with my parents, and I don't think I ever took the time to appreciate how beautiful this area is. And the smells—like earth and wet leaves. In the near distance, someone is having a campfire. I imagine a family gathered around a fire pit, holding sticks with marshmallows ready to make s'mores, which evokes a sense of nostalgia in me.

The humid summer heat coats the forest in mossy, polished textures, and the asphalt faintly shimmers in the fading light. The distant chirping sounds of insects in the forest are carried through the air, along with the gentle rustling of leaves in the light breeze. As I make the final turn across large boulders alongside the road, and the incline increases slightly, I navigate between the old granite posts. The crunch of the grated dirt road against my tires reminds me to decrease my speed to twenty-five mph. I pass the sign of the town lake association as I turn left onto the final dirt road leading to our home.

I can make out the lights of similar residences covered by the thick, plush foliage of the summer evergreens, sugar maples, and birch trees, which provide a natural privacy screen among the other lodgings on this lake. I carefully handle the slight decline as I pull up in front of our family lake house. I raise the windows and immediately feel suffocated, so I shut the car engine off and jump out quickly.

Standing in the driveway, I stretch my legs, lifting my hands above my head and rotating my torso back and forth. The evening air is cooler here by the lake, and the sound of nature around me makes me eager to get inside. I quickly pop the trunk to gather my bags. Memories of bears and ransacked bird feeders come to mind, as well as remembering being spooked when I saw red eyes staring out at me while I was on the porch reading in the hammock one night. The sound of what I thought was a child crying, only to find out later that it was a fox.

The automatic light flickers as I approach the covered entry, and I drop my luggage on the porch. I fumble for a minute with the lock as I finally open the front door and set everything down in the foyer. I don't bother turning on any lights as I leave the bags and walk toward my childhood bedroom. I can't see the lake now in the darkness, but I know it's there. It is a comfort as I fall onto my bed, managing to kick off my shoes in one slick movement. I shuck off my remaining clothing until I am clad in nothing but my undergarments. I do not bother getting under the covers. Instead, I bring them around me like a warm embrace, curling into myself. I veer around onto my side, nuzzling my oversized Squishmallow. This time, sleep comes readily as I fall into a dreamless slumber.

CHAPTER
FIVE

MANNY

"**M**ijita, can you please pass the bag over to me?" My little girl looks aimlessly at the bags before following my finger, pointing straight to the half-full planting soil.

Donned in her pink gardening gloves, she bites the side of her bottom lip in concentration. "I got you, Papá." She gives me a very hot-pink thumbs up.

My lip twitches as I watch her, my little princess, bring the bag over and dramatically drop it like its weight is crushing before depositing it at my feet. She wipes her brow with dirty gloves, leaving a streak of soil across her forehead. I already know where this is going.

"Papá, we've been working out here all morning, and I think

we need to reward ourselves with some pancakes." She crosses her arms together, ready to validate her reasoning. I firmly bring the remaining topsoil around the purple impatiens she picked out at Piney Woods Florals. Pressing it against the pretty purple bunch of annuals, I give her my best side eye, and she beams at me. Fucking beams. I swear this little girl has me wrapped around her finger. She knows it, no matter how gruff I am. She sees through my scarred and rugged heart that, at the moment, only belongs to her. I have no room for any more heartache in my busy life, especially now that I have full custody of Catalina. I've had enough lies and betrayals to last a lifetime.

I kneel with my hands on my thighs, resting there. Perspiration drips down the side of my face. Damn, it's already humid this morning. I point at her with my gloved finger. "I'll make you a deal." She pops her hip out, her hand resting on it, and I fight the urge to roll my eyes again. "You help me finish this up quickly," she assesses the remaining job, "and we can get some pancakes for breakfast."

She quickly notices what I do. There isn't much left. I would take her regardless, but she doesn't need to know that. I can put the mulch on myself. Spreading it around is easy, as it is just around the trees and this bush, where I am sprinkling in bits of color she chose for the yard.

"You got yourself a deal." She extends her little pink glove toward me, and I can't resist. When she reaches out, I grab her, pulling her toward me and, in the process, knocking her off-balance and catching her in a big embrace. I start to tickle her, and her laughter echoes and melts a little of my frozen heart. In my periphery, I see two women walking around the block, and one places her hand to her heart as the other woman waves at me.

"Hey, Manny, let us know if you need help with anything!"

The other woman chimes in on the conversation. "Yeah, any day or any night, Manny." The first woman hits her on the arm, and they both giggle as they power walk a little faster. They must see my face harden with disgust. They have no shame doing that around my little girl, and if they didn't get the picture before, then maybe the look I send their way will convey it.

They walk around this corner on the weekends and obviously are not here for the exercise. They are thoroughly done up with makeup to walk the block. I can't help but cringe at the thought of welcoming one of them into my home. No woman is allowed here except for my daughter, mother, and the one responsible for my sour expressions most days when I'm not feeling sorry for myself. The only woman I was devoted to, and look where that got me. If she wasn't allowed supervised visitation rights, then maybe not even her.

I try not to talk about it, despite my mom trying to get me into counseling because my marriage failed, making me, in turn, feel like a failure. I've learned that sometimes you can't fix what's broken, and I am utterly in a thousand pieces of brokenness. If it wasn't for my daughter, I wouldn't ever say her name. She has a fuck ton of baggage, and I was her devoted bellhop. I hate that it came to this, but she needs help, and I hope for her sake and our daughters that she gets her shit together.

I'm just about to grab my car keys when the phone rings. *Jefa.* The name flashes across the screen. I laugh at this because it is a nickname my father gave her long ago. It means "boss lady" in Spanish, and that's what she is. The boss. It's been a running joke in our home for as long as I can remember. I raise the phone to Catalina just as she is about to grab the doorknob.

"¡Espérate, mijita!" I lift my finger, indicating it should only take a minute, but she knows her grandma.

She sees it and groans, "It's never a minute, Papá." She harrumphs, plopping herself onto the couch as I hit answer on the phone.

"Bueno, Mamá." I don't have to wait long before she begins her onslaught of questions.

"Manny, have you made a posting yet?" That is the most important one, and I know I need to, but the thought of having someone else—a stranger—watch my daughter is too much to bear. "Honey, you know you need help." I nod even though she can't see me. I bring my hand to the bridge of my nose, drop it, and look up at the ceiling. I glance at my daughter, who is intently watching me. I am sure she can hear the conversation; her nose scrunched up. I don't want this conversation with her now, especially if it is within Catalina's hearing range.

"Mom, I promise to get a post at the rec center this week." She begins speaking to me in rapid-fire Spanish, and I can tell she is trying to stress the importance of my recent move. I moved here because my job has more work in this area, and I wanted a fresh start for my daughter. I tried to remove her from the toxic atmosphere her mother provided, where our families reside in the Merrimack Valley in Massachusetts. My dad has had a business there for years, but this area in the New Hampshire lakes region has experienced significant development since the pandemic, and most of my clients and work are now located in this region. It seemed like a logical choice to move her, but I don't have the support from my parents that I did back home. I only need childcare for the summer months. Catalina will be in school and the after-school program until I get out of work. Next summer, she will be old enough for the recreational program that the town's Parks and Recreation Department sponsors for school-aged children up to sixth grade. I'm golden if I can just get through these two months.

I hate to interrupt my mom, but Catalina glares at me, and my stomach grumbles so loudly that it could have been interpreted as an earthquake. A giggle erupts from the couch, and I spare a glance at her. She is covering her mouth to fight off the onslaught of laughter that is undoubtedly at my expense.

I mouth an "*I know*" to my daughter and continue with the necessary interruption. "Hey, Mom, I will have to call you back when I get home." I don't give pause because that will allow her a moment to interrupt and continue, and I'll be here for another fifteen minutes. It's not that I don't want to talk to my mom, but I need to have this conversation away from prying ears. My little girl is wise beyond her years, and I hate that her mother is responsible for that, and not in a good way. "We were just about to head out for some pancakes," I add quickly. "I just put my keys in my hand, and your granddaughter is famished." That is the only thing to break the conversation. Hearing her granddaughter is hungry gets my mom going.

"Oh, my sweet baby. Please take her to get something to eat,

Manny. I hate seeing her hungry."

Having heard that, Catalina jumps off the couch eagerly, shouting, "Bye, Grandma!" as she throws open the door, runs to the truck, and climbs in.

"Okay, Mom. Gotta go. She's already in the truck. Yes, I will post that. You're still coming to help me this week, right?" After I get the answer I need and before she can go into something else I don't want to discuss, I politely say goodbye, hang up, and close the door behind me, meeting Catalina in the truck. I hit the button to start the truck's ignition. My Bluetooth connects, and I hit play. "Master of Puppets" by Metallica plays, and Catalina starts headbanging. I look over at her briefly before checking both ways at the intersection, and she is in full-on heavy metal mode. I suppress the laugh at the dichotomy of her with her glittery outfit, which she picked out after cleaning up from planting flowers this morning, with the headbanging motions in beat and the music blaring through my truck's speakers. I love it and can't help but smile against my better judgment. She is the only thing that can break me from my resting dick face.

I ease into the tight parallel parking on the street across from Planet Pancakes, which has become our new favorite diner—the whole area has a small-town vibe that is very welcoming. Many are seasonal workers in the lake area, but the majority are locals who have lived in the town for decades or have had family homes in the area for generations. I chose a home in a neighborhood close to town, rather than a more rural area. I thought it would be a nice place for Catalina to ride her bike or go to the park. We are close to many amenities in town, and it was essential for Catalina to be close to school, where the bus picks her up right in front of the house. It is also within walking distance, which may be helpful if she continues to participate in sports and needs to get home. I did a lot of research when I bought the charming little three-bedroom cape on the corner.

As Catalina closes the door, I am already there to help her, and we walk hand in hand to the diner. I glance at her, and she tells me how happy she is. I know I made the right choice in moving her here. Catalina opens the door, and I grab the top of it to hold it open as we walk inside. It is packed, and there are a couple of booths by the window available.

"Hey there, how are you guys doing?" I hear the gravelly voice over the indie rock music playing in the background. This place is eclectic at its finest. From the trippy decor to the wild color scheme, I fell in love with it and the owner, who is quickly becoming a friend. Catalina throws her body into Odette, hugging the lithe-framed woman in an embrace. What can I say? My girl is a hugger.

"Odette!" she exclaims while Odette laughs gruffly, pulling my daughter in for a matching hug. Catalina lets go, looking up at the tall woman who almost rivals my height. "I was telling Papá for hours to bring me in for some pancakes, but he took for-evah," she says dramatically in her New England accent. Odette looks at me, patting her drama down on the back.

"Well, luckily, he brought you just in time because now you don't have to wait," she says, pointing at the booths I was looking at as we walked in.

"Business is good." I jut my chin outward.

Odette nods. "Baby, it's always busy in the summertime. The locals frequent this place, but the seasonal renters or lake house owners are all here every day in the summer, but you won't see me complaining." She waggles her finger at me. I see people watching our exchange and fighting to return the glances my way. I've heard the talk about the hot, divorced, single dad who moved into town, and I'm over it. I won't have them talking about me badly and my daughter hearing it, so I don't engage or date them.

Odette, a very perceptive woman, turns and grabs my daughter's hand. "Okay, baby, let me show you guys to your seat."

CHAPTER
SIX

NADIA

I bolt upright in bed to the sound of my phone ringing. "Who? What?" I scan the room, momentarily forgetting where I am. Then I plop back down, grabbing a nearby pillow that I hold over my face, shielding it from the glaring light that threatens to pierce my retinas from my sudden intrusion of wakefulness.

The ringing stops. "Thank God." I breathe a sigh of relief, my words smothered as I turn around. Just as I sink back into my pillow, the phone begins ringing again. "Good Lord, why? Why this early?" I look over at my alarm clock to check the time. Yep, it's still early morning. Disoriented, I rise from my bed and walk toward the source of this morning's auditory assault, rubbing my temples and cursing at the crick in my neck from falling asleep at that weird angle. I attempt to massage the pain that is shooting down into my shoulder, but I know I can't avoid this call. I also know who is calling without looking at the screen. Taking a moment to appreciate the picturesque lake view from my bedroom window, I answer, shouting, "Sorry!" before she can say anything. "I'm so sorry, Savannah."

I don't have to wait long for the verbal tongue-lashing that ensues. I place the call on speaker, heading to the bathroom. "Have—worried—I was?" The call cuts in and out, so I only hear half of her sentence as the call switches over, but her tone is clear.

"Sorry. What?" I cringe at having her repeat herself.

She emphasizes each word, making the single sentence sprawl out over several seconds. "Do you have any idea how worried I was?" Savannah's voice explodes through the speaker, this time loud and clear.

I chew on my lip and tilt my head back and forth before sighing. "I have an idea," but it sounds more like a question. As I use the toilet, I put the phone on mute, relieving my full bladder.

"Hello? Are you there?" I hear her snort into the phone. "Did you mute me?"

Flushing the toilet and washing my hands, I unmute. "I'm here. And yes, I was peeing." I grab a new toothbrush from the middle drawer, rip the package open, and apply some toothpaste to the stiff bristles.

"Fine, I guess that's allowed." She pauses, her voice softening. "How are you?" she asks, this time with concern etching her words.

I pull my hair around, one hand sweeping it over my shoulder as I spit into the sink. "Honestly..." I stop, thinking of what to say, taking a sip of water to rinse my mouth and spitting the remnants of mint paste into the sink. "I don't know." I sigh. "I'm going to figure it out, though."

"Right." She stops like she wants to say more, but thinks better of it. "I know you will. I'll be up to see you in a couple of weeks." She sounds hopeful.

I nod even though she can't see me. I stare at my reflection in the mirror. "Okay."

"We can go out, like old times, maybe?" She hesitates. "That is, if you want to."

I force a smile in the mirror. "I'd like that." The lie flows from my lips.

"Yeah?" she asks. Skeptical of the way I agreed so readily.

"Yeah," I reassure her. "Maybe that's exactly what I need. To forget and live a little."

"Definitely," she counters with more confidence. The relief from her on the other end of the line is palpable.

"Great. So what are your plans now?" Savannah asks. I look around my room. "Are you going to just hang out?" I could, but the thought has me breaking into a cold sweat. I start the shower. The steam billows around as I grab a towel from the linen closet.

"I think I'm going to keep busy, you know? Maybe get a job?" I bite my nails, waiting for her response.

"I think that's a good plan." I hear her remove the phone from her ear to address someone. She returns to the phone, and I hear more voices in the background. "Hey, I'll see you soon, lady. Call if you need anything at all," she insists before disconnecting the call.

I step into the shower and let the spray hit my face as steam envelops me. I pump shampoo into my hands and lather it through my hair, massaging my scalp and rinsing it through to the ends as the foamy suds slide down my shoulders and hit the floor in audible clumps around my feet. I rinse it and repeat the same motions with my conditioner and body wash, letting the familiar motions settle my nerves. When I'm done, I shut off the water and towel off, hanging it on my hook behind the door. The soft feel of the rug on my feet wraps them in a sensation of warmth as I look through my closet for something to wear, but then I remember I left my bags by the door. Frowning, I pivot to the dresser instead, opening the drawer to find a thong and a bralette. Nestled beside them is the lavender sachet my mom tucked in there. I inhale the fresh scent wafting upward, and it makes me smile at the memory.

After I blow-dry my hair, I stroll out to the foyer where I left my bags last night, bringing them into my bedroom. I rifle through one bag and find a skirt and crop tee. "That will do indeed," I say. "Great, now I'm talking to myself." *If I don't answer myself back, then it's okay* is the rationale I use as I grab my hair, pull it back into a messy bun, and sit on the edge of my bed to lace my white leather sneakers.

I stare at the scattered items on my bed and floor. I planned on putting my things away. Really, I did. But now, I have a particular craving for Planet's pancakes. I haven't had an appetite in the past weeks, but I find myself salivating at the thought of these tasty concoctions, which makes me antsy to get there.

I park the car along the front of Main Street and lock the door behind me, although I don't need to do that here. It's a place where everyone knows each other. During the summer, tourists flock to the area, making it a bit more crowded, but the honest, good people here wouldn't bother with a few coins in the cup holder. The door chimes as I walk through, and the song "Drive It All Over Me" by My Bloody Valentine plays in the background. Odette is at the counter. Her long braids hang mid-back against her tawny skin. Her hazel eyes are speckled with flecks of green and brown that darken or lighten depending on the outfits she wears. Today, they look greener as she wears a moss green knit halter and white skort. Her penetrating stare locks me in place before recognition hits, and a smile spreads across her face.

"Nadia!" she shouts excitedly as she drops her towel mid-wipe to hug me. I embrace her, and the familiarity of the act makes me ache at the loss of my parents. We always came here together. "Take a seat, sweet girl. I'll join you in a few minutes."

Odette brings over my stack of gingerbread pancakes along with a maple latte. I'm on my second latte when she slips into the booth across from me. I feel the zip of electric java flowing through my veins, licking my lips in appreciation and wiping away the excess froth. "God, that coffee is amazing, Odette."

She lets out a laugh. Her raspy voice is a welcome sound. "That it is my sweet girl." I know where this conversation is headed when she clasps her hands together, leaning forward. "So, tell me how you're holding up? You know I'm here for you, right?" I avoid her stare and look out the window at the kids riding their bikes along the path around the town square.

"Well, you sure don't beat around the bush, do you?" I snort, trying to mask the awkwardness. I feel her hand engulf mine and I swallow down the impulse to yank my hand back, instead forcing myself to keep it there. I don't want to hurt her feelings. I just don't want to be touched. These thoughts make me think that whatever happened to me broke me just a little.

She squeezes my hand. "Hey, Nadia. I am here for you." Her voice is soft and comforting as she punctuates the last word. I turn toward her and see the promise in her kind eyes.

I nod once but don't say anything about it. What could I say? "Do you need anything?" she repeats.

I clear my throat. "Kinda." I pause. "I need a job. I think it would help to keep me busy."

She smiles. "You plan on staying here this summer, then?"

I smile back at her, but it doesn't quite reach my eyes. "Yeah." I shrug. "I'm going to put in some applications." I pause, wondering if I should say anything, but this woman knows me, and I feel safe talking to her, a familiarity from the years coming in here. "I don't exactly know where I belong, but this seems like the place that feels more like home when I don't have one anymore."

She releases my hand and stands. Her movements are quick as she walks over to my side of the booth before plopping down into it and throwing her arm around my shoulder. She pulls me in, and my head instinctively rests on her shoulder. "Now, you know that isn't true, sweet girl. You always have a home here, with us, and with the townspeople who have known you since you were a little girl."

My throat tightens, and my words refuse to come, so instead of speaking, I simply nod my head. "Good," she says. "Now," she clasps her hands together, "tell me more about this job you are looking for."

"I'm not sure. Maybe waitressing at the Big Lake Tavern or working the bar there." I rest my chin in the palm of my hand. "Still up in the air. I think I will get settled first, and then Savannah will come to hang out with me."

Odette laughs. "Oh, gosh. You girls here all summer together?"

I shake my head. "Nah, she's just coming to visit when she can."

She pats my other hand, which is resting on the table. "Well, you always have a job here if needed."

The bell chimes above the door, and a man walks in, holding

hands with a little girl. Odette walks over to greet them just as the waitress stands before me, handing me the check.

"Do you want to take anything with you?" She glances over at the leftover food on the plates. Out of my periphery, I see Odette seat a well-built man and his daughter in a booth ahead of me. I try not to stare. I bet his wife will be joining him soon.

"No, I think my eyes were bigger than my stomach." I laugh. "I was so excited to be back here and got greedy ordering a little of everything, huh?"

The waitress smiles. "So, see you tomorrow then?" She gathers my plates up, and I pick up the check.

"Absolutely," I tell her, smirking. I take out my wallet and pull out enough cash to cover the bill plus a tip.

Standing, I place my purse across my body and give it a little stretch. I might have to walk around downtown to work off this food. My appetite has been almost zero these days, and even though I was hungry, I got full so quickly. I'm walking down the aisle when a crayon falls at my feet. I bend over, fighting the urge to expel my gingerbread pancakes all over the black and white checkered tiles and retrieve the red crayon from the floor. As I rise, I look at the little girl with big blue eyes and sun-kissed skin. "Hi there. I think this belongs to you." I tell her as I extend the crayon. She smiles at me, minus a few missing teeth, and I can't help but smile back at her. She is adorable.

I hear a deep voice speak. "What do you say, Catalina?" The intonation in his voice is warm and melodious, emphasizing the child's name with an accent. I turn to look toward the masculine voice when I am hit with the most stunning blue eyes I have ever seen, the same ones on the little girl across from him, who is undoubtedly his daughter. His deep, piercing eyes are like a clear blue sky—the calm before a storm. The bright color contrasts with his tawny skin, along with his curly black hair hanging around his face in a mop of ringlets. My gaze sweeps downward toward his chiseled jaw and the neatly trimmed facial hair that outlines his... frown? My eyes squint in confusion.

"Thank you." I hear the little voice speak, and it startles me. I realize that I was staring at her dad, her *very attractive* dad, who is *not* looking at me the same way I was looking at him. Embarrassment ensues, and my cheeks suddenly feel extremely hot. I abruptly turn to her.

"You're very welcome." Before it gets any more awkward, I bolt from the spot, waving at Odette as I leave the diner. Then I turn, walking down the sidewalk. I blow a puff of air at a strand of hair that has come loose from my messy bun. When I look in through the window to get one more look at the fine specimen of a man who looked at me with loathing, I see him staring at me. He doesn't smile at me, and I don't smile back.

CHAPTER
SEVEN

NADIA

I walk down Main Street feeling off-kilter. Instead of walking to my car and driving home, I pocket the car keys and continue toward the place that always makes me feel better, where I can get lost for hours and travel to a place without leaving the room. I look both ways before crossing the street and running up the few steps that lead to the familiar old brick building. The historical plaque out front dates the library's founding in 1880, and the soldier's memorial is below the dates. I touch it like I always do before walking in the double doors, paying homage to the fallen from our town.

The smell of wood polish and the musty aroma of books assault my senses as I scan the large room on both sides, looking for Penny, the town librarian. The door closes loudly behind me, and I hear a voice coming from downstairs. "Hi. If you need something, let me know." I smile, recognize that voice, and follow it downstairs to where the entire floor is dedicated to children's and young adult books. I carefully take the stairs, which someone built in a different era, because the steps are small and narrow. I stoop down to avoid hitting my head on the last steps with the low clearance area before I step onto the hardwood floors. I turn to the right, where the lift was recently installed for those unable to take the stairs. My mom worked hard to help raise the money for this vital necessity for our town library. This assistance has made it possible for those who could not climb the stairs to access the library's top floor or take the granite steps through the entrance to enjoy all that the library has to offer.

I see Penny reshelving returned library books with her cart and stops right before I reach her. She turns around. "Hi, do you need—" She stops mid-sentence and throws her arms around me. "Nadia, it's so good to see you here!" She pulls me back to look at her, and tears pool in her eyes. "I didn't think you would come after all this summer." I nod in understanding.

"I know. Honestly, I wasn't sure either, but I just couldn't stay in that house in the city any longer. It seemed like the right choice." She smiles.

"I'm so glad you did." She places the books she was holding in one hand back on the cart.

"I wanted to thank you, Penny, for attending my parents' funeral. Your presence meant the world to me. I was surprised at how many people from the town were there." Penny raises her hand and gently places it on my shoulder.

"Nadia, you know how much we adore you. Most of us have known your mother for ages. She did so much volunteer work with the library, and we will miss her so much." I raise my hands quickly before dropping them at my side.

"Well, I am here all summer, so you'll see a lot of me." I shrug.

"I'm so glad. Did you come just to say hi, or did you want to stock up on some reading material to enjoy in your hammock?" She waggles her eyebrows. I laugh at the gesture.

"Yep. That, too," I add. "You know that I'm a sucker for a good beach read from my favorite Nantucket authors."

"Well, you're in luck." She tucks her arm in mine, ushering me upward. "She has a new release I just put out front this morning. I don't think anyone has been in to check it out yet. I'll grab it for you." She halts. "Or is there anything else you want to look at down here?" She releases my arm. "Why don't you look to see if there's anything else you might want to add to that?" She walks up the stairs and pauses midway, arching her back to avoid the low ceiling. "And Nadia, I am happy you're here." She smiles one last time before disappearing up the steps. I hear the electronic chime letting me know another patron has entered. I search the YA section and pick up three Romantasy books about kings, queens, and cruel princes, then decide this is enough for now.

I reach the checkout section at the front of the library, and Penny hands a couple of kids some bookmarks to accompany their books. Each child has one book, and the mom mumbles something to the little boy she is holding. They walk out holding hands, and I place my books on the counter. Penny's eyes spark in amusement at my book selection. She hands the book over with a due date slip tucked into the front of the first book. She taps the book on top. "I loved this trilogy. So good." I stand there in shock.

"You," I point at her, "like Romantasy novels?" She laughs.

"Of course I do. I read many different types of books, Nadia." She says with a wink as she pushes the books in my direction. "Oh, and bonus points if there's a dragon."

I chuckle, clearly amused at envisioning Penny reading a dragon fantasy series tucked under the covers with a night-light illuminating the foil cover of the book. "Good to know," I counter as I pick up the stack and walk toward the front entrance.

"Nadia." I turn back to look at her. "I just wanted to let you know that a couple of people have nominated your mother for this year's Volunteer of the Year award. I didn't want you to be surprised if she won and was hoping you'd be around to accept the award if she did." I nod. I am fully aware of what this is and what it entails. I had helped my mom set up for the ceremony, where the volunteer receives a gift card to our local bookstore and a plant while they discuss the contributions that person made to help the library thrive. They also get their name on a plaque that displays the current and past members who have received this award for their generous contributions. It currently hangs by the front entrance.

"Of course. Just let me know if that's the case, and I'll be here," I tell Penny as I push through the door and leave with my stack of books in tow.

I skip down the steps and start the walk back to my car. More people are walking around with their dogs, throwing frisbees in the town center. I look up and see the man with his daughter eating at Odette's diner, Planet Pancakes, walking toward his truck up ahead. As he opens the door, I squint to make out the decal on the driver's door. "Torres Builders," I say. *Renovations and Construction* is added in script beneath the names in bold, gold lettering. I slow my pace, hoping he will drive away without noticing me. I hear the door close, and a few seconds later, I hear the engine start. *A diesel*, I think to myself, as I hear the deep rumbling of the start-up and rhythmic puttering of the motor.

As I inevitably approach his truck, I fight the urge to look up, but I must be a glutton for punishment. Because I can't help myself, I direct my sight and look into the driver's side front windshield. I almost halt in my steps when I see him staring at me. I refuse to look away as I approach his idling truck. A muscle tics in his jaw, and I lift an eyebrow in challenge. His lips twist upward in a snarl, and when I think he might open the door and confront me for my presence, for some reason annoying him, he twists his upper body to look behind him, breaking our eye contact. He pulls away from the parallel parking spot on the street without glancing again in my direction, and I don't bother looking back.

"What the fuck was that about?" I mutter to myself. He acts like he hates me, and I don't know why. What the hell did I do? I don't even know him or that adorable little girl who looked at him like he hung the moon and stars. How can someone look at another person that way without reason or knowing them? Frustrated with that weird encounter, I finally get to my car, toss my books into the front seat, and drive back to the lake house with one goal in mind—purging.

I take another sip of my latte and bob my head to the strong, repetitive beats that echo around me. "Not Like Us" by Kendrick Lamar plays through the Bluetooth speakers throughout my house. I jump onto the sectional couch and dance to the quick, rhyming lyrics, rapping with the countdown of the song as I jump off and run back toward my parents' bedroom. I lug out another bag of clothes that I have not so delicately loaded into a garbage bag and plop it down on the foyer flooring.

I look over and count seven bags of my father's clothes. For the first hour, I stood in the center of their room looking around, remembering when I would jump into my parents' bed when I was a little girl, after having a bad dream. My dad would pull back the covers as I got in, and my mom would rub my forehead, whispering about safety and love. How many countless nights did that happen?

I let one tear fall before I broke the trance, tore my sight away from the bed, and went into extreme purging mode. I opened the closet and threw my dad's clothes in first. I had no use for them. I didn't even check the pockets. I don't care. I just tossed everything into a bag, fighting the urge to smell his cologne just one last time. There isn't a point in torturing myself any longer about things like that.

Next, I entered my mother's closet and did the same thing. I don't want to keep anything here. The items in this house are only clothes they would wear here, and there aren't many summer clothes and even fewer winter ones. Occasionally, we would visit the lakes region for their winter events, such as the ice fishing derby or snowmobiling, but that stopped after I went to college.

The summertime here has always been our thing, and that's where the memories lie. I look in the bathroom and leave my mom's facial and toiletry products where they are. I clean up the counter and neatly place everything in the drawers, minus the toothbrushes and open toothpaste tubes, which I throw out. I shut off the light, feeling like I had a productive day.

After I drag the last trash bags out of the house, I go back inside, walk toward my parents' room one final time, and close the door. I close the door on the hurt, the memories that are too painful to remember, and lastly, the lies and betrayals that seem to linger in the air. The answers to those questions may never come, but I have

THE CRUELEST TRUTH

this nagging feeling that they, like all lies, will come to light and hurt those left to endure the pain when the truth is finally set free.

CHAPTER
EIGHT

MANNY

The look I gave her had to be done. I saw her talking to the waitress as Odette took us to our table, and it was the first time in a long time I looked at another woman besides my wife—my *ex*-wife. Referring to her that way is still hard. The words seem foreign on my tongue, and sometimes I forget, but she forgot about us long ago. Even that is hard to get used to. I'm barely twenty-six years old, and I have an ex-wife and a young daughter who is just turning five, although sometimes I question if she is going on sixteen. God, I hope she isn't like us as teenagers. I'm sure the little hellion won't get away with much around us— correction, around *me*. I'm not sure my ex will ever be able to grow up and stop being selfish. It's hard to see the woman I fell in love with anymore after all she's put us through: the addiction, the mood swings, and worst of all, the depression.

Even with the music playing, I can hear the girl from the diner's voice clearly as day. That laugh. That's what makes me want to get a better look at her. Maybe with me pushing her up against a wall, my cock in hand, ready to thrust into her. What noises will she make then?

It happens in slow motion. I see the red crayon fall, and then someone stops to pick it up. Her voice is low and soft, a melody carrying a tune toward me, and I watch her crouch down to speak to my daughter.

"Hi there. I think this belongs to you." That soft and sensual voice is a cruel awakening for me, causing whatever went through my mind to vanish, and the rugged exterior I show every female who tries to talk to me returns as she extends the crayon to Catalina. My daughter smiles at the woman, who is still crouching at my feet. Her kneeling before me makes my cock spring to attention. My gaze roams over her little white sneakers with pink stripes, roaming upward to those long legs that peek out from her almost too short skirt, where her panties are hidden from view only because I'm at the wrong angle. If I was in front of her, I'm sure I'd be able to witness how the thin piece of fabric would probably hug her folds. Upset with myself for having these thoughts, I speak almost too harshly, startling the woman as I watch her attention rise.

"What do you say, Catalina?" They can hear the intonation of my voice, probably from trying to calm the rising feelings of lust I'm trying hard to suppress. It hasn't been an issue for a while now.

That is until my world is nearly knocked off its axis when she turns to look at me, and I am hit with the most devastating, beautiful whiskey-colored eyes. The warm brown and reddish tones remind me of my favorite beverage, which I'd like to lap up, hoping to get drunk on her. I take in her appearance: delicate heart-shaped face, perfect little bow-shaped lips, and pointed chin. I notice her taking mine in, and I know she likes what she sees, which bothers me. Sometimes, the most beautiful package can have the worst surprise inside. My expression hardens, and a scowl makes my lips turn downward, snapping her out of whatever fantasy she imagines.

Her eyes widen, startled by my expression, before squinting in confusion.

"Thank you." Catalina wakes her from her trance-like state. She must realize that she was staring at her dad, and I hope she didn't notice the way I returned the sentiment, because I don't want to lead her on, just like I have turned down invitations for coffee or playdates. Yeah, that's the most common one, and I won't fall for it. I won't let them use my daughter as a means to get to me, either. I can tell she's embarrassed because her cheeks flush, as do her ears, cutely peeking out of her messy bun. She abruptly turns to Catalina to address her.

"You're very welcome." Before it gets any more awkward, she bolts from the spot, waving at Odette as she leaves the diner. I track her movements, feeling annoyed that she has affected me this way and angry with myself for wanting her. She turns, walking down the sidewalk, blowing a puff of air at a strand of hair that has come loose. I continue to watch her, unable to look away. It's like a disaster waiting to happen, and I have a front-row seat to witness it all. When she looks up, her eyes meet mine. She looks at me with loathing, mimicking me, almost making me laugh. I see her continue staring at me without looking away. She doesn't smile at me, and although I want to, I certainly don't smile back.

She disappears from my view, and I fight the urge to look for her and follow where she goes, tracking her path. Does she live in town? Is she from here or just visiting? Maybe her family just rented a house here, which isn't uncommon. Lots of vacation rentals are available here on the lake. The waitress comes to take our order, and I haven't even looked at the menu, so I decide to order what I had last time, not wanting to waste any more time. I know it's getting late, and Catalina must be hungry after only eating a bowl of cereal before we did the garden work early this morning.

Catalina orders a big Belgian waffle with strawberries and whipped cream on the side, and I order my usual, eggs Benedict. The waitress leaves, and another one comes over to refill my black coffee. I am easy when it comes to my beverages. I don't like the mocha caramel macchiato swirl, whatever shit. I am a black coffee, no frills, and especially no bullshit, kind of guy.

THE CRUELEST TRUTH

I'm not hard to please. Just don't get addicted to drugs. Ignore your daughter selfishly. Cheat on me. See, not too bad, huh?

From what I gathered, I'm not sure about the last one, but I know that my ex was into older men. She kept calling an older man to the point of infatuation. She didn't even try to deny it when I confronted her. Although she tried to explain, I was fed up at that point, and I didn't want to hear anything she had to say. The manipulation had worn me thin, and I was tired of seeing Catalina getting her feelings hurt. I kept thinking about all those times she'd been the last one picked up from daycare, staring out the window while waiting for her mom. She was the only one left with the daycare worker after hours, where they charged by the minute until I arrived. So many times, they gave us chances, until finally, we had to go in for a meeting. It was our last chance, so my mom offered to do the pickup for me to help out. The way the childcare specialist looked at me with pity initially, and then with protectiveness toward my daughter, was enough for me to make a change. I still didn't know if it was the right one until recently.

Six months later, here we are. It was a little easier to purchase a house in this area during off-peak time, and a client gave me a heads-up about this home. And I am grateful she did. The house was never listed, and we were able to agree on a cheaper price because it needed repairs. Only took a few months of work. I am a homeowner at a young age, and I own my own business with established clients, thanks to my dad. My parents are the reason I was able to finish college after getting my girlfriend pregnant. My parents helped with Catalina, and I finished my engineering degree. I owe them so much.

"Hey, Papá," my little princess interrupts. I look toward her, not realizing I had zoned out after scaring off that young girl who was just trying to be nice.

"Yes, mi angelita?" She beams at me, and I know I will say yes without a doubt, no matter what she asks me for this time.

"Can you sign me up for t-ball today?" I forgot about that. She loves baseball, the Red Sox, obviously, and I told her we would sign her up for the program I saw advertised in the town newsletter. This town has a newsletter that provides all the important information in a cute and concise format that comes in the mail to residents, letting them know of all the services available at the time.

"Mija, the recreational department isn't open today. I'll tell you what. I will sign you up first thing Monday morning, okay?" She looks at me, searching for the truth.

"Okay," she points her fork at me, "but don't forget." She stares me down, and I want to laugh at her imitation of my face when I get angry. Her lips pout, and her eyes narrow.

I almost want to laugh, but instead, I just nod. "Of course, Catalina, I won't forget."

"You promise not to forget?" I see the vulnerability in her eyes and the meaning behind it. Her mom always promised her things and never followed through. It breaks my heart to see that look of distrust, like she's just waiting to be left there after school, waiting for her parents, who said they'd be there.

"Never." She smiles at me.

"I love you, Papá," she says before returning to consume her waffle, and my heart breaks a little more for all the ways she was let down. I vow with everything in me not to be that person. I want to be someone she can always count on; nothing will change that.

We finish eating, and I wait for the bill to come. Odette comes over to chat with us as we wait. "Hey, honey, did you eat that entire waffle?" she asks Catalina, her eyes expressing surprise.

Catalina giggles. "Of course I did. I'm a big girl, and my Papá and I planted flowers this morning, so I was really hungry by the time we came in here." She readily broadcasts our business to Odette and half the patrons near us.

"Oh," Odette says, clasping her hands. "I love flowers. What did you plant?"

Catalina fully describes everything we did upon awakening this morning, down to the purple flowers we planted. "Look," she says, showing Odette her drawing. "See, here are all the flowers at our house. I almost lost my crayon and couldn't paint the door red, but that nice lady picked up my crayon for me and then ran away. Before I could ask her her name," Catalina says. I turn my head abruptly, but the movement doesn't escape Odette's notice. Her eyes light up in amusement. I turn away, trying to feign disinterest.

THE CRUELEST TRUTH

"Oh, that's Nadia. She's a college student at Boston University and graduating this year, but she stays around the lake during the summer. Her parents have a house, and her family was well-liked." I notice that she said *was* well-liked, and I can't help but wonder what they did to not be liked anymore, but if I asked, that would show that I'm curious. I also know that she didn't give all that information to Catalina, but it was all for my sake.

Odette leaves, chuckling as I give her a little wave. The waitress comes to drop off the check, and I am ready with my credit card to pay the balance. I drink the rest of my warm coffee, and after placing my returned card into my wallet, I stand, dropping some cash for the tip onto the table and striding behind my daughter as we leave the diner. I stop her as I take hold of her hand, stressing the importance of looking both ways before crossing a street, always being alert to sounds, and listening for vehicles approaching quickly from the roundabout ahead of us.

As I approach the truck, I press the unlock button on the key fob so she can jump in. After I assist her in securing her seat belt, I walk over to my side, swinging my long legs over and into the truck, closing the door behind me, and hitting the ignition button on the dash. As I look up, that's when I notice her. How can I not, because I can't help myself? I see her direct her sight, looking into the driver's side front windshield straight at me. She almost halts her steps when she sees me staring back at her. She holds my stare, refusing to look away as she approaches closer to my idling truck. I should drive off. A muscle tics in my jaw, but instead of being sensible, I lift an eyebrow in challenge. My lips twist upward involuntarily in a snarl.

"Look, Papá," and that breaks me from her hypnotic trance over me. I twist my upper body to look behind me, breaking our eye contact. I pull away from the parallel parking spot on the street without glancing again in her direction, and I don't bother looking back. Catalina forgets what she is going to say and begins humming a song I don't recognize. All I can think of is that I'm not interested in Nadia.

CHAPTER
NINE

NADIA

The following weeks consist of the same agenda—cleaning the house and sorting through my parents' remaining personal belongings. I'm on my last trip to drop off the items at Goodwill, and as I pull into the driveway, I see a familiar car. I park quickly and jump out, searching for the face I've been waiting to see for two weeks. That is when I spot Savannah in the hammock on the front porch. My smile widens as I run up the front steps. She jumps up from the stringed cocoon and into my waiting embrace.

"Love nugget, I was waiting hours for you." She laughs while rocking me back and forth. I can't help but laugh along with her, and God, it feels good.

"I couldn't wait until today," I tell her happily. "I thought you wouldn't make it out here until tonight, though." I look at her quizzically.

"Well, I left work early and decided just to leave. I had most things packed and ready to go, and I figure I could either borrow what I need from you or buy it here."

I nod. "Of course. Where are your bags?" I ask, looking around the porch as if they'd magically appear.

"Ugh, I didn't know when you were getting home, so I left them in the car."

I snort. "Why didn't you call me?"

Savannah rolls her eyes. "We really have to work on that snorting of yours. Well, it's called a surprise, silly goose. What else?" We walk to her car to retrieve her bags. "There's some in the trunk, too," Savannah yells over her shoulder.

"What the hell did you bring? I thought you said you could buy stuff here if you need to." She shakes her head in disagreement.

"Yeah. That's 'if' I forgot something." Savannah signals with one hand, making air quotes as she walks ahead of me. "I mean, I might have." I look at her as if she had grown another head.

"Really? I don't think you forgot a thing. I think you have your entire summer wardrobe in these five bags." We get the last of her items into the house, and I help carry them into the spare bedroom, where she usually stays when she sleeps over in the summer.

"Whew!" She plops herself on the bed. "So what's on the agenda tonight?" She waggles her eyebrows.

"Not sure. What do you feel like doing?"

She moves her head from side to side, contemplating the choices. "Dinner and drinks? Happy hour?"

"That could be dangerous," I reply.

She laughs. "God, I hope so." That was something we always told each other in college. When one of us had an idea, we'd go out, and things would always get out of hand. Hence, the "dangerous" comment. It's been a running joke after a fight broke out at a bar we were out at one night. Unlike some of our friends, we ran out, barely avoiding getting arrested. So the almost getting arrested part, hell no, but the dangerous fun, abso-fucking-lutley.

"I could use a coffee," Savannah yawns. "I'm so tired from

the drive from Massachusetts and could use a pick-me-up." She stretches out.

"I know what you need." She stands.

"Oh yeah, what's that?" she asks, almost unimpressed.

I smile widely. "An espresso martini."

"Oh." Her eyes twinkle. "Now, I think this is starting to become very dangerous indeed."

We blare "Red" by Taylor Swift as we dance around, trying on different outfits and making an absolute mess of my room. We ultimately decide on Savannah's outfit. She chooses a drop-waist mini dress, and I prefer a spaghetti-strapped romper.

Savannah loves wearing flip-flops, and I prefer sneakers for comfort. I tame some of my waves in a pull-through messy ponytail with some pieces crowning my face because my longer bangs don't fit into the whole pulled-back style unless it is in a higher bun. My chestnut brown, slightly tousled strands are thick and long, running a little past my mid-back. I place a little styling paste to tame the wispy strands that threaten to stand out from my forehead. My mom used to call them my baby hairs. It makes me happy to remember her telling me things as I stood beside her in this spot, doing the same routine with my hair. It makes me sad simultaneously, knowing that I'll never hear her say those words to me again.

I walk to the mirror, where Savannah lets her long blonde hair hang loose in large S-shaped curls, courtesy of purchasing a hair wand from her favorite social media app shop. That device is magical, and she sweeps her long locks into the heated roller with a button. After a few seconds of holding it in place, she releases it to give a beautiful wave that won't frizz on this cool summer night. She rotates her body side to side to appreciate the swish of her tresses. She moves her head downward and then flips her hair back as she abruptly stands upright. Those once tame curls become wild and voluminous. She smirks at the result in the mirror. "That's exactly how I like my men, too. Wild, but held in submission." She cackles, sipping her martini. I roll my eyes.

"Oh, please," I retort. "Don't even talk to me about that. Remember David?" She shudders.

THE CRUELEST TRUTH

"Do not speak his name again in my presence." She hisses the last word. "That was the worst vanilla sex I've ever had. The guy couldn't find my clit with the help of Siri and Apple Maps." My toasted coconut water goes flying out of my mouth at a poor attempt to stifle my laugh. "What the hell, Nadia?" She sniffs her arm. "Ew. I smell like summer and coconut, like bad-for-your-skin tanning lotion."

"Sorry. Sorry." I wipe the remaining spittle from my mouth. "That was hysterically accurate. I am so glad that he was *your* boyfriend." She shakes her finger in my face.

"Nope. Not my boyfriend, just a bad lapse in judgment," she counters.

"Sure, if you say so," I placate and laugh, realizing I am actually smiling and meaning it. I feel light and carefree. I feel like my age. I feel like nothing bad happened just a month ago.

It's time to do makeup, and I do it lightly with a bit of bronzer to highlight my naturally olive skin and a little gold sparkle for Savannah. A scant amount of lip gloss, and I think we are done. I close my all-in-one compact as I head to my closet to search for a wristlet to take with me on tonight's escapades. I yell out to Savannah across the hall. "You about ready, girlie?" She meets me out in the hallway.

"As ready as I'll ever be." She winks and saunters ahead of me. I lock the door behind us as we enter my car and head to the Big Lake Tavern.

We pull up to the tavern and walk to the sound of live music playing from the outside patio along the docks. The patio is dressed out in string lights, illuminating the space. The moon is full and reflects off the water. We thought about going to happy hour, but we needed some food after the time it took to get ready and a martini later. I approach the bar and decide to order some nachos. The bartender takes our order and cards us when we order some drinks. I proudly take mine out, as does Savannah, and show it to the guy who doesn't look much older than us. "Okay, ladies. What will it be?" he asks, smirking as we search the specials. Savannah takes her time; I don't have to think about it.

"I'll have a watermelon margarita with sugar on the rim, please."

He smiles. "Any preference for tequila?" he asks, and I shake my head.

"Nope, not at all," I state, my arms resting on the bar counter. Savannah oohs.

"I'll have the same, and no, just surprise us with the tequila," she says. The bartender nods and walks off. "I'm going to get his number," Savannah announces, but I can't stop the laugh that erupts.

"You don't waste any time, do you?" The nachos arrive and save her from having to answer. I'm about elbow deep in our large order with all the toppings possible when the margaritas arrive. I lick my thumb before the salsa drips off, landing on my outfit. I pick up my margarita and take a big sip through the straw. "Wow, that's good." I nudge Savannah, and she turns to her drink and takes an equally big sip.

"Wow. Good choice," she squeals. "You're not kidding. That is so good and strong, too." She fake coughs. I roll my eyes.

"He's not going to come over here and give you mouth-to-mouth, girl." But sure enough, Gage, the bartender noted by the name displayed on his tag, comes over with a glass of water for Savannah.

"My hero," she says, twirling a luscious lock of blonde hair around her finger. Gage blushes as she licks the sugar off the rim of the glass. I see his cheeks flush red, and then he averts his gaze. He coughs into his fist.

"Call if you need anything else," he says.

Savannah, the temptress, responds with a "Sure will, Gage," as the poor guy who doesn't stand a chance of making it out of here tonight unscathed walks away to wait on another customer at the end of the bar.

Savannah does, in fact, get Gage's number and spends some time chatting with him. "Hey, Gage?" He stops flirting with my bestie to look at me. "Are you guys hiring?"

"Yeah. You want to apply?" I nod my head.

"Yes, I'm looking for a job. I'll be here all summer, and I need some work."

"Okay, but do you have any experience?" he asks, and I think about it.

"Does nannying count?"

He chuckles. "If you can do that, you can wait tables. I'll tell Ryan you're looking. He's our manager and owner," he says hushedly, "but he doesn't want anyone to know that. Stop by or fill out the application online, and I'll let him know when I see him tomorrow that you are applying and to look out for it."

"Thanks, Gage. I appreciate that."

"Yeah, Gage," Savannah coos. "We appreciate that." I snort, turning around and hopping off my bar stool, crashing into a wall of muscle.

I almost fall back when an arm stops my descent, holding me tight, pressed against his hard, chiseled chest. I lean in, gravitating forward, as my nails press into him, grabbing for purchase. I jolt at the sensation as I look up and catch sight of those blue eyes that stared me down at the diner. His eyes narrow, and he lets me go before I can stand upright, regaining my footing.

"You should be careful where you're going, mi cariño." He leans in like he's going to tell me a secret only meant for my ears. His warm breath caresses my cheek, contradicting his icy blue eyes that narrow in on me like a hunter targeting his prey that he's now backed up against the bar. They almost smolder like the steam wafting from the most delicious cup of coffee as he stares me down. My breath hitches, and my lips part slightly. I want to say something, but being this close to him short-circuits my brain. I'm confused because I don't know what that word he called me means, but I feel sure it must be an insult because his muscles tense as he says it. And God, are there muscles underneath that tight tee that hugs his pecs much like the tension that hugs the air between us?

I don't engage or acknowledge his comment, but instead, I walk off and search for the nearest toilet. When I return, composed and ready to give him a piece of my mind, I search the bar for him, but he is nowhere to be found, and Savannah is now kissing Gage behind the bar.

Fuck my life.

CHAPTER
TEN

MANNY

"Fuck my life," I mumble under my breath, but my mom hears it with her laser-sharp hearing. I walk to the cabinet and shake the bottle, finding it almost empty. I frown, opening it and retrieving a couple of antacids. "Oh God, I hope it's not an ulcer." I clutch my upper abdomen.

She waves her hand, dismissing my antics. "You are too young to be worrying like this. You do too much." She tsks. "Have you heard from—"

"Don't bring her name up, please, Amá." I look around for my little angel, but she returned to her room to finish coloring her drawing. Like my mother, she has the same inherited bat-like hearing skills. "We don't know when she will be around for her supervised visitation." I glance at the clock and notice I still have a little time after breakfast this morning. "Honestly, Catalina hasn't even asked."

My mom frowns, making the sign of the cross and mumbling something under her breath before turning around to fold the remaining clothes in the hamper. I start to load the dishwasher, but I'm quickly interrupted by someone snapping to get my attention. My head pops up, searching for the sound.

"Leave it," she commands. "I'll get it after you leave for work." I place the pan back in the sink, arms up like I was caught red-handed, and walk away. Má always cooks good food when she is here, but all those spices do not help the queasy feeling in my gut that now churns from all the increased acidic bile that threatens to appear if I bend over or hiccup. I'm glad I don't have to bend to load the dishwasher after all.

Looking back at my má, I find her facial expression softens, and she walks toward me. I hate the look in her eyes. I don't want anyone's pity for my life choices. Those were mine and mine alone. I don't know if I regret it because it gave me the most wonderful gift—my daughter, Catalina. From the moment I held her at the hospital, I knew there was nothing I wouldn't do to protect this little girl. I'd give her all I could and more.

"Amá, you shouldn't have to stay here to help." I avert my eyes from hers. "I feel bad."

She places her hand on my cheek, looking up at me. "Mijo, I love taking care of my granddaughter. It is no trouble at all." My mother has been staying with us since I started this new job last week. I had a couple of weeks off, but couldn't put off work any longer. "Any hits from the post you placed for a nanny?" she inquires. I frown, thinking about the couple of women who came to interview. The most qualified one is a teenage girl who didn't have reliable transportation because she wasn't old enough to drive.

"The options are limited," is my reply. She continues folding Catalina's clothes, and I feel like I'm undoubtedly a failure. I'm exhausted, and with work and taking care of Catalina, I've been falling asleep when she does, around eight o'clock, and waking at five. I still feel unrested.

"Mijo, you are too stressed. Why don't you go out to have

drinks with the guys after work?"

I contemplate the offer, and the more I think about it, the more appealing it sounds. I nod. "You know what, Má? I think that it might be good for me to get to know my crew a little better. They have been asking me to go and hang out with them. I have to be up early tomorrow for Catalina's t-ball game, so it shouldn't be a late night," I inform her, but she just shrugs.

"Not a problem if you want to stay out, mijo. I'm here until you find someone." She picks up the hamper and walks to Catalina's room to put away her folded laundry.

"What about Apá?"

She snorts. "Your dad is a grown man who can care for himself." She pauses. "Plus, I like it when I'm away. When I return, I swear he appreciates me just a little bit more." She winks and walks off. I can't help but chuckle. I think that's where Catalina gets her sass. It's hard to remember any redeeming qualities about my ex, except that she provides half of my daughter's DNA. She also broke my heart, so there's that.

I shout "Bye, girls!" as I walk toward the door. "Bye!" is shouted in unison at my departure as I close the door behind me and leave for work.

The job site isn't far today. I'm working on a lake house renovation, which consists mainly of the decking around the back and down the steps leading to the dock. I find myself pausing multiple times during the day to take in the view and wonder what it would be like to own a house on the lake. I could shoot off fireworks with Catalina and maybe drink my coffee out on the deck while reading a sports blog about all New England sports teams.

Obtaining the permits for this job took some time. The homeowners were frustrated by the delay, but as a structural engineer, it is my responsibility to work closely with the town to ensure the blueprints are accurate and that the remodel they requested would be structurally sound, safe, and able to withstand the elements. The home sits on a one-acre lot, featuring a deck set against stone retaining walls and walkways accented with granite steps. Large pavers are interwoven sporadically along the walkways, leading to the dock, with a small sandy patch nestled along the water on the lower level.

This project is a big deal for my company, and I am committed to ensuring everything runs smoothly by enhancing the structural integrity of the existing building. I plan to build my bank account with the promise of good pay and future job opportunities, most of which will come through word-of-mouth, a common practice in this line of work. I want people to say, "He is reliable, trustworthy, and honest." Those are the qualities clients look for in a contractor. They want someone who can tell them what to expect and show up every day. I've lost count of how many jobs I have had to step in and finish because another contractor took half a payment and never completed the job. It gives us a bad name. I'm still mulling that over when I hear Luc's voice behind me.

"Manny, are you coming out with us tonight?" I turn to Luc, who is walking toward me, his tool belt slung across his arm. I nod, and his eyes widen. "No way. Ha!" He turns to yell at another employee, Luis, coming this way, as we are all loading up our trucks to get out of here. Luis hands Luc a twenty-dollar bill. "I told you I would get him to cave in at some point." Luc gloats, while Luis shakes his head and walks away.

"Alright, I'll see you there. I'm going to run home and shower quickly, then meet up with you guys."

"First round is on me," Luc says as he places his twenty-dollar bill in his wallet.

"Did all you fuckers bet on me not coming out tonight?" I ask Luc, a little irritated.

"Correction," Luc says, raising a finger in the air. "I bet you'd come out tonight, and I'm glad you are. You won't be disappointed."

"So, where are we meeting tonight, anyway?" I toss the rest of my gear into the truck and shut the door behind me.

Luc shrugs. "Where else? The Big Lake Tavern. It's the best for happy hour on Fridays." He pats me on the back. "Glad you're coming out, Manny." Then he hops into his truck and starts it up, the loud engine roaring to life, as he waits for me to back out first.

I climb into my truck and lower the window. "See you there," I call out, pulling out of the job site just as he reverses and follows, both of us leaving the parking spots the owners had told us to use.

When I get home, I see a note from my mom.

> Mijo,
>
> I took Catalina to the library to pick out some books, and then we are going for ice cream. I am making your favorite, arroz con pollo with a pot of frijoles charros, so don't worry about dinner. There will be plenty of food left when you get home.
>
> Amá

I groan after reading the note. I pick up the bottle of antacids and notice I'm almost out. "Too bad she doesn't grab me some more antacids," I mutter, shaking out the last few tablets. I strip off my work clothes and toss them into the washing machine, setting it to soak before the wash cycle kicks in. I take a shower, washing a day's worth of grime, and pull on a pair of jeans, but change my mind. Choosing comfort instead, I grab some black joggers, with a fitted black t-shirt, and white sneakers. It's Lululemon, and I don't care what anyone thinks. Those shirts are so fucking soft, and the joggers match, so zero apologies given.

I pull into the packed parking lot. Walking toward the tavern, I follow the thump of music that can be heard from the outdoor patio where I am greeted with panoramic views of the vast, blue lake ahead. Inside, the place is equally packed. I scan the crowd until a hand shoots up, waving me over. I lift my chin in acknowledgment and weave my way through the crowd toward Luc, Luis, and several other crew members as they lift their beers in a salute. They scoot down, and Luc jumps up, disappearing into the crowd as I slide into the picnic-style seating with my back to the patrons. A moment later, Luc plops beside me with a bucket of beers on ice. He twists the cap off, handing me one.

"Here you go, boss," he says. "Good to have you out here with us. We thought you were ignoring us."

I smirk. "Nah, bro. Just don't have a lot of childcare options."

He lets out a laugh. "Yeah, I know what that's like. Did you try posting up at the rec center?"

I take a swig of my beer. "Yep, I just posted it this week. I had a couple of interviews that didn't work out, with some people I knew in town recommending their niece or friend, but that was a disaster. I hope someone at the rec center will respond to this post. I need the help. As much as I love my mom and her help, I also need my space. I shouldn't even complain, but—"

His hand halts me mid-sentence. "Say no more. My mother-in-law stayed with us for three weeks to help. It was the longest time of my life."

I shake my head. "She's folding my underwear in quarters, bro. They, like, fit in my hand." I stick out my hand, and beer flies out of Luc's mouth.

"Stop, I'm dying." My hand is wet, and some guys were unlucky enough to get caught in the beer spray. I stand up and slide out of the picnic table.

"I'll grab some napkins," I tell the group that is cursing at Luc for his outburst. I see the bartender preoccupied with a young blonde-haired girl, and I decide to take matters into my own hands, leaning over to grab at a stack of cocktail napkins. "That should do the trick," I mutter.

As I step back, I collide headfirst into the intoxicating smell of lavender and roses. I find myself breathing in her heady floral scent, and the startled gasps from the woman lets me know she realizes I am a total hair sniffer. Groaning inwardly, I become painfully aware that I'm still holding onto her, and she has her hand pressed firmly against my chest. Her touch is warm and inviting, as I feel myself gravitating toward her. She leans in slightly, just enough as her fingernails graze against the fabric of my shirt and press gently into my pecs, causing me to jolt at the contact.

She looks up at me, startled, and I see those whiskey-colored eyes staring up at me like she did when she was on her knees at the diner. This is the second time now. Wait. Is she stalking me? My eyes narrow, and I release her before she can get her footing. I drop her like I've been burned, and boy, have I been burned before.

I lean in like I'm going to tell her a secret only meant for her ears. "You should be careful where you're going, mi cariño." My mouth is so close to her that my words caress her cheek, contradicting the frosty blue of my eyes that narrow in on hers. My body heats as I stare her down. Her breath hitches, and her lips part slightly. I can tell she wants to say something—anything, but being this close to her confuses me because my mind says one thing, but my body betrays me by acting out. What makes me so drawn to her? But I already know what it is—like calls to like. When I look into her eyes, I feel it. The same loneliness is there—the sadness and the betrayal. Whatever happened to this girl, she is just like me. She looks so fucking sad that I just want to grab onto her, hug her, but I know that would be a mistake. My cock twitches, and I know she feels it because she releases her hold on my shirt, pushing away from me and walking off. I miss the loss of her body heat instantly, and I fight the urge to pull her back, ridiculous as the thought may be. So, I stand there for a few moments, trying to get my emotions in check and for my cock to go down before I head back to the table where the guys are getting a little loud.

"Screw this." I motion to the bartender, close my tab, and walk over to the table of my fellow crew to say goodbye. I don't see her return from wherever she went, and I vow to keep my distance from her should I run into her again. I mean, how hard can it be?

CHAPTER
ELEVEN

NADIA

I let Savannah enjoy her night of margarita bliss, and I stopped at one alcoholic drink at the tavern because I was driving home. There's been enough car accidents in my lifetime, so I'm still very cautious when I get into any car. I try to block out what happened to my parents not long ago, and I don't think I'll ever feel the same after having survived them. It only takes one impaired person to ruin lives—those that they either injure or kill, but especially those left to live after the lasting destruction caused by that one bad decision.

Tonight, we decide to order pizza and stay in, watching movies and catching up. Once we get home, I make drinks for us. Savannah has her arm thrown around my shoulder as we sit cross-legged on the couch, with more margaritas in our hands but minus the fruit flavor from last night. "He was cute, right?"

I lick the salty rim that replaced the sugary one of the watermelon margarita yesterday. "Who? I mean, I guess if you like the whole," I move my hand around in a circle, envisioning his brooding presence, "tall, dark, and handsome look mixed in with some major alpha hole." I shrug. Midway through drinking from my glass, I feel Savannah's stare. I turn to her. "What?" I finish a big gulp, but it goes down hard.

She puts her glass on the coffee table before us and turns to face me completely. "Hold up." Her hand, which was on my shoulder moments ago, has her fingernails clicking together in front of me as she says it. "What the fuck are you talking about?" Her words sound cruel, but the twinkle in her eyes tells me she's not letting this go.

"Um. I don't remember. The alcohol is confusing me. Who are you talking about?"

She waggles a finger at me. "Nuh, uh. You are not getting out of this, and I know you have had just as much to drink as I have, so stop with the excuses and spill the tea." She squeals. "Who is this 'alpha hole' you are talking about?"

I place my drink on the end table and bring a hand up to my forehead, rubbing off the impending migraine that will likely ensue after Savannah attempts to coax every little detail about the stranger. I can't say that I am not intrigued myself. I bite the side of my bottom lip. "Well," I begin, "I saw this guy at the diner the other morning."

"Woah, hold up. What diner? I need you to be more specific." Her hand slices through the air.

I just stare at her craziness. My eye twitches. "Planet Pancakes. I went to see Odette."

She nods. "Okay, better. Now keep going, and don't leave anything out."

I roll my eyes. "Fine. So like I was saying, I was at the diner, and when I was leaving, this kid dropped her crayon, and I bent to pick it up and hand it back to her. You should have seen her, Savannah. She was so adorable. She had these bright blue eyes, and then when I turned to look at the guy sitting there—" Savannah cuts me off again.

"The tall, dark, and handsome alpha-hole?" She nods eagerly.

"Are you going to let me finish?" I throw my hands outward.

"Sorry, sorry. Yes, finish, please."

"Yeah, him. But he looked at me like he hated me or found me annoying, to say the least. I guess I saw him getting into the truck with his daughter when I returned from the library. I mean, I don't know if it was his daughter, but they both have the same blue eyes, so I assumed..." I trail off. "Then, I saw him at the bar while you were eye-fucking Gage or whatever his name was."

"Stop, you're not getting out of this by trying to redirect the conversation to Gage. We can talk about him later. So that was him again at the bar—the guy I saw whispering in your ear last night?"

I smile, but it drops from my lips as quickly as it comes—my brows furrow. "Yeah, that's him. I ran into him, and he leaned over to tell me, 'You should be careful where you're going, mi cariño.' I try to make my voice sound like his, but it just makes me sound like I smoked way too many cigarettes over too many years.

Her eyes widen. "Are you for real right now?" She squeaks into her hand. "Shut up." I look at her.

"What? He told me to watch out, so yeah, alpha hole, right?" She shakes her head, disagreeing. She places her hands on my shoulders and gives me a little shake.

"He called you 'mi cariño.'" My expression must show my confusion because she asks, "You don't know what that means?" Her eyes search mine.

"Nope, no clue. But I wish I knew some Spanish right now. It was Spanish, right?"

"Yes, it was, and my roommate had a Hispanic boyfriend. I think he was Mexican. Anyway, that's not important, but what is important is that he would call her mi cariño all the time, among other things. She married him, ya know. So devoted. Such a keeper." She lets out a dreamy sigh. I snap my fingers in front of her buzzed face.

"Savannah, focus." She lets out a hiccupped laugh. "Are you going to tell me what it means?" I beg her, now super intrigued.

The little vixen smiles, showing every molar in her mouth,

drawing this out excruciatingly slowly. "It means sweetheart. More specifically, my sweetheart or my love. Either way, I always heard my dormmate's boyfriend use it as a term of endearment toward her, usually before I chose to leave and give them some privacy."

"Huh. That's weird. Why would he look at me like he hates me and then call me his love?" I rub my finger against my lip, contemplating the rationale, but decide I have no idea what to think.

"Do you think you'll see him again? Maybe you should ask him what his problem is with you?"

I shrug. "It doesn't matter, and I don't know. He must live here, and I live here, too. Considering I ran into him twice today, I think the probability is likely."

She waves it off. "So about Gage." She clasps her hands together. "Isn't he hot?" But all I can think of is the stranger with eyes I want to get lost in. The way his body felt against mine, the hard planes of his torso that looked more like the result of manual labor than hours spent at the gym, but I could just be speculating. I wish I could feel his hands clasped against mine. I bet there are calluses. Savannah goes on and on about the bartender, but I only hear his voice over and over in my head whispering, "Mi cariño."

I wake up to the light beating through the window pane. I didn't close the curtains last night, and as I sit up, I notice that I didn't even make it to the bedroom. The stiff neck I'm sporting is another reason. I know I slept on the couch at an awkward angle. I look around and see Savannah strewn across the carpet with a faux fur throw from the sofa and a sequin pillow at her head. I laugh as I envision her waking up with the butterfly pattern's imprint on her cheek.

I bet that can't feel good right now, but I doubt she feels anything after all those margaritas. Speaking of the neon green liquid, I see our two empty glasses on the table. I grab them and carry them, placing them in the sink with a clink. I twist my hair into a loose bun instead of the ponytail I was sporting earlier last night, then brew a pot of coffee. While it brews, I wander into the bathroom to wash my face and brush my dragon breath away. Back in my room, I pull on a tank and shorts, ready to face the day.

When I return to the kitchen, Savannah sits on the island with a mug of black coffee. I burst into a laugh when I read the inscription. *When I think about books, I touch my shelf.* She lifts one eyebrow in the freakishly cool way only she can pull off. I sure as hell can't do that.

"Girl, your mom sure did have some pretty cool cups." She cackles. I smile, but it quickly fades when I realize she won't use that mug ever again. I have plenty of fond memories with her, particularly her passion for collecting obscure phrases on coffee mugs. "So, what's up for today?" she asks, trying to steer the subject away from my mom.

I go to the coffee pot and pour myself a mug that resembles a soup bowl, which I was told was popular in the 1990s. I pour some sweet oat milk creamer into a jar and froth it with a whisk before adding it to the top of my mug, sprinkling a little bit of local maple sugar onto the froth. She holds out her mug for me, and I repeat the same process, making her one similar to mine. "Here you go." I hand it over, and she lets out a sigh of contentment.

"So good," she remarks.

To answer her question, "I think I am going to get that application in and see if I can get the job at the Big Lake Tavern."

"Oh, that's good." She blows on her coffee, and I don't know if she's talking about the coffee or my job search. "Any nannying jobs here?"

"I'm not sure." I gulp my coffee, enjoying the dark roast mixed with the sweet creamer. "Ideally, if I could do both, that would be great."

"Do you need the money?" she asks, concern clear in her eyes.

"No," I say matter-of-factly. "Fortunately, my parents left me with money, so I can relax if I want to, but that's the whole point, bestie. I want to stay busy. If I stay busy, I don't have time to focus on my parents and the fact that they were supposed to be here and will never be here again to spend another summer with me."

She grabs my hand and squeezes it. "I know, sweetie." She pulls her hand back. "Then stay busy and enjoy this time at the lake house." And that's precisely what I intend to do.

I filled out the application online and have an interview with

Ryan, the owner, today. I am loading the last luggage piece as Savannah stands in the doorway. "I can't believe you are leaving already."

She nods, throwing her arms around me. "I know, I wish I could stay all week with you, but you know, responsibilities and all. I'll be back soon to visit and stay for a weekend. I'll let you know when I can get away again. It's not like I'm far away. Just a few hours and a phone call away if you need me. I'll be here."

"Thanks, girlie pop. You are the best friend I could only dream of having in my life."

She pushes away from me. "Always," she says as she walks away, striding to her car. Oh, and tell Gage I'll be back soon, too."

I laugh. "You know he's going to be sad that you left, right?"

She waves her hand in the air. "Yeah, sure he will," she says jokingly.

"Drive safely and call me when you get there so I know you got home safely."

She shuts the door and lowers the window. "I could, or you could just stalk me on the Find a Friend app to see where I am." She winks and then reverses out of the driveway, the tires crunching on the graded dirt road. She pulls away and drives off toward her home in Massachusetts. I watch her turn the corner and disappear. As I shut the door, I notice how quiet the house is.

"Fuck this." I grab my purse and fling it over my shoulder across my chest. "Let's go get that job," I say as I jump into my car and fight the memories that threaten to pop into my head of a different time, not so long ago, when voices and laughter filled this space. Now, all that remains is deafening silence.

CHAPTER
TWELVE

NADIA

"When can you start?" Ryan taps his pen against the table on the covered patio, peering across the lake. I sit up straighter, excited over the prospect of having a job and, well, a purpose this summer.

"Whenever you want me to. I can even start today?" Wait. Yikes, I hope that didn't make me sound too desperate. I am eager though, I just hope—ugh.

"Perfect." He interrupts my thoughts, making me snap my head upward in attention. "Mandy called out again." I nod in understanding, even though I have no idea who Mandy is. "I swear she is the most unreliable waitress I've ever had." I look at him, not liking how this conversation is going, but he smiles. "Amanda." He pauses, and I can tell he wants to say more. "Also known as Mandy.

My niece, by the way," he says. "God, I love her, but she gets away with anything around me. She just looks at me with her puppy dog eyes, and I melt. I'm a big marshmallow around her."

I chuckle because Ryan is in no way a marshmallow-type guy. He is a retired Marine, and it appears that he still lives by the same standards he was required to maintain on active duty. I heard he went in after age eighteen, retired twenty years later, and bought this place not long ago. Nothing is safe from gossip around here. My case in point.

"Here." He hands me some forms, and I take them from him. "I need you to fill this out and bring it with you this evening when you show up. Does six to closing work for you today?" He doesn't wait for me to answer as he is already walking away. He turns around. "Oh, ask Gage at the bar for a t-shirt. There's a few styles for you to choose from. He'll also let you know the dress code, but we are pretty relaxed around here." He sways his hand back and forth in mid-air.

I stand. "Thanks!" I elevate my voice at his retreating form before heading to the bar to chat with Gage, bringing my employment papers with me. He is waiting for a couple of guys to place their order, who appear to be on lunch break, and when he turns around, he sees me and waves. As I approach, he looks around as if looking for my trusty sidekick, but he is going to be disappointed. "Hey, there." I give him a small wave while I pull up a chair and sit at the bar.

"Hey." He smiles, and I decide to put him out of his misery.

"Savannah went home today. She has to work, but she wanted me to tell you she'll be back and hopes you guys can hang out." He looks at me, almost relieved at my words.

"I'd like that," he says. Changing the subject, he nods in the direction of my papers. "You get a job here?"

I wave my papers before placing them back down. "Yep, just have to fill this out."

"Nice," he says, wiping the counters where someone just vacated moments ago. "When do you start?"

"Um. That's the thing. Ryan told me to come over here to ask you about a uniform. I guess I'll start in a few hours." Throwing the towel under the bar, he goes to retrieve a box.

"Ah, yes—the uniform." He plops the box on the bar top and starts pulling out shirts. "Here are the styles." He pulls out a t-shirt, a crop top, a tank, and...

I pick one up, studying the size.

"Maternity shirt?" I ask quizzically.

He chuckles. "Yeah. We don't discriminate here. Besides, we have had plenty of pregnant wait staff. Maybe they just like the give in the shirt." He raises his hands in supplication. "Not for me to judge."

"Okay, point made, but I'm pretty easy. I'll just take the medium t-shirt if you have it."

He nods. "Sure thing. That's easy enough." He pulls out a bin and retrieves a shirt wrapped in plastic.

"Here." He tosses two shirts with the letter M in a black and white sticker adhered to the plastic wrap. I grab them and tuck them under my arm.

"Thanks, Gage. Are there any other dress code things I need to know about?"

"Nah, just wear the shirt, and anything goes with the bottoms. Shorts, skorts, skirts, jeans, leggings...Whatever." I stand from my chair.

"Perfect then." I move to step away. "Thanks so much."

"Anytime. See you tonight. I'll still be here."

I wave and walk off toward my car so I can go home before returning to work later for my first shift. I'm driving home when I realize I should get some caffeine before starting my shift. I'm passing Planet Pancake and pull into a vacant spot up front. Jumping out of the car, I race toward the diner before it closes to see if I can grab a to-go latte. I see Odette at the register and head in her direction.

"Nadia, love. What brings you here today?"

I wave. "Hi, Odette. I was hoping you could make me one of your maple lattes to go."

She chuckles. "Squeaking in at the last minute, huh? Only for you, my sweet girl. Give me a second." She goes over to the machine, grinds some beans, and taps them into the filter basket, where she attaches the group head, locking it in place. I pick up my phone to check the time and see a message from Savannah.

> **Savannah:** Just got home. I'm checking in, babe.

> **Me:** Glad you're home safe. Gage says hi.

> **Savannah:** OMG, is he there?

> **Me:** Nope, but I start working tonight. He seemed sad you left.

> **Savannah:** *sad face emoji*

"Here you are, Nadia." I pocket the phone and take out my wallet to pay. Odette places her hand over mine.

"Don't worry about it." She smiles. "And don't be a stranger, sweet pea."

I lift my latte in homage, praising the coffee gods and a little to Odette for making it. "I won't. I got a job at the Big Lake Tavern, by the way."

Her mouth forms an O shape. "That's great, sweet pea. Keeping busy? That's good."

"Yeah, that's what I was wondering. I want to get another job. Do you know if anyone is hiring for a nanny position this summer? I have something at night but am also looking for something during the day."

She seems to think about it. "Well, have you tried the recreation center in town? While the parents are at work, they have a camp for school-aged children during the day. They might still be hiring staff."

"That sounds perfect. I'll check it out."

She waves me off. "Glad to help."

I leave and drive home so that I can change and get ready for my first shift. The excitement of having a purpose this summer helps to lift my spirits.

I'm walking through the door when my phone begins to ring. "Ugh, fuck right off." I pull my bag off my neck and place it on the counter with my latte. "Stupid spam." I fish the phone out of my bag just in time before it goes to voicemail. "Hello?"

The voice on the other end of the line causes me to pause. "Hello. Is this Nadia Kennedy?" I sit on the couch before I can second-guess anything.

"Yes, speaking," I answer. I gulp, knowing that whatever Officer Stanley has to say won't be something I want to hear.

He continues. "Sorry to bother you, Ms. Kennedy. Is this a good time to speak with you? I have some updates on your parents' case, which I'd like you to know." I brace my head in my hand, waiting for the news. I blink back, the emotions threatening to leak from my eyes.

"Yeah, you can speak." He clears his throat.

"Look," he begins, "I just wanted you to hear it from me before anyone else, and I know you made it perfectly clear at our last meeting that you do not want to hear about the person who hit your parents, but I thought you still might like to know this information."

"Okay." I pause. "What is it?"

"We received word today that Mrs.—"

I cut him off. "I don't really want to know her name or anything else about her. Nothing about her makes her human because, in my mind, she will always be a monster. It's bad enough that I know what she looks like from the folder you showed me of her mugshot." I rub my temples.

"Right, I understand, Ms. Kennedy, but today was the sentencing, and it didn't go as well as we would have liked." I stiffen at his words.

"What do you mean it didn't go as well as you'd like? What happened?" I fight the urge to curse, but I know better than to raise my voice and rage at a police officer on the phone. I want to get the whole story, and I know he called to tell me the truth even though he didn't have to.

"There's no good way to say this, so I will just come out and say it. The judge went easy on her because it was her first offense. Despite her current addiction to opioids and other substances that came back on her toxicology report, she wasn't impaired at the time. Your father was driving recklessly, and that's what caused him to lose control of the car."

I interrupt. "But she was chasing them. Doesn't that prove reckless or something?"

"Witnesses on the scene contradict that and say that your father was the one out of control. Not to mention that his blood alcohol level was slightly elevated."

"Pfft. Oh, come on. You and I both know that if she wasn't chasing them, then my father wouldn't have felt compelled to lose her. And she made my mother cry."

"Although the latter is not a crime, I understand your grief."

"I can't believe this," I mutter under my breath. "So what does this all mean for her?"

"I'm sorry to say that her charge of vehicular manslaughter was downplayed, considering the circumstances, to a misdemeanor."

"No," I say into the phone. "No, no, no, no," I mutter again, gasping at my sudden loss of air.

"She could be out in thirty or sixty days, Nadia, but I doubt she will do over ninety days in jail." I slam my hand down on the table before me, tipping over the lamp.

"Seriously, that's it? For killing my parents. Ninety days, max? Where's the justice in that?" I question Officer Stanley.

"I'm so sorry, Nadia. We tried to lengthen the sentence, but we just couldn't. I feel like I failed you." I rub away the tears that pool in my eyes.

"I know you aren't to blame, Officer Stanley."

"Please, Nadia. Call me Mitchell."

"Mitchell, I know it's not your fault, but the system failed me. That's for sure. She will walk away free very soon, and my parents are never going to walk again because they are lying in a grave right now. A grave that doesn't even have a headstone at the moment. I'm sorry, but I just can't right now." I disconnect the call without another thought. I stand up and walk to where my latte is, probably cold on the countertop. I throw it away and crumble to the floor in a heap of self-pity. I don't know how long I've been sitting on the kitchen floor. I know that I have to go to work. I can't call out on my first shift, so I gather myself upright and walk to the bedroom.

I strip out of my clothes and turn on the water in the shower. I don't turn it on hot, but instead, I grit my teeth at the cold drops that land on my heated skin. I feel like I'm on fire and can't turn it off. I want to feel something, and the bite of the cold well water that shoots through the showerhead on full blast reminds me that I'm alive. I'm alive while my parents are dead.

CHAPTER THIRTEEN

NADIA

I show up to work at the Big Lake Tavern fifteen minutes before my shift starts. "Hey, you made it," Gage says behind the bar.

"Of course." I lift my hand in the air, palm out, much like the emoji Savannah and I always send each other.

He beckons me over with his hand, and I walk toward him. "Here, let me show you the ropes before Jen gets here to relieve me."

The shift goes by slowly. For a Sunday night, not much is going on. I had a couple of tables earlier, but now I sit, looking at the moon reflecting on the water as nightfall begins. This place is open every weekday until 10 p.m. and closes at midnight on the weekends. It's the perfect gig to keep me busy this summer before

I can decide what comes next.

I've been avoiding thoughts of home. My parents' home. I managed to clean out the lake house, but the house in the city still waits for me. Just the thought of sorting through their belongings is enough to throw me into a full-blown panic attack, so I decide to wait until after summer. When I go back, I'll also have to place their headstones at their final resting place. At least by the time I return to school for my final year before graduation, I'll have that behind me. The future may be unknown, but the path forward will finally be clear from the loose ends that tie me to that horrific time. A fresh slate, if you will.

I hear someone come up to sit beside me. "Here," Gage's replacement tonight says, "it's almost time to close. I thought you might like to split this beer with me." Jen pours a beer into two glasses and sets one down before me. "Do you like beer? I hope I didn't assume."

I wave it off. "No, I love beer. I always met my dad for oysters on the half shell and a Corona Light, dressed up with salt and lime. It was our thing when he wrapped up his work day in the summer— our Friday happy hour." I take a swig of the beer. I'm not sure why I shared that. It just slipped out, the way some memories do at times when we least expect it.

Jen smiles at me. "Oh, that sounds so nice." She takes a drink. "Is he here or back home this summer?"

My smile fades for a moment. "He's back home," I answer. I don't want to get into it with her because telling a stranger my entire story feels too personal. And technically, I'm not lying. He *is* back home.

Sensing that I don't want to talk anymore, Jen stands up. "Well, we should get the rest of this place closed up." Thirty minutes later, we are walking out, laughing about a story involving the owner's niece, Mandy. "You've got to meet her," Jen states. "She's a hoot."

I walk to my car, opening the door with the key fob. "Can't wait," I retort, sliding into the seat and starting the engine. The ride home is quiet. There is not much traffic on the dark country roads on a Sunday night. Everything is closed. Even the gas station on the way home is closed, as I glance down at the check engine light that should come on soon. I pull into the driveway, unlock the door, and step into the stillness of the house. It feels odd to be here. I drop my things on the table and strip down as I head to the bedroom. By the time I reach the bed, I'm already in a tank and sleep shorts. I pull back the duvet and climb in, letting the silence settle around me.

I don't have anywhere to be tomorrow, so I don't bother to set the alarm. I'm just winging it every day, hoping that, eventually, I'll stop feeling dead inside. But most of all, hoping that one morning, I'll wake up and actually feel alive again.

On Monday morning, I decide to go to the recreation center and submit a job application. I pull up to the red building, and before I see them, I hear the sound of kids laughing and screaming.

"Oh, the enjoyment of being young," I mutter. One girl has a clipboard and is marking something in pen, while the other guy has sunscreen in his hand and is spraying the arms of a little girl as she giggles. I enter through the town office building's side door, walking past the police station, which is also housed in this same building.

"That's interesting," I mutter as I walk around the building. "Well, I guess the kids are safe." I see the director of Parks and Rec sitting at her desk, and I rap my knuckles on the door. "Hello." She looks up at me.

"Hi. Are you picking up early?" she asks. "Tasha has the clipboard around the corner." She points to a young teenager, who I guess is Tasha.

I laugh. "No, I'm actually looking to see if you're hiring. I live here in the summer and was looking for some extra work. I'm a college student and do some nannying, too."

She stands. "Oh, I'm sorry, but we usually hire high school students, and most of them have gone through here as kids in the past programs. Others here are volunteers for community hours and are also in high school."

I nod in understanding. "Oh, okay. I just thought I'd ask. Odette mentioned that you might have something."

Her eyes light up. "Odette. Love her and her pancakes."

I can't help but smile. "I know, right? Me, too. She's been a family friend for years. She and my mom were close."

Deb comes closer. Her eyes squint in confusion, obviously trying to place me. "My mom was..."

She doesn't let me finish. "Raquel Kennedy. She was your mom." It's not a question.

I nod. "Yes."

"I am so sorry for your loss and the community's. She gave so much of her time volunteering at the library for the kids' programs, too."

I smile weakly. "Yeah, Penny mentioned that they were thinking of nominating her for the Volunteer of the Year award to acknowledge her for her lifelong commitment to the Friends of the Library organization."

She brings her hands to her chest, crossing them over her heart. "Such a kind soul."

I avert her hard stare and feel my throat tighten. Sensing how much I dislike the uncomfortable feeling, Deb moves me along and steers me toward the bulletin board. "I just wanted to show you this." She points to an index card hanging from the bulletin board by a pushpin. "We have this hanging, and it's been up this week. It's for a nannying job. The guy really needs help. Single dad with a cute five-year-old. The mom isn't in the picture, I guess."

Remind me never to let Deb know the rest of my personal history, I think to myself. "Oh," is all that comes out. I'm afraid to ask anything else.

She takes it down and hands it to me. "Here. Give him a call. I know he could most definitely use the help, and you might just be perfect for the job." She winks at me and walks off as I take the card from her, looking at it.

Nanny needed for my five-year-old daughter. Flexible hours are a must. Honest and dependable. Must have reliable transportation. Serious inquiries only. Needed ASAP. Please feel free to text me if you are interested.

It doesn't say how much it pays, but honestly, I'm not in it for the money. What I need isn't just a job, it's something to occupy my time, to quiet the thoughts that keep me up at night, and ease the loneliness I feel at the lake house. This could give me purpose and help someone who clearly needs it.

The number is listed below. It's a Massachusetts number, so maybe they aren't local, or it's probably a cell number like everyone else's. I shrug. Deb has returned to her office. I tuck the card into my jeans pocket. "Thanks, Deb," I call out, waving as I pass. She's on the phone but waves as I open the door, leaving the building.

I leave my car parked at the rec center and walk across the street. It's a short walk from here, and I don't feel like driving just to find another parking spot less than a mile away. I take out the paper and reread it. I am honestly a little excited about the prospect of nannying again. I plug the number into my phone and send out a text message.

> **Me:** Hi. I saw your posting for a nanny at the rec center. I am interested. Is it still available?

As I walk, I check my phone, but there is no response. *He's probably working*, I tell myself, sliding it back into my pocket. I jog across the street, scanning for a place that sells frappes. Ahead, a small crowd is gathered at a to-go counter with about five people in line. A woman strolls past, licking her cone. "Can you believe this is kiddie size?" she tells the man beside her. He's holding a cone with four scoops and carrying a cup in his other hand.

"I love this place," he says, licking the ice cream melting down his fingers. I smile, remembering the first time I came here and made the rookie mistake of ordering a small cone instead of the kiddie cup. Ever since, it's only kiddie size for me all the way. Today, I grab my vanilla frappe and head across the street to a bench in the middle of the town park. As I sit, a notification buzzes on my watch. I pull out my phone and see that my message has finally been answered.

> **Unknown:** Hi. Yes, I am still looking. Have you done any nannying before?

> **Me:** Yes, I have. I read the list of requirements on the card and can meet all of them.

> **Unknown:** Great! My daughter is playing t-ball and has a game Saturday at noon. Can you meet me at the town fields then?

> **Me:** Absolutely.

> **Unknown:** Text me when you get there, and I'll meet you.

> **Me:** Great. See you then.

With that, I pocket my phone and feel a surge of excitement. I'm still smiling when a young man comes over and sits beside me. I look over at him.

"Hi," I say, taking a slurp of my frappe. God, I hope my slurping didn't sound offensive. His lip quirks up. Yep, he definitely noticed the slurping. He has a cup of ice cream with rainbow sprinkles on top.

"Hey. I'm Parker." He gives me a little wave, and I chuckle at the cuteness of his gesture.

"I'm Nadia. Nice to meet you." I tuck a piece of loose hair behind my ear to keep busy.

"Are you from here?" we both say in unison and then laugh.

"You first," he tells me.

I shrug. "Well, I guess both?" I say it as a question, and he tilts his head waiting for clarification. "I come here every summer. We have a lake house that's been in my mom's family for years, and the rest of the time I live in Massachusetts."

He nods in understanding. "Ah, that sounds nice." He takes another spoonful of ice cream. "I'm just here for a couple of weeks. We rented a house on the lake. I'm from upstate New York."

"Oh, that sounds fun. Are you enjoying your time here?" He finishes his ice cream quicker than I'd like him to. He places the empty cup on the bench.

"Yes. Most definitely. It's a cute place, and the lake is immaculate. Really clean. I can see the appeal. I'm here with my family, and my brother's girlfriend came with us. I've felt like a third wheel for a couple of days." His eyes twinkle with amusement.

"That's a terrible situation to be in." I also finish off my frappe.

He tilts his chin up and waves at someone. "Speaking of, there he is with his girlfriend now." I give them a little wave, too, and Parker laughs. "Hey, do you think you'd maybe like to go out sometime this week? I'm only here for a little longer, but hanging out with someone would be nice." He stands and takes our trash.

"Ah, thanks for throwing that for me. And yes, I'd like that."

"What's your number?" he asks, taking his phone out of his pocket. He punches in the number I give him, and a second later, my phone vibrates. "There, now you have my number, Nadia."

I take out my phone and add the contact. "I'll make sure to use it, Parker." He smiles, showing his straight, pearly white teeth, which are only made possible by braces.

"Will do." He runs off, tosses our trash in a bin, and throws his arm around his brother. The girl with them laughs, and they walk off, disappearing into a car and driving away.

I can't wait to tell Savannah. Things just might be looking up for me: a new job, a potential nannying job, and a date with a cute guy. I feel like the universe is sending me good karma. Don't all good things come in threes?

CHAPTER FOURTEEN

NADIA

After a whole week of shifts at the tavern, I sleep in and finally drag myself out of bed mid-morning for a much-needed shower. I was so tired last night that I fell asleep on top of my blankets in a heap of limbs and pillows. But after that deep, uninterrupted sleep, I've got a little pep in my step as I dress with purpose. Parker texted me yesterday to see if I wanted to hang out today, and we said we would confirm the details later. He mentioned going out on the lake near the rental where his family is staying, and there's a cookout, too. He seems like a nice guy, and honestly, I could use the company.

I pour myself a coffee and take it onto the patio. I sit in an oversized Adirondack chair that overlooks the tiny lawn, abutting a sandy patch spreading toward the crystal clear lake. The sky is blue, not a cloud in sight. I hear laughter somewhere coming from the lake, but the view is covered by large maple and oak trees surrounding my property. Little waves ripple from motor boats sounding about, and spacious pontoon boats house families in the distance as they enjoy a leisurely ride along the teardrop-shaped lake.

I pull up my weather app, and it is a lovely day with temperatures hovering in the mid-to-high eighties. I hum in contentment, lifting my face toward the sun and soaking up the vitamin D as a gentle breeze blows my hair back like a nuzzling touch. My phone vibrates with an incoming text, and I turn to grab it off the chair's arm to see who it is.

I smile at the name.

Parker: Good Morning, Nadia.
Are we still on for today?

I bit my lip and can't help the smile that comes to my face.

Me: Yes. What time are you thinking?

I see the bubbles appear, letting me know that he's typing. A minute later, his response comes up.

Parker: How about 1?

I look at the time on my watch now and see that it's almost 10:30. I go through the mental checklist: I have to leave soon to meet the man about the nanny job, then drive to the town fields, where his daughter is playing softball...

I begin typing.

Me: I have to meet someone at the town fields for a potential nanny job. His daughter has a t-ball game. Would you like to meet me, and then we can leave from there?

I'm unsure about letting him know where I live. He seems like a nice guy, but I'm all too aware that things are sometimes not what they appear. Being alone has made me more cautious of my surroundings, and I value my privacy.

> **Parker:** That works. Can we meet you there at 12:30? That gives us time to get back here to meet everyone.

A second text comes back rather quickly.

> **Parker:** Is that enough time for your interview? I can get a ride there, and then can we drive back here together?

I rethink the timeframe and the interview. Would it take more than thirty minutes? What if the job doesn't work out, and it's a quick "no" from me? I figure it out finally, deciding that I doubt that the interview would take longer, and if it did, then I'd arrive a little early. That would give him enough time to tell me about the job, what he needs from me for hours, and what the pay is. I can see his little girl play, too, without meeting her yet. That last part brings a smile to my face.

> **Me:** Perfect! See you then.

I walk toward my closet and dress for the boat ride on the lake, but I also need to dress casually for the interview at the ball field. Looking at my choices, I pull out a cropped, ribbed tank that shows minimal skin, and I pair it with a skort along with my pink and white sneakers. I let my long, dark brown hair down and decide to tame some of the frizz with long curls tethered with glossy hair products that smell fantastic and keep the curls together. I spritz a little perfume that smells like roses from a favorite place on the West Coast of California and grab my tote, filled with sunscreen, a change of clothes, a towel, water, and everything I might need for a lake outing today. Looking at my bag for anything I may have missed, I decide I'm ready.

Shortly after, I arrive at the town fields and see many parents standing around watching little kids run around a small diamond. I find a place to park, grab my tote, and walk toward the chaos. I hear one parent screaming, "Timmy!" who is running the wrong way. A little boy stops, then starts running toward home plate, bypassing third base. Laughter escapes me as he makes it home, and a little girl crushes him in a hug. They are jumping up and down at the run that he undoubtedly will not get, but I don't think they are even keeping score.

"*Cute*," I mouth as I walk by the bleachers, taking out my phone to text the parent I'm meeting today.

Me: Hi. I'm here.

I look around, waiting to see if anyone looks like the person I'm supposed to meet, but no one glances my way. I am a little early, but only by ten minutes. I'm about to pull out my phone to text the Dad again, but then I see a shadow. Someone is standing near me. Before I can turn to look, I hear a voice ask, "Are you the one interested in the nanny position?"

I pocket my phone and simultaneously turn when I'm met with those familiar blue eyes. Oh, God. *No. No. No. No*, I think to myself. His voice is rich and deep, and I feel myself gravitating toward it just to hear him better. He looks at me expectantly, and I almost forgot he asked me a question. I mentally chastise myself. *Get it together, Nadia*. I fail at my attempt at nonchalance.

"Yes, sir. That's me." I immediately want to palm my hand against my face. His lip quirks up briefly, and I almost think I imagined it. He doesn't mention that I've seen him twice now, and one of those times, he called me his sweetheart and felt the outline of his cock when he held me, and neither do I.

"So," he stands beside me, angling his body forward, watching his daughter play, all professional demeanor. I look out onto the field and recognize her—the cute little girl who dropped her crayon.

He doesn't continue talking but fixates all his attention on his daughter. She is up to bat and then hits it off the tee. She throws her bat backward, almost hitting another little girl also in uniform who is oblivious to the game she is supposed to be a part of as she leans over to pick a dandelion from the grass. His daughter runs toward first base. Wow, she is a fast little thing. The ball goes out between second and third base and rolls past a kid as he takes off to retrieve the ball. She comes flying past second base, her little braids flapping in the wind as she continues running toward third base.

The ball is thrown to third base, but the girl drops it, and his daughter rounds the base, heading toward home plate. The player throws the ball toward home in an attempt to get her out, but it lands flat, between third and home. She scores a home run, and I jump up and down. I'm hollering loudly while fist-pumping the air when I suddenly realize I was too caught up in the game. That is when I feel him before I see him staring at me. He's not smiling at me, but he's not scowling either. I'll take that as my own personal win here. I raise my shoulder, shrugging.

"What can I say? I love a good game." His eyes are alight with humor as he looks toward his daughter, placing his hands around his mouth.

He shouts, "Way to go, Catalina!" His voice rises above the hoots and hollers. There's that voice again, the accent that sends shivers down my spine.

The feeling is quickly doused when a woman approaches him and stands there. *Is this the mom?* She places her hand on his shoulder possessively, and he doesn't move his arms entwined across his chest. "She's a natural, Manny," she purrs, and I can't help the snort that leaves my mouth. His head turns slightly my way. He doesn't engage her in conversation or respond to her comments. In fact, he just ignores her. I stand there awkwardly, wondering whether I should introduce myself or walk off. Feeling like an interloper, I lift my hand to get his attention and let him know I can meet him later if now is not a good time. However, before I get a chance, he tells the woman he needs privacy. She looks at me, her eyes narrowing, but when she glances up at him, that hostile look is gone, replaced with understanding as she nods.

"Of course, Manny. Call me when you get a chance, okay?" She runs her nail down his arm in a show of possession, and I roll my eyes. His gaze never leaves me, and he sees it all. I immediately regret it when his features harden. It is juvenile, and I hope I didn't ruin my chances of getting the job. Why do I even care? I bite the inside of my cheek, wondering if I should bail. He must sense my indecision.

He extends his hand. "I'm Manuel Torres, and that," he points, "is my daughter Catalina." He gestures to the little girl dancing, still high on her victory. I meet his extended hand in greeting.

"It's nice to meet you. I'm Nadia Kennedy." His grip tightens around mine, and I feel the roughness of his hands, the calluses of which I wonder come from manual labor. When I saw him, I suspected his muscles were those honed from hard work, not the gym. Well, maybe he does work out, too, but the man can sure fill out a shirt. I should not be checking him out that way. I need to keep my cool and act professional. That lady who came up to him may have been hitting on him, but I will be working for him, and I can't engage in these thoughts if I do. "Thanks for meeting me. I saw the ad at the town recreational department, and they told me you needed help with your daughter, Catalina. What hours do you need from me to help you?"

I see him relax when I ask him job-related questions, and he delves into the job details. I nod. "I can totally do that," I agree willingly. "I also work at the Big Lake Tavern in town, waitressing, but I can definitely work around your schedule. My hours there are pretty flexible, too." His shoulders slump almost as if a weight has lifted. "I'm only here for the summer, though." I lift my hand up. "I want to clarify that because I will leave and return to school in August." From what I heard from Deb at the rec center, I know he is a single dad.

"That's perfect," he quickly replies, unfazed by my concern. "I just need help during the summertime. The next couple of months, really," he clarifies. "The rec department doesn't take her age until next year, which is a temporary issue." He moves his hand back and forth. "Once she's back in school in the fall, I won't have this problem moving forward."

"Great, so do I have the job?" I ask.

He quirks his head at me like he's trying to figure out a puzzle. "Aren't you going to ask about the pay before you accept?" He eyes me suspiciously. I smack my forehead with my palm.

"Sorry, yes. How much does it pay? I was so excited about getting a job that I forgot to ask that." I don't need to tell him that I have enough money and that this is about me occupying my time so that I can forget about my present situation.

His lip quirks up in an almost laugh. "How does fifteen an hour sound?"

He seems to wait, probably expecting me to negotiate. I know I could ask for more money, but I want to do this, and he genuinely needs the help, so I accept with no counteroffer.

"Sounds good," I tell him, and I smile. He seems pleased by this and goes over the days and times he needs. It's pretty much full-time. He also asked if I would be available to drop off or pick up on the weekend if he gets held up on a project. I agree with all of it.

"Do you smoke or drink?" he asks out of the blue.

"Um. I don't smoke, and I do have an occasional drink." I can tell from his protective stance that this man has some boundaries in his life that he won't let someone cross, and I can't help but feel there is more to this line of questioning, but I don't ask, or maybe I don't want to know.

He nods. "I just don't want that around my daughter." He hesitates before going on. "Her mother had a problem, and I don't want her in that situation. I'm sorry, I should have asked that before." And there it is. I'm glad he told me. It helped me understand his situation and that of his daughter.

I lift my hand up. "No, I get it. That won't be a problem."

He exhales. "Good."

I see that girl still staring at me, and I notice that the game is finishing. He looks over his back toward the field. "So, can you start Monday?" I nod eagerly.

"Yes, that's perfect. Text me the address." He is just about to ask me something else when I feel someone come up behind me.

"Hey, Nadia. I just wanted to let you know I'm here to pick you up. I'll wait over there." He points to the bleachers across the field and walks away. I turn back to look at Manuel, but he isn't looking at me. He's looking at the retreating man who has just arrived to pick me up.

His gaze turns back to me. "Oh, and another thing. I don't want any boyfriends at the house. You come alone and in your car. You said you had reliable transportation?"

My mouth drops open. "I would never do that," I tell him, mostly just shocked at the question.

"I just have to make sure." His voice trails off as he turns, looking at his daughter. "It wouldn't be the first time," he says as he walks away. "See you Monday." I stand there, dumbfounded, watching him walk away. I notice more than I'd like about the man who will be my future employer. Most notably, his tanned legs that bulk out from his fitted shorts that cup his tight…

I catch that woman watching me, eyes flicking between us, as she lifts a curious brow. She mouths, *Game on.* That's it. I turn abruptly and jog to Parker, rising from the bleachers and walking my way, oblivious to my conflicting thoughts.

Parker walks beside me. "So, did you get the job?" He nudges me, and I look up and smile at his playfulness.

"Yes, " I reply proudly.

"That's great," he remarks. He looks back. "Is that your new boss?" He tips his chin up toward Manny, who is now walking away with his little girl, hand in hand, speaking animatedly to her father while he carries her hot pink, glittery bag.

"Yep," I say as I look back at him. Our eyes lock, his gaze piercing, leaving mine just as quickly and sliding toward Parker. I turn back, forward-facing.

"Interesting," is all Parker says.

"Indeed," I retort, as we reach the car and drive off.

CHAPTER
FIFTEEN

MANNY

I knew it was her before I approached the woman who haunts my dreams and recently made me shower for about ten minutes longer. Why is the world trying to punish me? Who did I piss off so royally that out of the few women who applied for the job, she would be the one to have checked off all the boxes for the nanny position and for me, too? She arrived ten minutes early, and it gave me the opportunity to watch her. I wasn't sure it was going to be her, but what are the chances? I'd say one hundred percent when I see her take out her phone, send a text message, and look around. A few seconds later, it comes through my phone, letting me know she arrived. I'm impressed. Punctuality turns me on. The thought almost makes me laugh. So much has changed since short skirts and toned legs turned me on. Now it's being on time. This woman meets both criteria. My sunglasses allow me to shield my eyes from being caught checking her out.

It also helps to mask my disgust at the shameless women who hit on me in front of their kids. A prime example is Sylvie, the crazy divorcée who has been staring at me for the past half hour. I'd like to avoid her at all costs. I heard from Luc's wife, Tessa, that she is very interested in me. Apparently, she cuts her hair, and being a small town, everyone is into everyone's business here. Although my divorce was finalized a year ago, it had been over for some time before that. My girlfriend at the time had been on birth control, but somehow she ended up pregnant. There was no point in pointing fingers or finding fault. We just accepted it, and I was fully present. I married and loved her even when it wasn't enough to make her happy. I didn't realize that she was taking prescription drugs and had become dependent on them. She had a shitty home life with an absent father and a self-absorbed mother who apparently taught her how *not* to be a good mother. She never had a chance.

I tried repeatedly, but she played the victim instead of helping me care for Catalina. I figure I was already doing so much of this parenting on my own that I could do it solo. I gave her an ultimatum: get help, see someone to discuss your mental health, and then, after you take care of yourself, we can work on us. Perhaps a rehabilitation program could help her get better, and then she could be a better mom to Catalina and my partner in this marriage, but she refused everything. All of it. Now, she is in rehab set by her drug court program with supervised visitation rights pending her therapist's approval and a clean track record. She tried to call me, but I couldn't even talk to her. I was so angry about her last shenanigans. I won't let her hurt Catalina.

I watch this woman, whom I've run into a couple of times now, and it scares me more than anything because I don't want to feel this way—to trust someone again, and be let down because it isn't just me now. I have a daughter to think about, and I don't want to subject her to yet another heartache—getting used to someone for a second time just to have them leave again, just like her mother did.

Before I realize it, I am walking toward her. I see her tense and still. I wonder what she is thinking. What will she think when she realizes it's me? She probably thinks I'm an asshole, and I haven't given her any reason to believe otherwise. Before I freak her out any further, I clear my throat and ask, "Are you the one interested in the nanny position?" I try to be cool, calm, and professional, and I hope it comes out that way because this woman makes me anything but those things I am attempting to convey.

She opens her mouth, stunned, but nothing comes out. I wait patiently for her to answer, fighting the urge to laugh, until she snaps out of it and says, "Yes, sir." I can't help the small smile that graces my lip as I attempt to suppress most of it so that just a tiny bit of my lip curls. It could be curling from disgust, not lust. That is a more accurate feeling for that unexpected comment. I inwardly groan at the thought of her calling me sir as I bend her over the kitchen table, pressing her face into the polished wood and entering her in one thrust from behind. I turn away, noticing that Catalina is up at bat, and I focus my attention on her and not my cock, which is already semi-hard, and increasing at the thought of getting some action. Nope, I can't have that, so I glance at Sylvie, and it starts to go down immediately, thank God. Her head straightens, noticing that I look her way, and I hope that doesn't give her the wrong idea.

Catalina gets a hit off the tee, and I see her take off like her ass is on fire. Suddenly, the woman beside me jumps in excitement at my little girl's run and claps for her so much that it makes me almost laugh. I briefly catch a glimpse of what my life would be like to have a partner present, watching her daughter's game and cheering for her. I cup my hands together for amplification. "Way to go, Catalina!" I scream. Clapping loudly, I find myself smiling, but it is short-lived as a woman approaches me and stands there. I spare a glance at the new nanny, and I can tell she is wondering if this is Catalina's mom. Sylvie places her hand on my shoulder possessively, and I fight the urge to remove her arm from my shoulder.

"She's a natural, Manny," she purrs. I hear the woman scoff beside me, and I glance at her out of the corner of my eye. I say nothing, silently wishing Sylvie to leave, but she doesn't. We just stand there in silence, the vibe becoming increasingly awkward. I decide to end this, telling Sylvie that we need privacy. She looks at me, her eyes caked with too much makeup—attempting to cover up her age—narrowing at the woman standing next to me, but when she glances up at me, that hostile look is gone, replaced with understanding as she nods.

"Of course, Manny. Call me when you get a chance, okay?" She runs her nail down my arm, trying to mark her territory, and I see her roll her eyes. My gaze never leaves hers, and Sylvie sees it all. My features harden at their juvenile behavior. I hate these games, but Sylvie means nothing to me. I can see her look around, wondering if she should bail, but I can't have that.

I extend my hand. "I'm Manuel Torres, and that is my daughter Catalina." She turns at my gesture to the little girl dancing, still high on her victory.

"It's nice to meet you. I'm Nadia Kennedy." My grip tightens around her small, soft hand. She's delicate, my hand engulfing hers. I don't want to let her go, as I reluctantly try to remain cool and unaffected. She licks her lips, and I track the movement of her tongue. Thankfully, she can't tell the shift beneath my calm exterior, my expression unchanged, even though my heart rate picks up from her touch.

"Thanks for meeting me," she starts. "I saw the ad at the town recreation department, and they told me you needed help with your daughter, Catalina. What hours do you need me to help you?"

Right, I mentally chastise myself. We are here to talk about the job. She's not here to see my daughter play in a t-ball game. It is merely convenient to meet up here. I slip into responsible dad mode, hoping she proves what I already think I know, so I review the job details, including the hours needed, times, expectations, and anything else I can think of.

"I can totally do that," she agrees willingly, and I feel an invisible weight lift from my shoulders. I imagine all those little pocket squares of underwear in my drawer and cringe at the thought of Amá still folding my underwear, or calzoncillos, as she calls them in Spanish. I shudder at the thought. She let me know that she works at the place I saw her when I bumped into her at the bar—the Big Lake Tavern. So she waitresses there, too, huh? Interesting.

I make a mental note. "I'm only here for the summer, though," she says. "I want to clarify that because I will be leaving in August, and I know you are a single dad. Well, from what I heard from Deb at the rec center." My head snaps in her direction, and I don't think she realizes that she said that last part out loud.

"That's perfect," I reply almost too quickly. I fight the urge to tell her that Debbie has a fucking big mouth, but so far, Nadia seems like a good fit, so I don't want to scare her off with my mood swings. I'm tired, I'm jaded, and most of all, this woman makes me feel like she gets me. I don't want for someone to get me because I can't get distracted. So I force myself to believe that it has nothing to do with her and all to do with my ex and her rehab program and how I need this to work out for the next two months. Two months and then she can leave, so I tell her that.

"I just need help during the next couple of summer months. The rec department doesn't take her age until next year, which is a temporary issue." I move my hand back and forth, feeling restless for some reason. "Once she's back in school in the fall, I won't have this problem moving forward."

"Great, so do I have the job?" she asks excitedly.

Something seems off with her. She didn't even ask about the pay. That's usually everyone's first question, but not hers. I can't put my finger on it. She immediately accepts the first amount I offered her, too—no counteroffer. I was waiting for it, and nothing. Nada. I feel like I am forgetting something vital, and then it hits me. I almost panic at the thought. I should have led with this. "Do you smoke or drink?" I know it sounds so out of the blue, but I hope she answers correctly. Otherwise, this meeting is all for nothing.

"Um. I don't smoke, but I do have an occasional drink." I nod. I was almost relieved with her answer, and figured I should at least try to explain the reason for my concern.

"I just don't want that around my daughter," I say rather brashly. Her nose crinkles slightly, and I hope I didn't offend her. I hesitate before continuing and opt for honesty. She'll need to know anyway if my ex comes for supervised visitation, although I doubt it would be during these two months she's around. But just in case, I continue to explain. "Her mother had a problem with—" My hand comes to my chin, rubbing at my facial hair. "And I don't want her in that situation. I'm sorry, I should have asked that before." And there it is. It's out in the open, and I hope she doesn't tell anyone else about my business.

She sets my mind at ease. "No, I get it." She raises her hand as if trying to calm an angry guard dog. "That won't be a problem."

I exhale, relieved. "Good." I notice her biting the side of her lip and try to ignore it. My eyes snap back up to hers, immediately cutting off any more thoughts I shouldn't be having about my nanny—I mean, Catalina's nanny. Who hasn't even started yet. "So, can you start Monday?" I ask. My mind feels like I'm giving it whiplash with my thoughts all over the place, in contrast to what my face gives off.

She nods eagerly. "Yes, that's perfect. Text me the address."

I'm just about to ask her where she lives and if it's close by— maybe she needs a ride—but we are interrupted by a man.

"Hey, Nadia. I just wanted to let you know I'm here to pick you up. I'll wait over there." He points to the bleachers across the field and walks away. I watch him go, then turn back to Nadia.

My cheeks feel hot at the thought of wanting to offer her a ride home, being vulnerable from the attraction I'm fighting for her, and it being for nothing because she probably has a boyfriend. Of course, she does. She's young and beautiful and does not have the problems that I come with.

I don't know why I snap at her, but I can't stop. "Oh, and another thing. I don't want any boyfriends at the house. You come alone and in your car. You said you had reliable transportation?"

I see her mouth drop open, and I know that I'm being an asshole, making assumptions. She looks stricken by my comments, and I wouldn't blame her if she just said to forget it. It's not worth putting up with my crap. "I would never do that," she tells me.

"I just have to make sure." I give her my bullshit answer, and my voice trails off as I turn, looking at my daughter, and continue walking that way. "Besides, it wouldn't be the first time," I say, walking away. "See you Monday." I know she continues to stand there watching me, and I hate myself a little more for treating her that way. But most of all, I hate how I want to keep her for myself.

CHAPTER
SIXTEEN

NADIA

W e pull into the driveway of the vacation rental Parker and his family have been staying at on the lake. Voices carry on the breeze, as does the smell of something grilled. If I had to bottle the smells and sounds of summer, it would be this moment.

He grabs my hand, takes my bag from my shoulder, and walks me around the back, wraparound porch. My sneakers echo against the sound of wooden planks, the noise alerting the two people he was with at the park when we met for ice cream that we have arrived. Shortly, his brother and his girlfriend walk up to us.

"Hey, I was wondering when you were going to show up," his brother says, hitting Parker on the shoulder playfully.

"Hey, Parker," the woman near his brother waves. She extends her hand to shake mine, beginning polite introductions. "I'm Jasmine. Welcome." She smiles at me.

"Hi," I reply, matching her smile. "It's Nadia. Nice to meet you, and thanks." I turn to his brother, and he shakes my hand as well.

"Hadley." His hand is soft and smooth, unlike Manny's callused hand. I remember the feeling of Parker's hand as he grabbed my hand and walked me back here. It was also smooth.

The door opens as a man and woman, both middle-aged, presumably Parker's parents, walk out of the house carrying drinks and more food for the table. The woman asks the man if there is enough food when she spots us and walks over. "Hi," she says as she places a bowl of potato salad on the table. "I'm Marlene, Parker's mom, and that's my husband, Bob." She points toward the man now operating the grill, and he extends his spatula in the air in greeting.

"Nice to meet you. Welcome," he speaks loudly over the sound of the lake activity before returning his attention to the food.

"So what do you all have planned for today?" she asks, setting utensils down along with napkins and wooden disposable plates to eat from.

Parker shrugs. "Not sure yet. We will play it by ear, but I think we'll take the pontoon boat out and cruise around the lake." Parker looks at me, and I shrug.

"That sounds good to me. I'm game for whatever."

Jasmine and Hadley also say the same thing. "I like to go swimming off the boat, too," Jasmine says as she looks at me. "Did you bring a swimsuit, Nadia?" she asks.

"I came over-prepared for everything, and that," I point toward my bag, "holds whatever I need."

Parker laughs. "I bet it does. It weighed about one metric ton."

I hit his arm. "Oh, stop, it wasn't that heavy," I say. "In my defense, I didn't want to assume and brought my own towel and sunscreen, too. See?" I stick my tongue out at Parker. "Very prepared."

Parker raises his hands against his torso. "Okay, yes, totally prepared," he mimics.

"Food's ready," Bob announces loudly. Parker's mother goes over to grab the tray of food covered in aluminum foil.

Bob is cleaning the grill and shutting things off when Marlene hands me a plate. "Guests first," she says. "There are some drinks on that table." She points to another table under the covered portion of the deck, which features an assortment of glass jugs with spouts. "We have lemonade and iced tea, along with an ice chest of seltzer water alongside it."

Parker stands up. "What do you want?" he asks, walking backward toward the beverages.

"I'll take an iced tea," I tell him. He points at his brother, who asks Jasmine if she needs anything. He just gives a thumbs up, and Parker turns around and grabs our drinks. He jogs back with a seltzer water can and my iced tea in a mason jar. I notice it even has a lemon twist in it. "Thanks," I tell him as he places the drink on my plate.

I scoop some potato salad, grab a hamburger and hot dog, and a spoonful of fruit. I rub my hands together in excitement. I haven't had a home-cooked meal in a while. I am about ready to tear this shit up. I watch Parker take a bite of his burger, and half of it is gone. My eyes widen, and a giggle escapes my lips as I notice his plate is loaded up with a couple of items of each, as is his brother's. When I look over to Jasmine's plate, she is eyeing my mine and watching me eat. I look at my plate and then at hers. She has a salad, which I passed on, and a hamburger patty without the bread on the side. A small scoop of fruit is also placed there, but not much.

I don't know what to say, but I can't help but feel a little self-conscious. Is she judging me? Her almond-shaped brown eyes assess me, but not maliciously. She speaks before I can ask, pointing at my food. "I wish I could eat all that. Sorry if I was staring." Her boyfriend pats her hand reassuringly. I still don't understand.

"I don't eat like this much," I tell her.

"Pfft, I would if I could. I'm just jealous," she says, smiling kindly.

Parker leans over to explain, "Jasmine has Type 1 diabetes." He looks over at her, lifting his chin.

"Oh. Since when?"

She takes a bite of her fruit. "Since I was like, five, I think. It was a scary time for my parents, I guess. I can't say I remember it much, just the feeling of being around strangers." Her boyfriend kisses her on the top of her head.

"That's why Jasmine here is going to be a doctor. To help other kids with Type 1 diabetes. Right, babe?" Hadley states proudly.

"Wow, I am utterly in awe of you. Are you applying to medical school soon?" I ask now, interested.

She beams. "I'm in medical school now at Dartmouth," she replies proudly. I pick up my napkin and dab at the area of mustard I can feel smeared on my cheek.

"That is such an accomplishment."

She looks down at her salad, smiling bashfully. "Thanks." She continues eating her food, and we all pass the time chatting.

Hadley and Parker's parents went inside the house to let the "kids," as they called us, eat and enjoy ourselves.

Once we finish eating, we clean up the mess and gather our belongings. I grab my bag to change into my bathing suit. "Here," Parker says, opening the back door. "I'll take you to the bathroom so you can change." He leads me down the hall. I look around and notice that the house is enormous. It is a lot bigger than it looks when you drive up. He points to the door at the end. "You can change here, and then just meet me out in the kitchen when you're ready. I will get us some beverages for the cruise around the lake on the boat." He winks as he walks away toward the voices coming from the kitchen. I walk in, close the bathroom door, and place my bag on the vanity.

I wasn't sure what to bring, so I opted for a more conservative approach. I grabbed the criss-cross pattern of cobalt blue and a vivid green color. The top is a sports bra fit to accompany the high-rise bottoms. I have a beach-white knit cover-up that I put on to walk out in, along with some flip-flops. I throw my hair into a high ponytail, grab my lip gloss, and apply one coat. Checking myself out in the mirror, I look over my shoulder. Satisfied with my appearance, I walk out toward the kitchen and see Parker placing two four-packs of beer in the small Yeti cooler.

He looks up at me. "Did you want me to make you a drink, or did you want wine, or..." He looks around.

I smile at his thoughtfulness. "I'm good with beer."

His eyebrow lifts. "You sure? I have some wine, and I am making

Jasmine a drink." I notice he has a little decorative sippy cup to which he adds lime seltzer and one shot of Hendrick's gin. He looks at me as he stirs it. "It's something she can have without all the sugar," he explains, and I nod in understanding.

"Gotcha." I point at the beer. "What kind did you get?" I ask, truly curious. "I love a good IPA or sour."

He laughs. "Good to know." He stirs the drink and closes the cap, placing a little straw in the holder. He lifts up the beer. "This one is from a local brewery in Maine. It's a hazy IPA."

I nod. "I like that one, but it's around 7% alcohol," I mention.

He nods. "Yeah, we only take two four-packs on the boat when we cruise around. We can drink more when we get back if you want."

"Sure, but I still have to drive home, too." I remind him.

He extends his hand for me to take. "Come on, let's go."

Hours go by, and we're still out on the pontoon boat, soaking up the sunrays, and breathing in the fresh lake air. My laugh comes easily as I enjoy the company of Parker, Jasmine, and Hadley. I've only had one beer, so I decide to take a swim. I peel off my swimsuit cover and toss my sunglasses beside it, then climb up onto the seat. I stand and spring off the side of the boat and into the lake. Even though the temperature outside is in the high eighties today, the lake water is cool against my warm skin. I'm bobbing in the water, pushing the hair strands away from my face that spring loose from my ponytail. As I tread water, I spit a little water out, tilting my head back and basking in this perfect moment. Parker is next to join me. I see one leg extend out as he goes under in a half-dive. I hear the splash first and then see him swimming in my direction. He pops up right before me, smiling, and I can't help but smile back. I've had the best day.

"I'm super bummed that you're leaving soon," I tell him. He comes closer to me and puts his arms around my waist, pulling me to him in a hug.

"Why is that, Nadia?" he asks, his smirk on full display. "Are you going to miss me?"

I throw an arm around him. "I'm definitely going to miss you, Parker," I tell him truthfully. The look I have for him is one of love, like if I had a brother, it would be him. I'd wish it was him.

"You know," he says, rolling his eyes. "There is this thing called a phone. You can call me anytime. I'm hoping we can stay in touch. We both go to school in the same state, you know."

I look into his eyes and see the sincerity there. "I'd really like that, Parker."

He nods, his demeanor turning serious. "Me, too." We are interrupted by his brother, Hadley.

"Hey, you two. We should probably head back soon. Are we still going out, Parker?" he asks.

Parker looks toward me. "You feel like going out, Nadia?"

I swim toward the boat, and he follows. I lift myself and climb up the stairs. Hadley is there to give me a hand climbing up, and Parker follows me. I grab my towel, which was left on the seat, and dry off. Parker approaches me, toweling off his hair and drying his chest. He looks at me expectantly, still waiting for my answer.

I shrug. "Sure, why not?"

He clasps his hands. "She's in!" he shouts to Jasmine and Hadley as he drives us back to the dock. I hear a hoot and a holler follow.

Jasmine brings her cup up in salute. "Yes, girl," she says. "It's gonna be hella fun."

Parker and I sit side by side as he throws his arm around me, making me laugh about the plans for tonight. For once, I feel like I catch a glimpse of the girl I was before my life changed after my twenty-first birthday, and I've missed her.

CHAPTER
SEVENTEEN

NADIA

I open my eyes in search of my phone. I can hear it, but I can't see it. My eyelids feel like they're stuck together. I sit up and roll over, flipping the covers around until I see it peeking out under a pillow. "There you are, you little fucker." I grab it and groan at the red battery line.

I see that Boss Daddy has sent me a message. I giggle.

> **Boss Daddy:** I wanted to know if you could stop by today so I can show you around the house and officially meet Catalina before tomorrow.

He sent that two hours ago, but I reply as if he just sent it.

> **Me:** Sorry. I was busy earlier and just got your message. Sure, what time?

I don't need to tell him I was asleep because I stayed out late. I remember reliving the events from last night after we left Parker's lake house rental. While I didn't feel the sparks fly when he kissed me goodnight, I had a good time with him, and I think we could be friends. His family is lovely, and I really enjoyed talking to Jasmine. She's incredibly smart and is genuinely a good person all around. They all are. I'm interrupted by my thoughts when Manuel replies to my text.

> **Boss Daddy:** I'm sorry for reaching out at the last minute. I should have thought of it the day before. Is 3 p.m. okay?

I look at my bedside clock, and it gives me two hours to get ready and be there.

> **Me:** Sure. I'll be there. See you soon.

I scroll up and see the message he sent after I accepted the job, which included the address and time for Monday. I plug it into my Apple Maps and know it will take about ten minutes to arrive. It looks like he lives near the center of town.

Sweet. I jump out of bed, pulling the duvet cover over and tucking it in. I put my phone on the charger and head for a shower. I grab a racerback athletic two-piece outfit to wear. It looks like a dress with a slit up the side, but it has shorts on the bottom. I love these outfits because they are practical and fun. It's an olive color that I pair with some sneakers. I look at myself in the mirror and debate whether to wear makeup, but decide to go light since I am just going over to meet Catalina. I still have to grab something to eat, and blow-drying my hair will take forever. I place some firm-holding hair products in and plait it. I twist the braid into a bun so it's out of my face. I grab my pearl earrings from the set my mother gave me and put on my Apple Watch. I look at myself in the long mirror, twisting sideways, kicking my foot up. Perfect.

I open the glass lid on the two remaining scones I bought from the bakery the other day. I take a blueberry one and plate it. I grabbed one of my mom's favorite mugs, which had the names of banned books. *"Lady Chatterley's Lover,"* I read aloud, laughing. I think that one is in the bookcase in the sunroom. I grab a tea bag of Earl Grey and pour hot water from the jug dispenser on the side of the kitchen pantry. Then, I begin to froth some sweet vanilla cream oat milk. I place my breakfast on the kitchen island, sit down, and grab my iPad from the counter, where I left it yesterday, to do my Wordle for the day until I have to go.

Ten minutes later, I'm still driving. "Where the hell is his house?" I mutter, circling the center of town. Of course, it's a one-way street, so every missed turn sends me back through the roundabout. Then I spot a white truck. "Shit, there it is." I take the second exit this time and stop at the stop sign. The GPS was telling me to go through this street, but there is no entrance there, or maybe there was at one point, and it didn't update. Alas, technology. I debate whether to park in his driveway or on one of the streets, but decide to pull up next to his work truck, with his company name displayed on a decal on the side doors. I look at it like I did that day at the diner.

I close the car door and walk on the pavers that lead to his well-maintained lawn, which has pretty decorative purple plants along the walkway. The house is immaculate and well-maintained. It's a small cape with white paint and black shutters, except for the door. It's yellow, which seems odd when I imagine this man painting it a bright sunny yellow, so at odds with his demeanor. I knock on the door and wait. I look around at the other houses, which seem to mimic this one. There are also cute plants, nice green grass out front, wreaths on the doors, and welcome mats. I turn back toward the door and knock again. I see movement in the window and walk over to it, where I see a little girl waving at me. I wave back, and a second later, the door opens.

I look, and Catalina is staring up at me. "Are you here to see my dad?" she asks. I smile at her and bend down to talk to her at her level.

"Yes, but I'm actually here to see you." Her eyes widen in surprise.

"Are you a friend of Mommy's?" she asks almost hesitantly, and I don't know how to unpack that question or answer it. She glances backward quickly, and I sense this is a problem for them.

"No. I am your new nanny," I tell her quickly, trying to ease the rising tension. She grabs my hand, almost knocking me off-balance.

"Well, why didn't you say that, silly goose?" she says, pulling me into the house and closing the door behind us. "My daddy said my new nanny was going to be here tomorrow. Are you Ms. Kennedy?" I can't help but laugh.

"Yes, my name is Nadia Kennedy, but you can call me Ms. Nadia, okay?" While Catalina and I are making introductions, I see movement in the hallway. Manuel is walking this way, oblivious to the present company his daughter just invited into their home. I immediately want to say something, but I also want to run outside his door and wait there. I feel like an intruder and am second-guessing myself for allowing his daughter to invite me in. What on earth was I thinking?

He walks toward us, drying his wet hair with a towel and wearing only a pair of jeans. His bare feet peek out from underneath the hem. My gaze roams to the way his thighs fill them out and upward to his muscular torso, which is on full display. When I saw him at the town fields with his daughter, the shirt that previously covered them was pulled taut across those firm pecs, hiding them. They did not do him justice because he appears even bigger now without it. Ink is spread across his torso and down his arms. I imagine myself tracing that tattooed line with my finger, maybe my...

He snaps his head up, sensing he is no longer alone. His eyes meet mine, and then he looks at his daughter accusingly. "Catalina," he draws out her name. "I told you not to answer the door and let anyone in."

She swings back and forth, sticking her pointer finger in the air. "Nope, Dad. You said not to let Victoria's stalker mom into the house."

I turn my head away from her, trying not to laugh, but I fail miserably. Manuel sighs. She takes that as a win.

"This is my new nanny, and she's not a stranger or a stalker. Are you, Ms. Nadia?" She beams at me.

"I am definitely not either of those things, but..." I look at Manuel briefly before continuing. I think your dad was trying to tell you that you shouldn't open the door for anyone unless he tells you to, okay?" She looks at me with clear blue eyes, and I can't help but smile. She nods.

"Okay, Ms. Nadia, I promise," she says. I look back at Manuel, and he is watching our interaction. As if remembering, he is still half undressed. He points to the hallway he just came out of.

"I am going to finish getting dressed." He reaches to scratch behind his neck. And I track his every movement, of the way his pecs ripple with the movement and his bicep bulge as he extends his arm backward. "I'll be right back." I watch his retreating form and can't help but remember the way he stared at me at the diner. It was almost cruel. He seems to have a good relationship with his daughter, which is all that matters. He is just my employer, and I'm not here to pass judgment on anything.

When he returns, he is dressed in a navy, fitting t-shirt and sneakers. I like his shirtless form better with his bare feet peeking from underneath. "Hey, I'm glad you could make it today, and I apologize for the short notice."

I wave it off. "Not a problem. So, what is the schedule like?" I look around the house. "Do you have anything that I need to do?"

He seems to think about it. "Not really. What did you do with the other kids you took care of?" he asks, almost like he has no idea about childcare.

"Have you had a nanny before?" I ask.

He nods. "One, but it didn't work out." He looks at his daughter briefly, and I realize he doesn't want to tell me now, or maybe he can't. I look at Catalina, who watches and listens to everything we say. I decide to change the subject.

"So, Catalina, what do you like to do? Do you have anything that you want to do tomorrow when I come over?" She immediately runs off to her room and brings back a coloring book.

"I like to color and draw. I like playing outside on my swingset and going to the library to get books," she says, smiling her gap-toothed smile at me.

"Oh, that sounds fun. I know everyone at the library, too." I look at Manuel. "Is it okay to leave the house with her, or..." I trail off, watching him frown immediately.

"Please, Dad, can we?" Catalina asks, and I'm wondering if I shouldn't have put him on the spot.

I mouth, "*Sorry,*" and he shrugs.

"Sure, just stay close to her and don't let her out of your sight, please." I gaze at him, puzzled.

"Okay, that's not a problem. I will take care of her."

He wants to say more, but stops. "Catalina, can you please give the adults some privacy to talk?" He points to the table for me to sit, and I pull out a chair and sit as he does the same across from me.

She grabs her coloring book and begins to leave, but Manuel touches her arm and pulls her toward him, stopping her from leaving. "I'll call you in a minute so you can say goodbye to Ms. Nadia and show her your room before she goes. Sound good?" She seems to forget she was being dismissed, nodding excitedly, and then she runs off, shutting her bedroom door behind her. It's evident that Manuel didn't want his daughter to hear whatever he has to tell me, and I can't help but wonder what it is.

Once he hears the click of her door, he turns toward me. His posture is stiff, and his intent is serious. His striking blue eyes are fixed on me, obviously assessing what he should tell me. I inhale slowly, calming my breathing while waiting for him to speak, but he sits leaning a little forward. I want to do the same, but fight the urge to meet his advance and remain perfectly still. He brings his hands up onto the table and laces his fingers together. I want to look at them and see the ink there on his corded forearms up close, but I don't do that either. I don't think I could hide my thoughts from him, and considering what he said about "Victoria's mom, the stalker," I don't want any labels added after mine.

He clears his throat. "I'm only telling you this because it is important and, although personal, it is relevant to the care of my daughter," he begins. "I also trust that you will keep this to yourself. This is a small town, and we like it here. I don't want everyone knowing my business." He waits for me to speak.

"I understand. I won't say anything to anyone." I know this is what he wants to hear, and I mean it. I want him to trust me and feel safe enough to continue with whatever it is he needs to say next.

"I am recently divorced, and my ex-wife, Catalina's mother, is not currently in the picture." I must have a puzzled look on my face because he elaborates. "She had some issues with alcohol and substance abuse, which led to our divorce. I have full custody of our daughter, and she is allowed supervised visitation only, pending her rehabilitation program." His lips purse at the latter part of his explanation. It's almost as if he wants to say more.

"Oh," I answer, now understanding his issue with the questions regarding whether I smoke or drink. She must have seen her mother drunk or impaired on something, and he doesn't want that around his daughter again. "So, will she come over when I am here?"

"No. She..." He trails off, not wanting to or deciding how much to tell me. "She ran into some problems with her mental health and won't be around for a while. She might not be around this summer at all, or if so, maybe toward the end, so it shouldn't be an issue, but I will let you know."

Trying to lighten the somber mood, I joke. "Okay, so no other women should be allowed in the house, like stalker moms." He watches me, not speaking. The silence stretches, and I instantly regret the comment. I didn't mean anything by it.

He leans forward, and I sit upright, my relaxed back posture going ramrod straight. His gaze sharpens. "I don't allow any women into my house." He leans forward. "Ever. If I fu—take someone to bed," my breath hitches at his catch of the word, and I swear his pupils dilate, his gaze dropping momentarily to my mouth, "it won't be here. So don't let anyone in." He leans back, and now I have a visual of him fucking someone, and I can't get that visual out of my head. His words and actions take me aback, and for unknown reasons, they slightly turn me on.

I gulp, maintaining eye contact because I won't let him get to me. "Got it," is all I can come up with. "No women in the house."

He stands from the table. "Good. I'll get Catalina so you can see her room and tell her goodbye." With that kind of dismissal, I know that I am in deep shit.

CHAPTER
EIGHTEEN

NADIA

I toss and turn all night, and when I wake up, it's to the face of my new employer. I keep hearing that phrase repeating on a loop in my mind. *"If I fuck someone, it won't be here, so don't let anyone in."* The way his upper lip curled slightly when he caught himself had me clenching my core. I immediately replaced it in my head with the word "fuck." I imagine he would have said that if he knew it wouldn't scare me off. I also know that right now, if I push a finger into myself, I would be soaked. I hate that he got to me, and I hate that I am affected by him this much. *It's only for a couple of months*, I keep telling myself. *I can do anything for a couple of months, right?*

I am stuck with this visual of the handsome man who haunted my dreams last night, and I know how undoubtedly fucked I am.

I push the strand of my damp hair against my forehead, which is equally slick. Tossing my hand over my eyes and groaning at the feeling of being left unsatisfied, I throw the covers off, kicking them off with my feet.

I don't waste any time. I get ready quickly—no one to impress here. Not wanting to be late, I brew a quick Nespresso capsule of espresso with a splash of non-dairy milk on top. I don't bother to mix it in. I just pour it into a stainless steel mug as I grab my bag and jump into the car, putting it into reverse and cruising down the road to Manny Torres' house with a million thoughts floating around in my head and not a single one relating to my job as the nanny.

Those thoughts don't stop even as I pull into his driveway. The truck is outside, and I park alongside it, barely giving it a second glance as I grab my things and practically skip to the front door. Before I can even knock, the door swings open, and I'm met with the scowl of the man who performed effortlessly in my dreams with a standing ovation. My ovaries would have been doing cartwheels if it was real, but as I see how he regards me—the permanent scowl of his face—I know that is far from becoming a reality. Besides, he is my employer, and I will be leaving in a couple of months. Nothing could happen between us, and nothing would last even if it did. So, I take his scowl and choose to ignore it.

"Good morning," is all I say as he steps aside and lets me in. I know I'm on time, but I ignore him when he glances at the clock. This is a summer gig to do a little self-discovery before I finish my last year of college, nothing more. I drop my bag on the floor and place my coffee mug on the counter. I look around, but I do not see Catalina.

As if reading my thoughts, Manuel goes to the kitchen, grabs a stainless steel mug from the cabinet, and fills it with black coffee. I notice he doesn't add anything to it. I continue to stay silent, waiting for him to say anything, something that will break the palpable tension. I wonder if this is really worth it, but then I think of what I would be doing otherwise, and I continue to wait for his instructions. He finally speaks and puts me out of my misery.

"Catalina is asleep. She will wake up soon, and then you can make her something to eat. I stocked the refrigerator with her favorite items, so feel free to get yourself acquainted with everything. Just please stay out of my office and bedroom. Everything else is okay." I nod once again. He stays there staring at me, but I still don't comment. He saunters over to me slowly, and I watch him. He's close enough to touch me, but just then, he leans over and grabs his lunch box from behind me as I fight the urge to lean into him.

As he grabs hold of it, he says, "I'll be home at five," before pulling away and picking up his to-go cup on the way out. I hear the door click shut and walk toward the window. The shades are open and the curtains pulled back. I watch him look behind in the rearview mirror as he reverses out of the driveway. As he puts the truck in drive and our eyes lock once again, I watch him pull away, and I don't know what I'm doing.

"What are you looking at?" A little voice startles me, and I jump back, clutching my hand to my chest.

"Oh, gosh, Catalina. You scared me," I tell her breathlessly, and I convince myself that it has nothing to do with her dad.

She laughs. "Sorry to scare you. I heard the door close and knew you would be here already." I regard her and smile brightly. "My daddy wouldn't leave me alone. I was so excited I could barely sleep," she tells me.

I nod in agreement. "I know, I couldn't sleep either," I tell her, but it was for totally different reasons. "Come on, Catalina, let's get some breakfast." I take her little hand and place it in mine as we walk to the kitchen. I open the refrigerator and take a peek. "Wow, your dad wasn't kidding, was he?" The fridge is stocked with fruits and yogurts. There are also several juices and bottled waters. I open the cabinets and see cereals, canned vegetables, and a whole lot of rice. "Oh, I should bring over my rice cooker," I tell Catalina.

She claps her hands. "My papá loves rice, but especially when my abuela makes it." I smile, thinking of Manuel and his mother.

"I bet she's an amazing cook, huh?" I tell her, and she licks her lips.

"I miss her," she says sadly, "but I'm glad you are here with me."

I chuckle. "You know, Catalina, I am glad I'm here, too." I clasp my hands in front of my chest. "Okay, what do you want to eat?"

She looks at me. A sly smile spreads across her face, and I know she's already plotting something I should say no to, but here we are. She takes off running to her room to get dressed.

I don't know how she did it, but here I am with her booster seat in my car heading to Planet Pancakes. With all that food stocked in the fridge, I thought we could have some yogurt parfaits with granola and the local honey I saw on the counter by the coffee maker, but nope. This little girl is very persuasive. So I park the car and walk over to the other side, opening her door. Taking her hand in mine, we walk inside. The cosmic chime echoes through the semi-packed diner. Odette looks up from the register, smiling at me. Then, when she glances down at the little hand I am holding, her smile widens, and she nods. She steps around the counter.

"Well, if it isn't my two favorite girls," she coos, pulling at one of Catalina's little braids.

Catalina, the ever-vocal little girl, places her hand on her hip. "Mrs. Odette, can we please sit on the soft blue couch?" She points toward the back, where the mural of the planets is located on the back wall. "Can we please, please, please?"

Odette bops her on the tip of her nose playfully. "Well, wasn't that a mouthful? Of course you can, kiddo." She grabs two menus and leads us to the back, where Catalina requested to sit. She looks up at me, motioning with her hand that she wants to tell me something, so I lean over slightly.

"My daddy never lets me sit over here," she attempts to whisper, but it comes out as a hushed shout as she drops her cupped hand from her mouth. She fist pumps the air as she catches up to Odette.

I stand back up. "Oh?" is all I say in question as I follow them, and I can't think of why that could be. I mean, I know that these seats aren't the most user-friendly for children, but what is the harm? And then I halt when I see that girl from the park, the one who had her hand down Manuel's chest in a blatant show of intimidation. The pieces start to click together. Maybe this is where they always sit. Maybe Manuel doesn't like to sit here because of them.

Determined not to feel unnerved, I sit on the velvety soft couch, and Catalina sits close to me. Odette leaves our menus and walks off, but I know when she returns, it will be with my usual latte. I do hope she knows what Catalina wants. Catalina hops off the couch and returns with a coloring book and crayons. She sits on the floor near the table, her little legs crossed over one another, humming to herself. I feel their eyes on me and try to avert my gaze anywhere except there.

True to form, Odette returns with my maple sugar oat milk latte in a celestial-looking mug, and Catalina has the cosmic delight, which I know to be a combination of fruit juices topped with an orange slice and maraschino cherries. Catalina giggles with delight and claps her hands as Odette places it in front of her, and I can't help the smile that creeps onto my lips, seeing her sheer delight in something so small. I haven't felt happy in a while. The innocence of this little girl soothes something deep in my soul. She remains happy despite her parents' divorce and her mom's absence. I feel like I could learn a little bit from this youngster.

I bring the hot brew to my lips and take a sip, reveling in the bliss, that is, until I see a pair of purple and hot pink Brooks sneakers in my periphery. I resist the urge to roll my eyes, not wanting to start a conflict with anyone. Taking a slow, steady breath, I place the coffee mug on the table and look up to see the woman from the ball field staring down at me, one hand propped firmly on her hip. She glares at me, and Catalina must sense the awkwardness of her presence because she stops coloring, looking from the woman to me, worry etched on her brow. The woman—I think her name is Sylvie—looks at Catalina with a fake edge of sincerity.

"Cat, is everything okay with this woman? Does your daddy know you're here with her?" I'm about to respond, but she doesn't give me a chance, extending her hand to Catalina. "Do you want me to take you to your daddy, Cat?"

I stand ready to fight this woman off, but Catalina looks at her and replies, "No, thank you, Ms. Sylvie. Ms. Nadia is going to take me home after breakfast." Sylvie just stands there with her mouth open and I watch her try to say something and then stop, until finally she stands taller, pushing her chest out, her boobs lifting higher than they already are.

"But I thought your daddy doesn't allow anyone over to your house?" she huffs in question. Before I know why I said this, it just comes out, my finger pointed in the air like Catalina told me the first day when I went over.

"Nope, he doesn't want Victoria's stalker mom over." I laugh, and Catalina drops her crayon, her eyes widening. I hear a cough, and someone gasps behind the woman who has now gone rigid.

"What did you just say?" She tilts her head, and I know I have said something that I wasn't supposed to because the other two women at the round little bistro table are trying to smother their laughter. One is beet red, choking on a mimosa that went down the wrong way, and the other is handing her a glass of water with her face averted.

I hear a *humph.* Then Sylvie turns around abruptly and heads out of the restaurant. We watch her retreat, and Catalina looks at me, her hand covering her mouth, trying to stifle her giggles. The chime echoes above the door, and I don't have to look to know that she is gone.

"What?" I say, looking at Catalina. "What did I say?"

"That's Victoria's mom!" She bends over sideways, cackling, clutching her belly. I hear a chair scrape against the wooden flooring and see a woman come up to the table, and I don't know what to do. I stand, already thinking I will apologize, but before the words, "I'm so sorry," leave my mouth, I hear laughter from the other woman sitting at the table of three, and she walks over toward us. The woman extends her hand out to me.

"Hi. I am Tessa, Luc's wife. He works with Manny." I shake her hand, not understanding the introductions.

When the other woman doesn't introduce herself, she says, "I just want to say thanks for giving me the best laugh of a lifetime. Sylvie has never been put in her place, and I know you didn't intend to do exactly that, but she needed to hear it because we have been telling her for a while to lay off."

The woman looks over to Catalina, who is pretending not to hear, but I can see her taking everything in. The girl may be young, but she doesn't miss a beat. After they leave, I sit there and hope this doesn't get back to Manuel. I wonder what he would say if it did. *Please don't let me lose my job* are my last thoughts before my gingerbread pancakes come, and I forget all about Sylvie and my big mouth.

CHAPTER
NINETEEN

MANNY

After he got off the phone with his wife, Luc ran over to tell me what happened at the diner this morning. He is crying hysterically with laughter. "I'm telling you guys, my wife said it was epic. She just stomped off and left the restaurant." He slaps his hand on his thigh, still hooting with laughter at my expense.

I groan. "Oh God, I hope she doesn't say anything to me about it." I rub my temples.

"Are you kidding?" Luc throws his arms up in the air briefly before pointing a finger at me. "That girl probably did you a favor. Maybe that woman will finally get it into her head that she is a stage five clinger."

I shake my head. "I don't know why. We were never in a

relationship. I only made out with her once, and I never even slept with her." I don't mention that I might have if I hadn't gotten that phone call from my mom saying that Catalina threw up. I rushed out of the bar so fast that I didn't even say goodbye. My daughter did me a solid without realizing it. I thought that that incident was enough for her to leave me alone, and then, realizing how she was, I just avoided her advances after that. I was lonely and feeling sorry for myself at the time. After a drink, it seemed to intensify those emotions, and I vowed to lay off the alcohol. After my ex had her addictions and I saw what she struggled with, one of us had to remain sober for Catalina, and I was more than willing to take up the role. I was never a big drinker anyway, just a beer or two when I went out with the guys. Since I didn't have help with child care after my divorce and essentially became a single dad overnight, that wasn't too much of a problem anyway.

I should give her a raise. I have been trying to get that woman to back off for months. Maybe this little slip will do it, and she will take the hint because whatever I have said to her and my actions of ignoring her have not worked thus far.

Entering the house seemed quieter now that my mother is gone back home. No one is here to greet me at the door like my mom did when she helped out with my daughter. Once she knew that I had secured a nanny for Catalina, she left that morning. I can't say that I blame her. She raised her kids and has done more to help me than anyone. My father missed her too much. She does so much for him. She even gets his high blood pressure medication out for him with his meals. She doesn't have to do that, but she does it because that is who she is. She is a nurturer, and I am lucky that she instilled that same characteristic into me. I also feel the need to take care of everyone, despite how challenging it can be at times. I don't ever complain. I just do it unless it causes my most precious thing in life—my daughter—distress. I never want to put her through that kind of ordeal again. I pray that my ex gets her shit together for Catalina's sake as well as her own.

I almost think no one is here, except Nadia's car is in the driveway. I search my small cape-style home and don't find anyone.

I head upstairs to remove my work clothes when I see them outside. I stare out the window, watching them draw. Set up with little easels, Nadia shows Catalina how to use watercolors. I see purple spots on the easel and assume she is painting the flowers under the tree. I decide to jump in the shower and change while I can. Five minutes later, I'm down the stairs and opening the back door that leads out onto the little stone area I have set up with outdoor furniture and a fire pit. I walk out in my grey sweats, t-shirt, and sliders when they turn around to see me stride over to where they are cleaning brushes and putting their things away.

"Hey." I look at Nadia and then at my daughter. I stop in my tracks as Nadia gives me a little wave. Dropping to my knees, I open my arms wide. My daughter leaps off her chair and straight into my outstretched arms.

"Papá!" she exclaims excitedly. "I missed you." I smile and kiss her on her cheek.

"I missed you, too, princess." She beams at me, and my heart melts a little. I look over her shoulder, and Nadia is watching us. She quickly averts her eyes back to cleaning up. I clear my throat.

"How was your first day?" I continue to study her, but her eyes don't meet mine.

"Good," she replies noncommittally. We had a good day." She continues to wipe the excess water from the brushes, rolling a paper towel around the bristles, and placing them into a plastic container alongside the other brushes.

"Do anything fun?" I continue the interrogation, but she doesn't take the bait. Catalina, however, doesn't waste any time telling me they went to Planet Pancakes for breakfast. Nadia stiffens as she packs up the watercolors and empties the murky water onto the grass. "Oh," is all I say. Catalina giggles. She cups her hands to hide her words, but it has the opposite effect, amplifying them. We should really work on that.

"We saw Victoria's mom there," she says and glances over to Nadia, making a sorry-not-sorry face. Nadia stands there looking at me, waiting for me to say something. I look at Catalina's hands and frown.

"Sweetie, why don't you go and wash your hands and get ready for dinner?" I say, and she walks off, nodding, but then turns around and runs over to Nadia.

"Thank you, Ms. Nadia. I had a lot of fun today." Nadia grabs onto one of her braids and gives it a little tug.

"Me too, pickles," she replies, and my girl beams. Pickles? I don't get it, but I'll ask later.

She wraps her arms around Nadia's legs in a quick embrace and then darts off, yelling, "See you tomorrow!" I hear the door slam, and then there is silence. Nadia stands there, looking around at the passing cars on the street. I walk a little closer, my hands in my jogger pockets.

"So," I say, and her eyes snap to mine. "I heard what happened today at the diner." I let the words hang there, gauging her reaction. I want to believe it was innocent, but I'm not sure. I saw the looks the women gave each other at the ball field and Nadia's snort when Sylvie made that comment to me. I don't like Sylvie, and what Nadia said didn't bother me at all. But on the drive home, doubt crept in, and I couldn't help but wonder if it was intentional. My ex was extremely jealous and would often cause a scene. The woman was nonstop drama, and I don't want to fall back into that same pattern in any form. While Nadia is technically just our nanny, I don't like this sort of behavior around Catalina. The girl has been through too much already, and I won't let that kind of negativity around us again.

She rubs at the dirt with the toe of her sneaker, deliberately avoiding my gaze. I can't have that. I need to see her face when she tells me because I want the truth, not just her pretty words. So I take a step closer, narrowing the distance between us, but she turns her head away. Gently, I lift my hand to her chin and guide it toward me. She closes her eyes, breathing in deeply, waiting for something. Maybe it's for me to tell her she is fired. I have no idea what she is thinking, and I know I shouldn't be touching her like this, but something about her stance now screams defeat. She seems like her mind is so far away and she just looks so fucking sad. My hand drops to my side, and I place it back into my pocket because I fear I will do something stupid. I'm just about to speak when she beats me to it.

"I'm sorry." She looks up at me. "I didn't know that was her, and I am horrified at my behavior." She shakes her head. "I get nervous, and when I get nervous, I sometimes say something stupid. This case is the perfect example." She covers her face with her hand. "God, I am so embarrassed, and I didn't and wouldn't say anything like that or ruin your chances with her on purpose. I just want you to know that."

I raise my hand to stop her from speaking any further. "First," I lift one finger, "you didn't ruin anything between us. You and I are fine." She looks up at me, and I know that isn't what she meant, but I wanted to clarify that for some reason. God, I am a jackass. Of course, she doesn't think like that. I'm just a single dad. She is in college, for Christ's sake. Backtracking, I attempt to make it better. "You are still our—I mean, Catalina's nanny." I think I grimace at the slip. "Second, I am also not interested in that woman. In fact, I feel like I should buy you dinner for helping me out with that problem. Hopefully, she gets the hint." I see her eyes widen, and then I realize I have no business saying things like that. I counter with, "We sometimes do little cookouts on Fridays. You are invited to hang out and stay to eat with us if you'd like or not..." I look away, but something comes to me about what she said a moment ago.

"I'd like that," she answers without hesitation, surprising me and making me look back at her. She has a smile on her face, and I wonder what her story is. My eyebrows furrow as I stare at her.

"You said something that struck me as odd." Her smile dims, and I hate that I made her lose it.

"What?" she says, truly not understanding, but I know she acted that way for some reason, and I want to know why.

"You said that you got nervous." She swallows. "Why did you get nervous, Nadia?"

"She tried to take Catalina's hand and wanted to take her away from me and take her to you. To your house," she elaborates further. The house I told her no one is welcome in. As I purse my lips at Sylvie's audacity, my mouth forms a thin line. Nadia tries to clarify quickly, "I wasn't going to let her take her anywhere, but the woman was persistent and I just got nervous trying to use humor to deescalate the situation." She throws her hands up in the air. "How was I supposed to know that that was Victoria's mom?" Her voice rises in pitch, her hands land around her waist. His head hangs down in defeat. I bring my hand to my chin. I can't help the laugh that flows out. I drop my hands to my thighs and let out a long laugh. I'm wheezing. Tears spring to my eyes as I cough and try to stop, wiping the tears that pool around the corners.

"Fucking hysterical," I boom and then try to stop, but Nadia is looking at me while I lose my mind, and it must be contagious because she begins to laugh, too. We both stand there eyeing one another, and I break the silence. "I wish I could have seen that, and that woman is batshit crazy in case you can't tell. I never want my daughter to go anywhere with her, so thank you." Nadia nods.

"I wouldn't let Catalina out of my sight. She is my responsibility when I am watching her, so I want you to rest assured that she is safe with me." I smile, knowing that this woman is kind and passionate about taking her role as nanny seriously.

"Thank you, and I can see that. Maybe I should have been clearer with Sylvie, and that's on me." She tries to say something, but I cut her off. "If she says anything about it, I will set her straight, don't worry. The woman is no one to me, and I won't have her treating you poorly. If she says anything to you, especially in front of my daughter, I want you to call me even if I am at work, and I'll handle it, understand?"

"Thanks, Manuel. I don't like how she tries to use a little girl to get to you."

"She's not getting me, Nadia," I tell her, but the silence that follows hangs awkwardly between us.

She picks up the remaining items and heads toward the house. "I'll put these away and see you guys tomorrow at the same time."

"We'll be here," is all I say as I watch her walk away. But I stop her before she opens the door. "Oh, and Nadia?" She turns around to look at me, giving me her full attention. "Call me Manny." She nods, smiling widely, and I don't think I have ever seen anything more beautiful. The sight leaves me wanting more of those smiles, so that I can replace the sadness that usually paints that pretty heart-shaped face. This time, when she turns back to walk away, she leaves, and I hear the start of her car along with a slight squeak of her brakes as she drives off. I stand there, staring at nothing, consumed in my thoughts of a nanny I can't let myself want.

CHAPTER
TWENTY

NADIA

Watching Manny walk toward me in the grey sweatpants that hung low on his prominent hips was like watching my own striptease. Freshly showered, his hair hung in curls framing his beautiful, chiseled face. His bright blue eyes pop, matching the blue t-shirt that clung to his body, like he hadn't entirely wiped off all the water from his shower. I had to avert my gaze to avoid ogling my boss. He is so hot, and I understand the lengths Sylvie went to try to snag his attention. I, however, draw the line at using his kid to get to him. She has no shame in doing something like that. I wonder if he slept with her or gave her reason to act like she does.

He never gave me permission to call him Manny, so I still referred to him as Manuel. I was so excited when he asked me to stay some time for dinner, but I honestly don't know if that is a good idea. Blurring the lines of our professional relationship seems risky. Sure we are both young and single, but there's also the fact that I'll be leaving soon, and besides, he doesn't come off as emotionally available either. As I drive, my phone rings, and I see Savannah's name flashing across the screen.

"Hey, bestie! What's up?" I roll up the window and turn on the air to hear her better.

"Hi, honey! So, what's the plan for the Fourth?" she asks immediately. I hear a honk and wonder where she is. If that is the sound in the background, she must be in the city. Boy, do I miss Boston.

"Are you just getting off from work?" I ask, raising my voice over the excess noise filtering in through her phone.

"Yeah, you?" she replies quickly.

"Yes," I respond without further elaboration. I haven't told her about the nanny job and it being the same guy from the bar who called me his sweetheart in Spanish, but she would definitely get a kick out of hearing about that. Maybe I'll wait to tell her about it when she comes over on the holiday weekend. "Are you still planning on coming up that weekend?" I ask, hoping that she will say yes, so I don't have to be alone for the first time. My parents and I had such a celebration with fireworks on the lake, and we would grill all kinds of things with an American flair of cold sides such as potato salad, deviled eggs, orzo pasta, and homemade sorbet. My mom would use the slushie machine to make a bunch of frozen drinks, and I was looking forward to having some frozen margaritas.

"Hell yeah," she says, breaking me out of my thoughts. "I wouldn't miss it for the world, but I'll probably take Friday off and make it down that night or maybe in the morning. I think the traffic will be bad that day, getting out of the city." I hear her yelling at someone before picking up the phone again. "So, what's new, chickie?" she asks. I want to tell her about Manny, but that will be a longer conversation, so I choose to be brief.

"I got a nanny job, so I started that."

"Wow, that's great!" she exclaims. "So, now you have two jobs?"

"Yep, keeping busy." That's all I say, and then the silence hits. It's like she wants to ask more but doesn't.

"I'm glad, but bitch you better have time for your bestie when I get here." I can hear her attitude and love that she is always there for me, and I'll always be there for her too.

"Of course," I say. "You don't even have to ask," I tell her because it's true. There is nothing I wouldn't do for her. She is my family and the only one I have left.

"Okay, girlie. I will see you next week. Love you."

She laughs, and I reply without thinking about it. "Love you, too, Savannah." She disconnects the call, and I turn up the music in the car. A favorite song of mine comes on, The Killers, "When You Were Young." I lower the window, letting the cool lake air in as I turn up the music and sing along with the lyrics. This is when I am most carefree, and I momentarily forget about the tragic turn of events in my life. As I round the final curve toward the lake house, the song fades out. I pull into the driveway and cut the engine. My phone chimes, and I notice Parker has sent a message. I grab my bag and punch in the code on the front door. Once inside, I disarm the alarm and set my things down on the foyer table. Pulling my phone from my bag, I walk to the kitchen at the back of the house. Opening the fridge, I sigh. "Yogurt and eggs. Great." Sarcasm laces my words as I close the refrigerator door, pondering my options. I don't cook much, and tonight I'm definitely not in the mood for eggs. The phone buzzes again in my hand as I finally check the messages.

Parker: Hey! Want to join us for dinner tonight?

I don't take long contemplating the lack of options for dinner before replying quickly.

Me: What were you thinking?

He answers immediately as if he is waiting for me to respond.

Parker: Nothing fancy. Pizza and beers?

THE CRUELEST TRUTH

"Sweet," I say, even though no one is there to answer or hear me.

> **Me:** Perfect. Where to?

The bubbles appear and then disappear.

> **Parker:** Sorry, we were arguing about Italian versus Greek style pizza and where we want to go.

I make a face. Well, that's an easy one.

> **Parker:** Can you meet us at City Pizzeria on Main Street, or do you want me to pick you up?

I'm already walking out the door.

> **Me:** I'll meet you there. See you in about ten minutes.

> **Parker:** Nice. See you soon.

I pull up ten minutes later and park my car along the common and jog across the street. Through the window I see Parker, Hadley, and Jasmine talking animatedly. And as I approach closer, Jasmine catches sight of me. She points, then waves, drawing Parker's attention. He turns, his smile wide showing his pearly white, straight teeth. I'm suddenly grateful I met him that day at the park. He's a genuinely good guy, and I hope we can remain friends after he leaves next week to head back home to New York. He just doesn't make my heart stutter the same way as Manny does when our eyes meet. I sigh, knowing I have to keep those feelings under wraps.

As I walk into a little pizzeria, the smell of parmesan cheese and garlic assaults my senses, and I inhale deeply. I walk up to where my new friends are sitting and slide into the booth next to Parker. There is a beer waiting for me. The local IPA on tap. "Ah, you shouldn't have." I smile and rub my hands together. "But I'll gladly take it. Yum." I take a long pull from it, and the hazy, citrusy, bitter hops make my mouth water for another swig. So I oblige myself by taking another big drink. I hear Hadley laugh and Jasmine giggle. I can't see them because my face is currently in a twenty-two ounce beer.

"Love me a woman who appreciates a good IPA." Parker winks at me, and I know he didn't really mean it that way, but still, he puts his arms around me and pulls me to him. I lean in, and he kisses the top of my head. It feels more brotherly than romantic. After we peruse the menu and argue about items like pickles or pineapple pizza toppings that should never be on a pizza, we order "Brett's favorite pizza," which has pepperoni, sausage, mozzarella, and dollops of ricotta cheese on top. I lick my lips in anticipation of the tasty treat. It'll be ooey goodness like none other. It's my favorite pizza on the menu, but I don't mention it. I've been coming here since I was a little girl, and I am glad that the owner isn't here tonight, but just a local seasonal worker at the counter. There are no waitresses here; you have to walk up and order, or get your beer at the bar.

The pizza is ready, and Hadley slides out to grab it. There are paper plates and napkins along with it, and the metal plate is already in a box, so if we don't finish it, it can slide straight into the box. I doubt there will be any leftovers with the guys here, but I can also pack away a couple of big slices, too. Hadley drops into his seat, and Parker hands me a slice. I accept it gratefully, biting in before I realize just how hot it is. Steam rises, and I wave a hand in front of my mouth, trying to cool it down between breaths. The cheese makes a little appearance on my chin as I swipe it away.

Jasmine just watches me with amusement. "I think I'll give it a few," she says, grimacing.

I take a sip of beer, swallowing hard before grinning. "Probably a smart move." Across from us, Parker and Hadley are completely unbothered, inhaling their hot as fuck pizza across their singed taste buds.

"So what are your plans for the Fourth?" Parker asks in between bites, wiping his mouth with a napkin.

I shrug non-committedly. "I'm not sure, but my bestie, Savannah, is coming up from Boston and staying with me for the weekend."

"Oh, that's cool," Parker says. "Are your parents doing anything fun with you guys, or are you two just doing your own thing?" The bite of pizza suddenly feels like a rock going down. I know it isn't Parker's fault. We really don't know each other, and it is an innocent question. Still, I reach for my drink, washing down the lump in my throat as I set the slice aside. He senses the shift, his eyes flicking between Hadley, Jasmine, and me. They all go quiet, patiently waiting for my reply. Not wanting to look at Parker, I glance out the window, placing my focus on nothing in particular.

"It's just me," I say quietly, then lift my eyes to meet Parker's. "My parents, they..." I twist my hands together nervously, and Parker reaches out for me. His hand envelops mine. "They died a few months ago." Jasmine lets out a soft gasp, while Hadley mutters a quiet curse under his breath. But Parker pulls me to him, his words silent for only me to hear.

"I'm sorry, Nadia. I didn't know." I draw back slightly to look at him. The sorrow in his eyes devastates me, and when I look around at his brother and Jasmine, I see the same sentiment mirrored in theirs.

"I know. It's been an adjustment, but I'm doing better," I say, offering a small smile. "Thank you for inviting me out with you guys. It means more to me than you will ever know." Parker reaches across the table and gently takes my hand. Jasmine leans forward, grinning, and asks about planning a party.

Just like that, the heaviness lifts, and they cheer me up like I've known them for a lifetime. Sometimes people enter your life at the most unexpected times, and I believe they came into my life exactly when I needed them. Meeting Parker that day over ice cream was meant to be, and happened when I was at my lowest. When Savannah couldn't be around, he has been there, and I can't wait for them to meet my best friend. I think they will get along perfectly. We sit there enjoying our pizza, and the tension over telling them about my parents' death is gone. It's just pizza, beer, and the promise of friendship that is more than I can ask for. We make plans for the Fourth, and for the first time in a while, I have something to look forward to.

CHAPTER
TWENTY-ONE

NADIA

The week passes by, and soon Savannah will be here to celebrate the Fourth of July with me. I told her about my new friends here, and she is eager to meet Parker, Jasmine, and Hadley. I spent time with them this weekend, balancing it along with my other job at the tavern.

As I pull up into the parking spot next to Manny's company truck, I can't help but wonder why he's been distant, barely offering more than a quick hello and goodbye. When he gets home, he immediately excuses himself to shower. I tell him I'll see him tomorrow as I let myself out, but he doesn't even glance in my direction. It stings, and I can't help but wonder what I did or if maybe this is just his way of setting boundaries, of keeping things strictly professional. After all, I'm just here to care for Catalina, nothing more than the nanny.

Yet, despite how logical it all seems, a part of me can't help but feel the loss of something I thought was there. While I can understand him setting these boundaries, a part of me is disappointed. I still fantasize about him when I am alone. It isn't Parker who comes into my mind when I close my eyes, but the all-consuming image of Manuel Torres.

I'm wiping down the counter in his kitchen when Catalina walks in with her little backpack. It has butterflies and wings outlined in sparkly glitter. She has her shoes on, and I watch her approach me, wondering what will come out of her little mouth. I don't have to wait long.

"Ms. Nadia, can we go to the library today?" she asks, and I know she already has everything planned. I toss the rag into the sink and wash my hands, then dry them off with a sheet from the roll of paper towels. Throwing the trash away, I lean over the counter, watching her. I nod once, and the jump she does makes me wish I was that age and so...springy? I smile, matching hers.

"How about," I lift my finger to my lip, touching it a few times, "we also have a picnic in the common area after the library? That way, we can read some of the books while we eat?" I shrug, and she squeals in delight at my plan. "Are you ready?" She puts her backpack on her shoulders and heads to the door. "Wait," I tell her. "Let me pack a lunch for us."

I noticed a little cooler that hangs on the hook and grab it. I open it and look inside, seeing it's pretty clean. For good measure, I take a disinfectant wipe and clean the inside before placing a couple of sandwiches in it. I cut up some strawberries and grab a seltzer water for me and a juice box for Catalina. I add some napkins and a package of hand wipes before I zip it up, and we walk out to my car. Catalina slides into her car seat and buckles herself in. I start the car and watch her in the rearview mirror. "Are you all set, sweetie?" I ask and she smiles.

"Yes, Ms. Nadia. All buckled," she replies proudly. I smile, pulling away from the house, steering toward the town's public library. When we arrive, I take her small hand in mine as we walk to the quaint children's section. I set my bag down on a tiny table and begin pulling out chairs, the legs scraping softly against the floor as Catalina gazes around with eagerness.

"What are you thinking of getting?" I ask as I watch her pull out a few books from the nearest shelf on display, featuring a story about a couple of little raccoons on the front cover. I walk over and pick up the book. "Oh, I love this one. It's great." She smiles and places it on the table. I walk over to the one with a little pig and spider on it. "How about this one? I love this story, too."

She glances at it and puts it down, frowning. "I can't read it," she says. I place my hand on her shoulder.

"Don't worry about it," I tell her. "I can help you with it." She looks up to me, and uncertainty lines her expression.

"Will you read it to me?" she asks, hesitantly.

"Of course I will." She twists her hand together, and I notice this is one of her nervous tics. It lets me know something makes her uncomfortable, so I proceed cautiously. "Do you not want me to read it to you, Catalina?" I ask her, wanting to know what has her so bothered. She looks up at me with her little blue eyes that have a slight sheen to them.

"My mommy always promised to read to me, but she was always asleep in the room, and my daddy said she was sick." I look at her and bend my knees, dropping to her level. I don't know how much she knows about her mother, and I don't want to make her out to be a bad person. I don't know her and what she went through, but I do know that I could never not be present for my kid. So I make her a promise that I intend to keep.

"I promise I will read it to you," I tell her softly. "You can always wake me up if I fall asleep, but I won't do that on the job, so I am guaranteed to read it to you. In fact, why don't you get a couple more books? I can help you with your reading, and maybe by the end of the summer, you can read it to me," I say enthusiastically.

Her face lights up, and her smile broadens, and I will make it my mission never to see this little girl sad as long as I am around. I know that Manny is a great dad with her, but she must miss her mom. I miss mine more than anything, and if I can help Catalina, I will without hesitation.

After carefully selecting books, we check them out with my

library card and walk out hand in hand. Catalina's spirits have improved, and I gently steer the conversation away from her mother. I know the topic brings her sadness, but as much as I want to protect her from that pain, I also understand that sometimes she may need to talk about it. I want her to know that she can always talk to me about this or anything else.

We walk down the street to where I parked the car, and I pull out a blanket and a cooler from the sturdy plastic beach bag that I used to take on trips to the Cape. It's tough, easy to clean, and perfect for picnics like this. We find the perfect spot to settle onto the grass while the sun warms our skin. I tilt my head up enjoying the rays as a light breeze blows my hair, bringing with it the smell of freshly mowed grass. Catalina eagerly opens one of her new books, plopping herself stomach-first onto the blanket. I grab the sunscreen out of the bag and stand up, beckoning Catalina upward with me.

"Okay, kiddo. Before you get too comfortable, come over here," I tell her. "Cover your face." She does, and I spray her arm and neck with sunscreen. I spray the part in her hair and her ears. Then I rub some on her face. After I am sure I have covered all areas, I do it myself. I hand her a wipe, and we disinfect our hands before taking the food out and grabbing our sandwiches. I put the cut-up strawberries between us and put the tiny straw in her juice box, squirting a little on my leg. She laughs as I hand it over to her. "There." I take a napkin and bite into my sandwich, ham and cheese on rye.

Catalina hands me a book, and we start on the first chapter about an unlikely friendship between a pig and a spider. I see a shadow fall over us, and I didn't even notice someone approaching as we were so wrapped up in our story that I startle when I hear the voice over my own. I stop mid-sentence, and Catalina jumps up.

"Daddy!" she screams, and he catches her in his arms.

"Oye, mija," he says, laughing as she kisses him. He drops her back down and watches me. I place my hand over my brows to stop the sun from getting into my eyes. "You didn't even hear me walk over here, did you?"

I shake my head, feeling like I failed in some way. "Sorry, I was reading and I wasn't paying attention." He doesn't scold me or say anything negative about it. He just nods.

"What were you guys doing?" he asks, looking over at the set-up of books in a bag and our picnic lunch, probably already guessing by the looks of it.

"Catalina wanted to go to the library, and I thought we could make a little outing of it, so I packed lunch for us, and I'm reading to her." He nods, and a sad expression clouds his face, before it disappears just as quickly.

"She likes that," is all he says. He hitches his thumb behind him. "I just had lunch. When I was walking to my truck, I noticed you and Catalina sitting here. Thought I'd come over and say hi." He smiles, and it is breathtaking. I want all his smiles, and I want him to look at me like that. I don't know why I say it, but it comes out before I can think twice.

"Do you want to sit with us for a bit?" I move over and then hesitate, wondering if he will laugh at or reject me, but he does neither. He watches me. He fixes his eyes on mine, leans over, and sits all while holding my stare. Catalina jumps into his lap, and I've never been jealous of a little girl before. It makes me smile at its absurdity. It breaks our connection, and I look away. She talks animatedly about the books she borrowed from the library, showing them to him, and he listens patiently, giving her his full attention. He asks me about my day with genuine concern, and I find a simple joy in our conversation. It flows easily, like we've done this before. Suddenly, I can see myself in this type of life. With a husband who looks at our little girl like she's his whole universe, and is equally interested in my day. If I am happy? I startle from my thoughts when he takes a strawberry out of the Tupperware and takes a bite.

"Give me one, Papá." Catalina opens her mouth, and he places one of the sliced berries in it. She smacks her lips loudly. "Juicy," she says as she wipes her mouth with the back of her hand. I hold out a napkin to Manny, and he wipes the juice from her hand before she wipes it on her shorts.

"Give a strawberry to Ms. Nadia, Papá," she says innocently, and I face Manny abruptly. He watches me and then grabs a berry from the container. He brings it up slowly, the connection of our stare unbreakable as he lifts it toward me. I watch him as he leans forward, and I follow suit, like a tether bringing us closer together. Then he is there to meet me as he brings the berry to my lips. I open my mouth, sticking out my tongue slightly, and his finger grazes the tip as he places the decadent berry in my mouth. His breath hitches when I close my mouth ever so slightly on his finger before he can pull it out. His daughter, oblivious to what is happening to us, continues to flip pages of her book. I chew the berry, and he watches my lips. A little juice runs down the side of my lip and he reaches up and wipes at it with his finger that was almost in my mouth a moment ago, before he takes it and sucks on it.

It's my turn to pant, trying to expel the liquid fire threatening to melt me from the inside out. My cheeks are hot, my core is clenched, and I am so damn close to combusting from this all-consuming lust as thoughts of him begin to swirl in my mind. He wipes his finger on his pants and lifts Catalina from his lap as he stands just as abruptly. He kisses her cheek, telling her he will see her at the house soon. He doesn't say goodbye to me and leaves without looking back. I feel the redness heating my ears, and it's not from the lust that surely evaporated the moment he stood up and couldn't get away fast enough from me. Instead, it is replaced by pure embarrassment. I just hope that it didn't cost me my job.

I scoop up the berries as fast as I can, wanting nothing more than to toss them in the trash. I'm not sure I'll ever be able to look at another strawberry without thinking of Manuel Torres. Catalina quietly gathers her books and tucks them into her little bag while I shake out the blanket and fold it into a neat square. I place it in the bag along with the rest of the supplies we brought. Slipping the bag onto my arm, I reach for Catalina's hand, ready to make our way back to the car.

That's when I feel someone watching me. I notice Sylvie sitting on the park bench. She observes me with a smirk, and I know she witnessed the moment Manny jumped up, desperate to get away from me. And from the satisfied curve of her lips, she seems to be enjoying my humiliation. I can't help but realize that I am attracted to him just like she is. Except, she isn't watching his daughter. I am.

Shame floods me, thick and suffocating as I fight down the embarrassment. My skin burns hotter than the afternoon sunburn, I'll surely be sporting later. I walk away, clutching Catalina's hand, more embarrassed than I was a minute ago if that is even possible. I vow not to let Manny Torres get to me again, because I don't know if I will be able to resist him. I'm not sure if I could withstand the rejection. But one thing I do know is that after everything I have been through, he has the ability to destroy me.

CHAPTER
TWENTY-TWO

MANNY

Seeing her there with my daughter punched a hole straight through my chest. I always envisioned my wife and I doing something like this with our daughter. She would take her to the library, and then I would see them having a picnic, and I would join them for lunch. None of that came true, but I fantasized about it. As I walked toward them, every step was heavier than the last, and I couldn't help it because I wished it was different. More so, I wish this was my life.

The way Nadia is with my daughter is everything I wanted for my ex to be. She was reading to her, and it broke my heart. Her mom always promised to read her a story before she went to bed. When Catalina would walk into the bedroom to collect her promise, her mother would be passed out, high from some pain pill or anti-anxiety medication, telling me she just couldn't cope. Sometimes I would find her asleep and Catalina by herself, sitting on the floor while her mom was passed out on the couch, claiming she didn't feel well when I tried to wake her or ask what was wrong, but she never really felt well. The truth of the matter is that she was sick. Mentally. She refused to get the help she needed, and we all suffered for it, especially Catalina. All the lies and broken promises became too much to bear, and I knew I had to get out of that marriage. Not only was I unhappy in it, but it was hurting my daughter. I couldn't stay in a loveless marriage for my daughter's benefit just because I wanted her mom in the picture. She wasn't acting like a mom. She wasn't present. Not even a little bit.

I am ashamed of the way I acted toward Nadia. I let my feelings run away from me, and instead of confronting my problems, I ran away from them. I have avoided her all week, but maybe I can make it up to her by asking her to have dinner with us. Catalina likes her, and she is the only stable woman figure in her life now. Well, besides my mother and younger sister, but they are both out of state. I just hope it isn't any more awkward after this. So, when I get home today, I will ask her if she wants to stay and hang out a little while I grill outside for Catalina and myself. It is the weekend of the Fourth of July, and I am off tomorrow. I know there are a lot of fireworks and parties on the lake. I am already prepared to take Catalina to see the local fireworks planned in town.

Pulling up into the space next to Nadia's car, I open the door and grab my things from the seat. I stopped at the butcher store and picked up some marinated steak tips and stuff for a salad, and of course, I have some rice I can make to go along with the meat. I open the door and find that it's unlocked. I roll my eyes, ready to comment about the importance of keeping doors locked even though we no longer live in a city, when I abruptly stop, watching the scene unfold before me.

Nadia is wearing one of my aprons that says *The Grillfather* with my name in the middle. Below are the words: *The Man–The Myth–The Legend.* My daughter has her arts and crafts apron on, and by the looks of it, has been put to good use. Her face is speckled with flour, and I think it is even in her hair. But what really gets me is the loud music playing in the background from my little speaker that Nadia has logged into on her Bluetooth. The sounds of an old song that I can only recognize because my younger sister would watch the movie all the time, is about a little girl who wore a red ribbon in her hair and had awful parents who paid no attention to her. "Send Me On My Way" by Rusted Root echoes through the kitchen, and I stand there watching them together. Catalina shakes her hips back and forth while Nadia sings into a wooden spoon. Her voice is terrible, and I have to stifle a laugh because it sounds like someone who is in tons of pain trying to sing. They are scooping dough onto a baking sheet, and when the song finishes and the cookie sheet is in the oven, Nadia looks up to see me standing there transfixed on them. Her eyes go wide, and at the exact moment, she jumps back with her hand on her chest.

"Geez, you creep much?" She exhales, laughing and blowing at the pieces of hair falling out of her messy bun. But I continue to "creep much," standing there watching her. Her cheeks heat, and she runs a hand, moving the strands just to smear flour across her face, and I smile. A genuine smile that makes me all warm and tingly inside. The kind of smile I have always wanted, because the excitement in my daughter's voice as she runs over to me, is priceless. It's a gift, and this woman whom I have ignored all week and treated poorly, though no fault of her own, has caused this transformation in Catalina, and I am beginning to think that it isn't only her who is changing for the better, but me, too. I barely have time to put the groceries down when Catalina launches herself into my arms, and I catch her with one arm as I walk over to the kitchen. I'm a mess from work today, but they are too. I place Catalina down, and Nadia is looking around awkwardly. If she were my wife, I would kiss her with every emotion I feel at seeing her with our daughter like this. It's all I ever wanted for her—for us.

"I wasn't expecting you home this early, and I still have to clean up, but after you get out of the shower, I should have mostly everything back in order," she says nervously. I ignore her comments and advance closer.

"What did you guys make? It smells good." She smiles.

"We just made some Toll House chocolate chip cookies, but

we added a few butterscotch chips to them." I smile, and she looks away shyly.

"That's my favorite," I inform her. She starts to collect the dishes, placing them in the soapy water.

"I know," she says softly, almost too low for me to hear, but I did. I heard her say it, and I can't help but think that maybe she wanted to make them for me. So I proceed to ask her about tonight.

"Well, since you were so kind as to make my favorite cookies, how about I grill for you? I planned on grilling tonight because I have tomorrow off, and I thought maybe you'd like to stay for dinner?" I pause before continuing, and she looks up at me, meeting my eyes. "With us." Just to clarify, in case she doesn't understand. She searches my eyes for something, and I don't know what she is looking for, but I want to give it to her. If she asks me for something, I want to make it happen because I have come to love her smile and see the loneliness or sadness that always lingers. After all, when she smiles at me, I feel it, too. The loneliness and despair, hell, maybe even the failure of my marriage, seem to dissipate, and I think perhaps I can find someone who looks at me like that. Like I am her whole world, and in turn, I can look at her the same way. To have a partner in this life, a true partner where we share things with one another, and also the responsibilities. We fight our struggles head-on as a team and find comfort in the fact that someone else has your back and is there to lift you up when you fall. To be the comfort you seek and the love you live for.

She nods, and the blush that creeps up her cheeks is adorable. "I'm going to go shower, and then I'll start on dinner, okay?" I fight the urge to touch her. To reach for her arm just to feel the way her skin pebbles underneath my touch.

She nods. "Okay, I'll clean up here and help Catalina get changed. Hopefully she didn't drag the flour into her room." She grimaces.

"Don't worry about it. That is something we can clean. I've seen her happier these past few weeks than I have in a very long time. She can get as dirty as she wants."

She scoffs. "Sure, you say that now."

I bite back a grin and shake my head as I turn away, making sure she doesn't catch the smirk tugging at my lips after her sassy remark. I walk off toward my room, shutting the door behind me. I don't think she noticed I still had my lunch bag in my hand, but thankfully, it did just enough to hide the very obvious tent in my pants. Watching the blush creep up her neck to her cheeks made me wonder what else might be that same pretty rosy hue. The image makes me damn near salivate at the thought of just one taste. I drop the lunch box on my chair by the closet, and press my palm over the ache straining against my zipper. It's almost painful now. So many times, I stroked myself to the thoughts of her and the feeling of her lips on my finger when I gave her that strawberry, wondering how that mouth would feel on my cock instead.

I toe off my shoes and strip off the rest of my clothes. My socks are next to go, and when I pull off my boxer briefs, my dick stands at attention and I give it a good tug. I feel the liquid that coats the tip and I bring my thumb to circle it, bringing sticky liquid up as I bring my hand over my cock, twisting it at the end and repeating the stroking motion. My head falls back, and I let out a moan. It's been too long. Reluctantly, I release myself and step into the shower, letting the hot water pour over me. My body is exhausted, but my mind is worse. Leaning a hand against the wall, I breathe in deeply, letting the ache in my chest surface from the conflicting emotions that bother me more than they should. I tilt my head back, allowing the water to cascade over the ringlets atop my head and stream down my body, wishing it could rinse away more than the sweat and grime from my workday. I lather the soap slowly, my palms working in deliberate circles across my chest. Each motion is meant to help me stay in control, but I know that notion is a losing battle as I bring my hand around to my painful erection, knowing that I need to release the ache she stirs in me.

No matter how hard I try to fight the thought, it keeps creeping back in, and I begin to wonder what it would be like to take her to my bed in this house. To have her writhing underneath me. I pick up the pace and stroke myself to thoughts of her spread out on my bed, flushed and breathless with her pretty pink pussy glistening from her arousal. The excitement I stirred in her is clear as she stares up at me like I am her whole world, and the same awe and need is reflected in my eyes, where I'm unable to look away. The moment I visualize parting her legs to take my thick cock waiting angrily at her wet entrance, I start to unravel. I kiss her, entering her in one thrust, almost ready to come from the anticipation alone. It's something I've wanted and have been fighting the feelings of since the day that I saw her in the diner. I draw out a few more pulls and I throw my head back as warm, hot cum coats my hand and the shower wall in front of me. I place my hand against the wall, steadying myself as my ragged breaths become more regular and the haze before me vanishes. The tension ebbs from my muscles, and my shoulders finally relax under the hot stream of water. I let the water wash over my face, trying to clear the truth I've been avoiding. I realize I don't know how much longer I can continue pretending I don't feel something for her. And for once in my life, I want to do something for myself.

CHAPTER
TWENTY-THREE

NADIA

Manny walks out of his room, freshly showered and flushed. He must have taken a very hot shower. I find that cold showers are more my speed right now, to cool me off from the thought of this hot man that I try hard to purge from my mind every night and waking moment. He makes it difficult when he comes out of the shower looking like every fantasy comes to life. He's not only lovely to look at, but being a good provider for his family and being a good dad just adds to the whole package. Catalina comes running out of her room, and the smile on her face as she skips over to me is priceless.

"Are you staying for dinner, Ms. Nadia? My papá is an excellent cook," she singsongs as she pops up onto the stool of the island in front of me. I lean forward.

"How can I refuse that kind of offer? And well, you know that I love to eat." She giggles.

"You eat a lot, Ms. Nadia." She cackles, and I fake being upset.

"Now, that isn't very nice, Catalina." I shake my finger at her, smiling. Manny comes into the room with his pants hung low and I want to see exactly what he is sporting under that. I notice his cock twitch and I look up to see him walking toward me. *Oh God, he saw me looking at his junk.* I want to run and hide. Maybe I can make an excuse about dinner, but the smirk on his face as he approaches me tells me he isn't really upset at all. I stand there stock-still as he reaches out to me, and I stiffen as he lifts the apron off my head and pulls it up.

"Oh. Sorry," I say. "I forgot to take it off." The truth is, I didn't want to take it off because it smelled like him, and I tried to imagine what it would be like to snuggle up to that smell every night. When I turn out the lights in our bedroom and pull back the covers, I get into bed and he wraps his broad arms around me, snuggling me in with all that manliness and smothering me with his heat. Curling up into the safety of Manny Torres would be like a dream come true.

My arms fall flat at my sides. He already has the apron on and is tying it around his very lean waist. I move over to where the package of steak tips is and pick up the bag. Catalina is coloring but stops to watch me. As I remove the steak tips from the grocery bag, Catalina speaks loudly with her little hand up.

"Ms. Nadia, Papá doesn't let anyone handle his meat." I swirl around to look at the man whose meat I have in my hands, and when I look up at him, he has his head turned around, trying to suppress a laugh. My eyes widen in shock at the dirtiness of his thoughts. The corner of my mouth twists upward, and I also turn my face from Catalina. I cough.

"I'm sorry, Mr. Torres." My expression lets him know that I am not sorry at all. "I didn't mean to handle your meat." I walk over to him and hand him the package. His hand covers mine, and his eyes are alight with a playfulness I haven't seen on his face before as he brings me a little closer.

"It's okay," he says. "Ms. Nadia can handle my meat anytime."

I drop my hand like it was lit on fire, but he just holds my stare. I look to Catalina, still coloring, oblivious to our heated stares and hidden innuendos.

Without glancing at us, she comments, "Well, my papá must really like you, Ms. Nadia, because he won't let anyone touch his meat."

This time, I place my hand over my mouth and have to walk away. I head straight for the door and walk outside, muttering, "Excuse me, I'll be right back." By the time I walk outside, I am bent over laughing so hard. I hear the door close lightly behind me, and when I turn, I see Manny walking over with the steak tips on a disposable plate. His eyes find mine, and the smile on his face is breathtaking. He doesn't say anything else to me, but lights the grill and leaves the meat there as he waits for it to heat up, returning inside.

I follow him and see him now over the stove browning some basmati rice with a bit of oil in the skillet. He adds some spices that he ground in a small molcajete.

"That smells good," I breathe in, and the scent hits my nose. "What is it?" He turns back to look at me and smiles, showing all his teeth.

"Just a few ground spices of cumin, salt, pepper, fennel, and garlic." He then scoops them out of the mortar with the pestle, and they fall into the pan. It sizzles around the oil as the rice cooks. He adds some bell peppers and onions, along with hot water and tomato sauce, which are added next. He places a cover on top of the skillet and then sets the stove to a low simmer. Watching him take out things for a salad, I set up and offer to make it. He smiles down at me.

"Okay, that sounds good to me. I'll go take care of my meat outside." He smirks.

I don't know what compels me to continue with the inappropriate playful banter, but before I can think better of it, I respond, "Let me know if you need any help with your meat." He stops before he reaches the door and hangs his head down. I see him rearrange his package in front of his pants before he opens the door.

"Maybe later," is echoed through the screen door. It shuts, and he walks outside. I stand there staring at the lettuce and wonder what the hell got into me. Why am I flirting with this man, and more importantly, why is he flirting back?

Manny did not, in fact, need any help with his meat. He brings it into the house wrapped in foil. He walks up to the stove and removes the cover from the rice to check it out.

"Perfect," he says as he puts the cover back on and removes the stovetop from the heat. I have the salad ready in a wooden bowl, and I made a quick dressing of olive oil, orange juice, apple cider vinegar, garlic, lemon juice, and cracked pepper. I placed it in a mason jar and sealed it with the cover.

Catalina helps to do her part and sets the table for three people. She places the third plate down and looks longingly at it before walking away and grabbing the napkins and utensils. I saw the exchange, and I know that Manny does, too, because whatever smile he had on his face is gone, and I'm wondering if this was a good idea after all. I don't want to replace her mother, and I am only the nanny after all. This is the trouble with finding your employer attractive and both of you being single. Also, I don't want to cause this little girl any more grief. Manny turns around and brings the bowl of rice to the table, places a spoon in it, and the meat is also in another bowl next to it. I grab the salad from the counter and bring it over, placing the two wooden spoons to toss it before getting my dressing from the counter, shaking it thoroughly before putting it alongside the salad on the table.

"Okay, Catalina, let's go wash our hands and get ready for this amazing dinner your dad made for us." She nods, and I follow her to the bathroom, washing my hands right after. When I return to the kitchen, Manny and Catalina are waiting on me, and I immediately serve myself a portion of each. Manny looks at the jar of dressing quizzically, and I explain. "It's just a simple dressing that I made from scratch."

He nods. "Nice," is all he says as he pours some on top of his salad. Great, so now we are back to one-word replies. The dinner is tense, and I don't know how to return to the playful tone we took with one another before we saw Catalina looking at the third place setting, where she was undoubtedly thinking about her mother. Manny looks around.

"What do you want to drink?" He gets up and goes to the fridge. Catalina has a glass of milk that I poured for her already, but I don't know.

"What do you have?" I inquire. "I'll take anything." Manny's eyebrows rise in disbelief.

"You want a beer?" he asks. "I'm having a Corona."

"Yes, that's great," I reply. He looks hesitant.

"You like beer?" he asks like he doesn't believe me.

"Yes," I state, nodding to confirm in case there is any confusion that I do, in fact, like beer. He nods approvingly.

"Well, okay, then." He hands one to me and pops the top off with the Yeti opener that is screwed into the wall by the fridge. *Nice spot*, I think to myself. Catalina breaks the tension.

"What are you doing for the Fourth of July, Ms. Nadia?" she asks as she scoops some rice onto the spoon. I also notice half of it falls onto the floor when she brings it to her mouth. I grimace at the thought of Manny having worked all day and now having to clear up this mess. I should offer to help with the cleanup. Manny watches me, waiting for my response. Is he truly interested in my Fourth of July plans? Of course he isn't. I sigh.

"Well," I tap the edge of my napkin to my mouth to dab at the piece of food with marinade from the steak tips. "My best friend is coming over to my house, and we thought that we could watch some of the fireworks from our back patio on the lake."

She stops eating mid-bite. "You have a lake house!" she shrieks excitedly. I smile, seeing that happiness on her face. I nod, and I hear Manny groan.

"Now you've done it." He places his elbows on the table, leaning forward like he is about to watch a telenovela live and in person. Before she even says it, I know what she will say.

"Papá, can we go over to Ms. Nadia's house, please?" She raises her voice excitedly. Manny looks at the happiness on his daughter's face, and before he can protest or tell her no, I speak up.

"Of course you can, pickles," I tell her, and she beams at me. Manny turns to me, and I shrug. "What?" He searches my eyes for any reservation I could have about having her over, but he won't find it there. "She's welcome anytime," I tell him, and he nods once.

"Can we go for the Fourth to see the fireworks?" she asks, and Manny holds his hands up.

"Catalina, Ms. Nadia has plans with her friends already, but maybe you can go over next week while she's watching you." He looks over at me for confirmation, and I nod.

"Of course you can. That sounds perfect. You think of something you want to do, and we will do it." That seems to appease her, and I take a long drink of my beer, finishing the remaining liquid in one long swallow. I place it back on the table and look up to see Manny staring at me.

"You really do like beer, don't you?" he asks, and I tilt my head to the side.

"Why would I tell you I like beer if I don't?" I ask curiously.

"Want another one?" he asks, and I nod yes. He gets another one from the fridge and one for himself. Popping the top on both, he hands one over to me. I quickly get my napkin and tuxedo wrap it before placing it back down so that the condensation doesn't pool along the glass. He sits still, observing me with those calculating eyes.

"I find that sometimes women tell you one thing and then it isn't true at all," he says.

I'll chalk it up to him being in a terrible relationship. "That is one hell of a generalization, so I am going to let that slide. Instead, I'll give you one truth."

He looks at me and smirks. "Please tell me. I'd love to hear one of your truths."

I continue. "Well, maybe you've just been looking at the wrong kind of woman."

"You know, Nadia..." He takes a drink of his beer, and I see the liquid moving along his throat as he swallows one long pull. A little dribble of golden liquid falls on his lips, and his tongue peeks out to lick it away. When I look back up to his eyes, they are fixed on mine, and I can't help but feel cornered, like an animal being hunted down with nowhere to escape. Because when Manny looks at you, his total focus is on you. "I think you may be right."

CHAPTER
TWENTY-FOUR

NADIA

"Hey, girl!" Savannah rushes up to me, and I fall backward onto the couch, still holding onto her legs. It seems like the girl is going to fall, but how could she when her weight is all on me? I push her off, and she falls to the side, laughing.

"What the ever-loving fuck are you thinking?" She kisses me all over before jumping off, running over to the refrigerator, and taking out a water bottle.

"I'm thinking that I wuv you," she says before twisting the cap off the water. I stand up, watching my best friend guzzle down a whole bottle of water. She pants.

"Are you done, or do you want to drink up the lake while you're at it?" I smirk because that's our thing. We specialize in absurdities of grandeur.

"Got to stay hydrated, you know. I can't throw back drinks like I used to without proper hydration." She places her hand on her hip and pops it out sideways, attempting to emphasize her point.

"You could have killed me back there," I point to the couch where she threw herself at me in more of a koala bear tackle.

"Pfft." She snorts. "Quit being dramatic. Plus, that was like an hour ago."

My eyes bulge out. "It was literally like three minutes ago." But she isn't hearing any of it.

She walks to the door. "I'm gonna go grab my bags now." She saunters out and returns with enough stuff for a week's trip.

"Are you going to stay longer this weekend?" I ask, wishing she doesn't have to leave immediately, but she shakes her head, crushing my hopes for some company.

"Nah. Sorry, babe. I have to get back to work on Monday morning bright and early." I frown and am truly disappointed, but I know that this summer internship is what she has been working for, and I start mine in the fall, again, so I get it. They were so excited to have me there this spring for tax season that they invited me back and offered me a job pending graduation. To live in the city and work in Boston is expensive, but Savannah and I plan on sharing a space and I hope it works out because I really want to be able to have my career and now that I have to rely on myself for everything, there doesn't seem to be any other choice. Commuting in will be easy, and I love that my parents have their home so close. Well, my home, now. I guess. It was like the best of both worlds, being close to the city, but not having to hear the hustle and bustle of city life that comes with it.

Being out here at the lake house has been nice, but in less than two months, I will have to face the adult responsibilities I have been avoiding at my parents' home and in returning to college for my final year. Savannah walks toward the guest bedroom that she has claimed since we were kids.

"I'm going to shower," she states as she starts peeling layers. "I want to get the road grime off me. I was in such a hurry to get over here this morning." She grabs a towel and a face cloth, disappearing into the bathroom. She'll be in there for about an hour. The girl doesn't even wash her hair, and I swear she stands under the shower for about half an hour without doing anything. It's kind of nice, I have to admit, but I don't take many hot showers, so I don't see the point. It makes my skin kind of blotchy, to be honest, and I just wash, rinse, and towel off. I've never seen the need to take longer showers, but maybe if I had someone to share it with, I would think differently.

My phone rings, and I follow the sound's direction. I see it perched on the kitchen island, and I rush over to take the call when I see Parker's name flashing on the screen.

"Hello," I answer, and I hear a lot of commotion coming from the other end of the line.

"Hey, Nadia. What are you up to?" I walk around to the fridge and grab the ingredients for some frozen daiquiris.

"Oh, just grabbing some stuff for some frozen concoctions." I pull out some fresh strawberries for garnish and place them on the counter. "I have yet to try out this amazing slushie machine. My friend Savannah just got here, and we are going to hang out. The fridge is stocked and the alcohol will soon be flowing."

I hear a chuckle come from the other line. "Well, I was going to see if you wanted to come over here, but it appears you already have plans."

"Parky-poo, you guys are more than welcome to come over here with us and celebrate." I hear him shout over to someone whom I assume is Hadley and Jasmine.

"Hey, you guys want to go over to Nadia's house?" I don't hear the response, but he responds quickly. "Give me the address."

And I do. Savannah is just getting out of the shower, and I have managed to get the slushie machine working. I place a strawberry garnish on it and hand it over to her. She waggles her finger at me.

"Nope, where is my rum coater?" she says, but it comes out more like rum coatah. Her Boston accent is thick tonight. I laugh, mimicking her action with her wagging finger.

"Nope, it's not going to happen, sweets. I have friends coming over, and you have to pace yourself, or there will be no swimming or boating activities for you." She pouts but meekly acquiesces.

"Okay, but after, I am getting one." I nod. "Now tell me about these friends of yours," she asks, and I begin to tell her about Parker and how I met him.

"So you have had these friends for a couple of weeks and met Parker having ice cream?" she asks, and I nod. "Do you like him? Is he cute?"

"I like him very much and he is very handsome." I pause.

"You're just not into him?"

"I'm just not attracted to him. He has become a great friend, and honestly, he hasn't even tried anything more than a quick pec. I think he just likes me as a friend, too. He's fun and sweet, but there's absolutely no chemistry between us." She searches my eyes and sighs.

"That's too bad," she comments. "I really want you to meet someone." I look around, not meeting her eyes. She puts her hand on my arm. "Wait. Stop. I know that look, Nadia, when you are trying to avoid the topic." Her smile widens, and she smacks me on the arm, sloshing the alcohol from my drink. I jump up with my drink like she is at risk of spilling it all, and she might if I have to sustain another of her hits.

"Dang girl, that is straight up alcohol abuse. Look." I point at the offending spot on the leather couch that is sliding onto the floor.

"Whatever, get a napkin or just top it off, but you," she tries to stab at me with her pointed pink fingertip, "are not getting off that easy." I grab a napkin to clean up the mess and sit back down, taking another sip of my now full drink. She is staring at me intently.

"What?"

"Ugh, don't act like you don't know what I am talking about!" she shouts. "Spill the tea, babe. I'm dying here. Please, put me out of my misery. I know how picky you are, and if you have found someone that piques your interest, then I want to know all about this mystery hottie." She exhales, having gotten that all out in one solid breath.

"Well," I begin, building the suspense and trying to decide how to tell her this story. So, instead of being subtle, I just blurt it out. "I am super attracted to the father of the girl I nanny for." I stop and wait to gauge her reaction, but she says nothing.

"Explain," is all she says as her eyes narrow.

"He's single—" I start, and she cuts me off.

"Bitch, from the beginning." And so I do. I tell her about the first time I saw Manny Torres at the diner with his daughter and how he looked at me like he hated me. I tell her about the second time I saw him at the tavern, and he bumped into me, calling me that term of endearment. Her eyes bug out.

"No way!" she screams. "That is the same guy?" She shakes her head in disbelief. "What are the chances, right?" She sits up, crossing her legs underneath her. "So, you answered the ad and then what were your thoughts when you met him and found out it was him?" she asks, fully invested in this story.

"Well, I was shocked, and then there was this girl who is like a stalker mom who now hates me." I take a sip of my drink, and she laughs.

"Oh, my God, you have had quite the little adventure over here, while I was working my ass off for near to nothing." She huffs. "Okay, now tell me more. Does he like you? Are there feelings?" Her eyes light up, and mine do, too, when I tell her about the meat innuendo and how he had to adjust himself as he walked out the door.

"Honestly, Savannah, I feel like the sexual tension between us is at an all-time high, but I think that both of us are afraid to act on it for fear of things ending poorly. I mean I am leaving in less than a couple of months and he is a single dad, recently divorced with a shit ton of baggage from his ex." I take a sip of my drink. Savannah seems to think about it for a little while, and as if having a breakthrough moment, she snaps her fingers.

"Got it," she remarks coolly, flicking her hair back over her shoulder. "Why don't you fuck his brains out before you leave, that way, it can't get weird because you won't be Catalina's nanny anymore, so there is not a chance of it ending poorly at that point?" She acts like she has it all figured out.

"Well, for one, maybe I don't just want to fuck his brains out. Maybe I feel something for this man, and I really like his little girl." My smile softens at the thought of Catalina and how she wants a mother figure in her life.

THE CRUELEST TRUTH

Savannah watches me with a mixture of sadness and understanding. "Nadia, you are leaving soon, right? This is temporary, and I know you have been through a lot, but maybe this is all too soon. It seems really complicated, and I don't think complicated is the best route for you." She bites her nail and looks away. I know she wants the best for me, but I don't want easy. I want passion and love. I want someone to look at me the way Manny looks at me. I want the family. I want it all, but instead of voicing all those things aloud, I decide the easiest way to end this conversation is to agree with her.

"Yeah, maybe you're right," I tell her, but she is too smart for that. She is watching me keenly and I am a shit actor, but I continue. "I have been through a lot, Savannah, and I am pretty lonely. Maybe that's what it is." Her smile softens, and she leans her head briefly on my shoulder.

"Oh, Nadia, you are amazing, and I know that good things are coming your way. Just be patient and please don't rush into anything like this, okay?" I meet her stare and nod once. "Good," she says, and the doorbell rings. I jump off the couch, wanting this conversation to be done with, and this is the perfect timing.

"Well, that's probably Parker, Hadley, and Jasmine." I walk to the door. "I can't wait for you to meet them."

All talk of Manny halts once the introductions are made and my old friend meets my new ones, but the thoughts of him stay with me as I ponder Savannah's words and wonder if this is me blowing things up and thinking that what happened between Manny and I are more than what they are. As I look across the lake and at my friends joking around, pouring drinks, I start the grill and begin to think about Manny and Catalina, wishing they were here with me, too.

CHAPTER
TWENTY-FIVE

MANNY

I sit on the grass with Catalina in my lap, looking up at the setting sun. The sky is illuminated in red, orange, and purple hues as dusk begins its journey into nightfall. Families with similar items are piled along the grass at Pleasant Lake Park. The gates opened at 6 p.m. this evening, and the fireworks will begin shortly. The town has an organization that focuses solely on planning the Fourth of July celebration to make it as epic as possible. It is filled with nothing but families, as well as those who are either visiting in a vacation rental or residing in their summer lake homes. The town also uses the funds it makes here, by selling items and charging admission at the entrance, to support youth programs and offset family costs, such as the t-ball program my daughter participates in. There is plenty of parking across the street in a large, open field, but the spots fill up quickly, so we have been here a while to get a prime location. I just hope that Catalina stays up to watch it. If she falls asleep, I'll also bring items for that, so either way, we are prepared.

The look of joy on her face last night when we had dinner with Nadia was something I had missed seeing. I don't want to bother Nadia, and I hope she didn't feel obligated to have my daughter over to her lake home because I'd hate to impose. Will her parents be there, too? The truth is, I don't know much about her, but I'd like to. As if conjured from my thoughts, I see Catalina spring up from the blanket and run over to Nadia. She is with a friend, and before she has time to react, she almost loses her footing as Catalina wraps her little arms around her legs, locking her in place.

"Oof," I hear her say as she stumbles forward. The young woman beside her steadies her arm and then realizes what happened. She drops down to meet her and extends her hand out to her. Nadia makes the introductions and searches around the crowd with a worried look. I stand, and her sights hone in on me as I walk over to her to retrieve my daughter. Nadia has now entwined her fingers with Catalina's and is walking toward me along with her friend, who has a shit-eating grin on her face. I don't know what that means, but I'd like to know if Nadia has said something about me to cause her to smirk this way. It's highly suspicious.

"I found something of yours," Nadia says playfully, swinging Catalina's arm back and forth as my little girl giggles. The woman beside her doesn't wait for an introduction and boldly steps forward.

"I'm Savannah, Nadia's best friend." I take her hand, shaking it, my eyebrow quirks up at Nadia, and she just shrugs her shoulders.

"I'm Manny, and this is my daughter Catalina." I tilt my chin toward my daughter, who is mesmerized by Nadia and very much ignoring me. I understand the feeling, because I am just as enthralled by her, and it's getting harder to deny. As Savannah is about to speak, a guy taps her on the shoulder. She swings around, almost annoyed, until she sees who it is.

"Gage!" she exclaims. The guy is clearly pleased to see her reaction to him. He looked hesitant when he tapped her on the shoulder to get her attention, and I knew it would go one of two ways. That would have been embarrassing to witness if the events had turned out differently. He points to where his friends are, and Savannah looks like the cat that got the canary when she returns her focus to her friend. She whispers something to her and then laughs. "It was so nice to meet you guys, but I think I'm going to follow this guy around for a bit." Gage couldn't be happier as he begins to drag her away. "Don't do anything I wouldn't do." She doesn't even try to be discreet as she winks at her. Gage looks to Nadia, clearly not seeing anyone else but her friend.

"Oh. Hi, Nadia. See you at work later."

"Hi, Gage." She waves, a little unimpressed as Savannah strolls off, blowing her an air kiss, but not before looking in my direction sternly.

"Take care of my girl, Manny," is all she says as she strolls away, enveloped by the crowd. Nadia still holds Catalina's hand, but now she looks uncomfortable. "I'm sorry if I am—"

I don't let her finish that thought. "Here, I have another blanket. Please join us." Catalina jumps up excitedly, and Nadia just gives me a cute little lopsided smile as she plunks herself down on the blanket I set up for her right next to me. She crisscrosses her legs, and Catalina sits right on top of her. I stifle a laugh, and Nadia makes a sound as my daughter smothers her. I don't have the heart to tell her not to, though. She looks so happy. Nadia smiles brilliantly at her, placing her arms around her and engaging in conversation about the fireworks that will soon be going off. She rests her chin on her head, like it is the most natural thing in the world.

I watch them both together, and I can't help but feel like a failure. Maybe I should have tried harder to help my ex so that Catalina wouldn't be attaching herself to her nanny. I also wonder if perhaps it was always going to fall apart. I tried to love her, but do you really have to try so hard to love someone? Shouldn't it come naturally? She didn't even try to love me back, and I don't think she had the capacity for anything that didn't revolve around her. I longed for the feeling of needing to be around them constantly because you enjoy their company, not because you have to. For them to feel the same way and make you feel desired and wanted.

I had neither of those things. Although I had women come on to me, I would never have cheated on my wife, even though our sex life was almost non-existent. I was devastated when I heard she had been texting an older man. She didn't even try to explain. She just retreated into herself, shutting me out completely, and I lost it. I couldn't handle her anymore. Frankly, I didn't want to.

Nadia looks over her shoulder as she squeezes Catalina further and gently kisses the top of her head as she rests her delicate chin there. Music starts playing, and I know the fireworks are about to start.

"Come on, Papá!" Catalina beckons me over with her little outstretched hand. I scoot closer to her side and place myself in line with Nadia. My knee noticeably touches hers as she glances over. I see goose pimples cover her legs, and look over at her.

"Are you cold?" I ask. "Do you want a blanket?" She peeks in my direction and shakes her head no, without answering me. The sky is getting darker, and the first set of fireworks erupts in the sky. Catalina squeals in excitement.

"Look at the pretty colors, Nadia!" She points to the sky illuminated in red, orange, and yellow. The booms continue. "Papá! Isn't it the prettiest thing you have ever seen?" she asks, and Nadia rests her chin on my daughter's head again, looking at me with a lazy smile spread across her face. My heart leaps in my chest, and I realize I am looking at my daughter's nanny with puppy dog eyes. I swallow the lump in my throat as the realization hits me.

"Yes, mijita." I nod, agreeing. Nadia is watching me, her focus razor sharp. "It is definitely the prettiest thing I have ever seen." Nadia's eyes widen, and her sudden intake of air lets me know she got the meaning. Because I wasn't looking at the fireworks. I was looking at her. I don't know what I am doing, and it might be the worst decision I have made yet, and Lord knows I have made a few already, but I can't help what I am starting to feel for this woman.

Since the first day, she affected me at the diner, even though I hated myself for it. Now, my daughter sitting in her lap gives me hope that someday, I can have a love that lasts, where someone picks me first, and I can be the husband and lover I know I can be—a family for Catalina and maybe more siblings for her to call a brother or sister. I never wanted to believe it could be a feeling I could ever want to have again. Maybe it won't be with Nadia, as much as I like the possibility, but I thought I was closed off to the idea. I can only pray that it could be with this woman, but I don't think I can take the rejection if I lay out my feelings for her and they are not reciprocated. So it might be best to keep things low-key. I can't push us on her. I can tell we are each harboring tons of baggage, so I decide to see where this could go. If it does go in the direction I'd like, then so be it. I decide not to fight it.

The fireworks have been going on for fifteen minutes, and I know that we don't have much time left. I place a blanket over Catalina, draping it over her, Nadia, and half of my leg. I rest my hand on the ground under the blanket, and it grazes Nadia's. She stiffens and looks at me, but I don't move. I just stay there and watch her, feeling this unspoken connection to her. There's an urge to touch more of her, but I don't act on it. The jolt of electricity that I felt from one slight touch, causes another kind of fireworks to spark in my chest, igniting a feeling I don't want to ever end.

She gives me another one of her smiles, and I return it with a slight smirk, lifting the corner of my mouth before turning my head forward facing. Then, unexpectedly, I feel her soft, yet deliberate touch. Her fingertips trail slowly down my arm before her hand settles gently over mine. I tilt my head sideways to look at her, meeting her stare. She sits there unmoving, awaiting my reaction. But I give her nothing, as I turn my head away from her, eyes lifting to the sky, just as the fireworks erupt for the final minutes of the finale.

Before she can lift her hand away from mine, probably second-guessing herself, I intertwine her fingers with mine and rest them there. Neither of us acknowledges the action or moves from the spot, not wanting the moment to end. The gesture and simple act just prove that she feels the same way I feel about her. The confirmation is clear in our joined hands. And as the last fireworks blast into the sky, so does my resolve and fight against what this could mean and the road ahead of us if we choose to pursue our feelings. I send those thoughts of self-doubt and negativity into the air along with the last explosions across the star-lit sky. When the smoke clears and the crowd's cheering erupts, I glance over to her. My thumb rubs in a circle over hers, hoping that whatever this is doesn't blow up in our face.

After the fireworks end, Nadia helps me with Catalina. She is asleep, and we patiently wait for the crowd to dissipate before we make our way out of the park. She holds onto Catalina as I continue to gather up all the supplies, carrying her until I load up the last of the blankets, fold them, and put them away into the bags I brought for us. I offer to take her, but she just holds onto her and tells me to lead the way. We walk to my truck as a unit, and I feel the ease with which we work together. There is no drama, just us.

I want to pretend that we are a family and that she is my wife, carrying our daughter to our truck, but I know it is foolish to even dream of the idea of us, in case it doesn't work out. It is a dangerous and slippery slope. And I am already poised at the top of the hill, ready to fall over it in a lovesick, foolish fashion.

As I walk over to the truck, I unlock the door with the key fob and place the items in my hand on the ground near the front tire. I open the door and pivot to Nadia as she leans into me and hands over a sleeping Catalina. I buckle her into her five-point harness car seat, ensuring it is secure, and move the little seat belt rest cushion up by her cheek so she can lean into it. Nadia is already putting the bag on the front passenger seat when I move around the back to lower the truck bed and place my cooler of snacks into it. I go over to the driver's side to start the truck and walk back over to Nadia, who is looking anywhere but at me. I don't know how to act at this point. I begin reaching for her when Savannah comes up out of nowhere, ruining the moment. Any further chance I have to show Nadia that I want this to happen just as much slips away. But I know, without a doubt, I would've kissed her.

"There you are!" She throws her hands up. "I was looking everywhere for you." Nadia looks remorseful.

"Sorry, babe. I was just helping Manny get Catalina to the truck. Pickles was out like a light." Savannah's eyes widen in surprise.

"Pickles, is it?" Nadia looks embarrassed, glancing away from her friend and back at me. I also wondered about that name, but I hadn't asked her out of a lack of curiosity. It was just in the way that her eyes softened when she used the name to refer to Catalina. It looked like she was remembering something too intimate a feeling to share with me, especially since we had a bit of a rocky start.

Meaning, I was kind of a dick to her. I don't know what transpires when they look at each other, but they seem to have a silent discussion. I look to where Catalina sleeps and realize I must get my daughter home.

"Do you guys need a ride to your car? I need to get this one home." I hitch my finger over to where she naps in her car seat. This stops whatever exchange was occurring between them, and Nadia looks at me, shaking her head.

"We are parked over there and have plans tonight anyway." I look at her, my thoughts bobbing as I swallow the questions I want to ask, but I have no business asking. Where to? With whom?

So instead, I say, "Okay, drive safely, and I will see you on Monday morning at the house." She looks at me, also appearing to want to say more, but Savannah tugs at her arm, and she smiles sadly, giving me a little wave.

"Alrighty. See you then." She walks off with her friend, leaving me to go home alone with my daughter in tow. I wish she was sitting in the front seat of my truck, going home with us tonight.

CHAPTER
TWENTY-SIX

NADIA

I stand frozen, watching Manny pull away from the park and join the caravan with the other cars in line. For a moment, I thought about chasing after him because my heart felt like it was moving forward along with his truck, all while my feet stayed planted in that same spot. Every part of me screams to run after him, to pound on his window, and to beg him not to leave. As much as I hate to admit it, Savannah is right. We have plans. Parker's name flashes on my phone, and I show it to Savannah. "Yes!" she grins, fist-punching the air with a joy I can't quite match.

She grabs my hand, guiding us back to the car. "Let's get out of here," she says excitedly, as our steps quicken with each stride. As I let her lead me, I cast one last glance over my shoulder, but I know it's stupid. He's gone.

THE CRUELEST TRUTH

We reach the car and climb in, falling into a comfortable silence as the line of cars crawls forward, inch by inch, across the grassy field from where we parked and now wait in line. Luckily, most people left before we did, since I was helping Manny pick up his belongings and pack up his truck. Next to me, Savannah flips down the visor. The mirror's soft light illuminates her face. She rummages through her cosmetic bag, touching up her makeup with quick, practiced strokes.

I decide to break the silence. "So...what's up with Gage?" I ask, trying to sound casual. Out of the corner of my eye, I notice Savannah's cheeks flush pink.

"We made plans to meet up later," she says, her voice a little too nonchalant, like she was trying to play it cool. "I already texted him with our plans, and he is fine with meeting us at the tavern." She huffs, but continues. "Even though he didn't sound too keen on going to hang out where he works since he's not, you know," she mimes air quotes, "'actually working tonight.'" She snorts.

I laugh at the comment because, yeah, I get it. "Same," I retort.

Savannah stops chatting and returns her focus, outlining her lips with a liner. "Oh, yeah, how can I forget?" She deadpans.

I can't help but giggle, the sound bubbling out before I can stop it. There's something so endearing about how much effort she's putting in.

"What time are we—" I cut her off as I read my new message.

"They are already on their way. He says he will get us a table."

She throws her makeup bag into her purse. "Nice," she comments before changing the music I'm streaming on my playlist. "I Don't Want To Wait" by David Guetta and One Republic starts, and she begins dancing in the front seat, singing along with the repetitive chorus. Her hands are over her head, fingers snapping as she sways along with the beat. I can't help but join in on singing and hitting the steering wheel in rhythm to the song as we drive down the rural road to the tavern. My mood picks up, and I'm ready to let loose and have some fun. That's what I tell myself, but oh, how I wish I were in my pajamas envisioning myself sitting on Manny's patio with a glass of wine in hand and maybe snuggling up on the couch with a movie, hoping to get to know him more...

intimately, maybe? My cheeks flush at the thought as I enter the tavern's parking lot and place the car into park.

I grab my phone and wristlet, walking shoulder to shoulder with Savannah as we approach. We hear the music playing on the patio surrounding the lake. We can see people who live or rent homes on this lake shooting off their own fireworks, giving us an extra show tonight. I look around until I spot Parker, Hadley, and Jasmine at a table. As we walk toward them, Parker's gaze finds mine as he jumps up to walk over to meet us. He hugs me, and I hug him back.

Ugh. How did he know I needed one? He has become a good friend in the past two weeks, and I am sad he will leave tomorrow. Things happen for a reason, and he was there at just the right time when I needed someone the most. Although we haven't discussed our relationship, I'm confident that he doesn't feel anything romantically for me either.

I step into the picnic-style table, alight with electric candles, giving off a light glow that matches the stringed lights draped along the pergola above us, encompassing most of the area. Savannah looks around eagerly for Gage, while Parker is already standing ready to grab us some drinks when he notices we don't have any.

"What do you ladies want to drink?" he asks, and Savannah gives him a wicked smile.

"I'll take a margarita, please," she says, and he nods, then looks at me.

"Surprise me?" I state playfully. His brows lift, accepting the challenge.

"Be careful what you ask for, Nadia." He waggles his finger at me, laughing as he leaves to grab our items. Savannah leans in and whispers in my ear.

"I like that guy."

I nod in agreement. "Me, too. He's great."

Savannah gasps as two hands reach around to cover her eyes from behind. "Boo," Gage says as he gives her a quick peck on the cheek, and she turns around, laughing, to face him.

"You're here!" she exclaims excitedly, moving over to allow Gage some space to scoot in. He waves at everyone, and she begins to make the introductions. Hadley grabs a Corona from the bucket of beer on the table and offers one to Gage, which he gladly takes.

"Thanks." Condensation runs down the bottle. He places a napkin around it and removes the lime, which is acting as a temporary stopper for the beverage.

"I love a good Corona fixed up with salt and lime," I comment, and Gage grunts his agreement as he licks the salt off the side of the beer bottle, then takes a couple of hard swallows. Savannah watches his throat bob as he guzzles the cold liquid. I have to turn away because of how hot it looks to see them so into each other, and Jasmine gives me a quick look as if to say, "*Same.*" Hadley is oblivious as he looks for his brother in the crowd of people.

Hadley lifts his chin upward, and Parker stands before us with a margarita for Savannah. Savannah grabs it eagerly, releasing a little squeal of delight as she brings it to her lips, smacking them in blissful happiness. I look at Parker as he places a frozen swirled beverage before me.

"Ta-da," he says animatedly. I lift a brow quizzically, and he just shrugs.

"I know you like piña coladas and strawberry daiquiris, so I decided to get you a mixture of each. It's called a Miami Vice." I sit there, stunned that he knows I like them, but we had some amazing ones the other night at the lake house when I tested out our brand-new slushie machine. So, I lift it to my lips and take a sip. I take a bite out of the strawberry, and my taste buds explode at the flavor. I pull the strawberry away, looking at it.

"It seems to have been soaked in some liquor, too."

Parker nods. "Regan's bitters." He explains as I lean my head on his shoulder. He kisses the top of my head. The way he kisses my head doesn't scream romantic gesture, but I begin to second-guess myself as I quickly lift it off his shoulders, looking up at him. He smiles brightly at me, bumping me on the arm with his, as he takes his seat. He takes another drink of his beer, playing off his thoughtfulness, and my smile widens.

"You're the best, Parker." Then I wonder how lucky I got to find someone like him. Savannah sees us and smiles back, clearly watching the interaction.

Our conversation is lighthearted, and we make plans to get together again when the school year starts, since we don't go to school far from one another. It looks like he has something on his mind that he wants to tell me.

"Nadia, I want to talk to you about something," he begins, and he seems pained. It makes me pause. I hold a finger up.

"This looks like it might take a while," I say, looking around. "I really have to pee first." I stand up and notice Hadley shaking his head at his brother, but I can't analyze it now. My bladder is going to burst, so I excuse myself to go to the bathroom, and Savannah says she has to go, too, but when she makes a move to leave, Gage stops her to ask a question.

"I'll meet you in there," I tell her, unable to stop as I haul ass to get to the bathroom. I had to go like an hour ago, but I was distracted by a good time. Now, like a little kid who was having too much fun to stop and go, I find a stall to relieve my poor overdistended bladder from exploding. When I come out and walk over to the sink to wash my hands, I hear a familiar voice that grates on my last nerve like the sound of nails on a chalkboard.

"Great, I just can't seem to find a place you're not at, can I?" I turn to see Sylvie, the woman who is after Manny. I haven't had the pleasure of engaging in conversation with her since the run-in at the diner, and I was hoping to avoid her for a while longer, like maybe forever, but I knew it would happen sooner or later, especially if I hung around Manny and Catalina more often.

So I turn to her, fed up with our few interactions. "Can we just not?" I say, grabbing a paper towel and throwing it into the trash. I turn to walk away, but she stops me. I place my hand on my waist. "If you have something to say, just say it already. I have friends waiting for me." I'm impatient and don't like this woman. I certainly don't need this in my already fucked up life.

She stands there coolly, acting like her banged-up cuticles are more interesting than my words. "Well, I was just thinking to myself about how clueless someone can be." I make a noise that resonates from the depths of my throat in a very unladylike fashion.

"That's rich, coming from you," I counter, and her eyes snap up to me.

"Oh, really, so you like sloppy seconds?" she asks, leaning forward.

"Oh, please." I roll my eyes. "Manny was never yours."

With that, she steps back in shock. "You're dating Manny? I thought you were just the nanny?" She looks into my eyes, searching for the truth, and whatever she sees angers her. "Well, then you also get my sloppy seconds." She walks closer to me with the intention to hurt me with whatever she is going to spew with her venomous words. "Has he ever had you pushed up against the wall as his tongue thrusts into your mouth, all while his hardened cock thrusts against you? It's so stiff, ready to erupt, trying to push out of his pants as he fucks your mouth with his?"

I step back, trying to rid myself of the picture she paints, but I can see it vividly—them together—and I want to vomit. My emotional distress gives her the motivation to continue. "One hand on my head to steady me in place as the other palms my tit in the most delicious way." She emphasizes her last three words as she licks her lips like she is remembering it and savoring the experience all over again. I know she isn't making this up, but reciting it from memory. It cuts so deep I want to scream. "When he is going to push me to my knees—" I turn about to walk away, but her following words stop me. "But I wasn't only talking about Manny, you stupid fuck," she says. "I was also talking about the guy you are just hanging out with, all lovey-dovey out there." She shrugs, laughing evilly. "He was just making out with some girl by her car and sending her off just before you got here."

I step back, affronted, because I didn't even think this was about Parker. I thought she was only talking about Manny, so why does it still hurt?

"What?" I say in confusion because it can't be true.

"Oh," she says, acting sorry, but definitely not sorry if the broadening smile on her face indicates anything. "You didn't know?" She shakes her head. "Well, let me enlighten you then," she continues. "The CliffsNotes version was that she came here, found him, cried, he hugged her, he left with her, and then he made out with her, practically dry humping her against the car before she left." She places her hand against her chest, where the hardened organ resides. "He looked longingly at her trail of dust as she disappeared. And then," she pauses for emphasis, "he stood there and took out his phone."

A single tear rolls down my cheek as I listen to her and envision the scenario in my head. Was that when Parker texted me? As soon as she left, I came here. Did other people see? She looks pleased as if she can hear the rolling thoughts in my mind, as her words cut me up so much. The door opens, and the blaring music of "Don't Look Back in Anger" by Oasis drifts in through the small space, threatening to invoke a meltdown from me of epic proportions.

"What's going on?" I hear Savannah's voice rise as she walks into the bathroom, seeing me upset.

I run out of there as fast as my legs can carry me, leaving them behind. Arriving at the table, I quickly reach for my bag, already grabbing my keys. Parker sees my face as Savannah pushes through the crowd, approaching the table hot on my heels. She grabs me and reaches for my hand, taking the keys in one swift pull.

"Go!" she shouts, pushing me toward the exit. "I'll meet you at the car, but babe, you are not driving home like that. I'll drive."

"Nadia, what's wrong? Talk to me!" he shouts above the music as I run out of there with him trying to follow me, but I see Hadley stop him, telling him to wait.

I don't hate the thought of Parker kissing another woman, but of how he didn't trust me enough to tell me. I'm fucking tired of secrets. I vow no one will do this to me again. Ever. The worst is hearing Manny make out with that woman who is utterly repulsive, and then first looking at me that time at the diner with hatred when I didn't deserve it. But I'm done. I'm so done with it all.

As I reach the car, I lean my forehead against the cool glass of the window, my arms hanging limp at my side. I just stay there for a moment, letting the night envelop me in its warm embrace. Then I flinch, hearing the crunch of gravel under approaching footsteps.

I turn slowly, my heart already sinking, and find Parker standing there. The look on his face is one of defeat and regret, conveying everything without a word. I know that what that cruel woman told me was true, and at this moment, I wish he thought of me better than that to confide in me. I look like a fool. It's not that I wanted a relationship with him, but I wanted the trust of friendship. What am I saying? I am hurt, but not for the right reasons. The thought of Manny with that woman makes my blood boil.

"I was going to tell you," Parker starts, his voice rough, but before he can say more, Savannah steps up behind him and shoves him backward, putting herself between us. I catch a glimpse of Parker's face. His glassy eyes hold more than just guilt. It wasn't just an act. He means it. But it doesn't matter anymore.

"Save it, Parker," Savannah says sharply, her voice trembling just enough to betray her raging anger. She backs away, and I turn away, too, leaving him standing there with all the words he should have said to me sooner. I slide into the passenger seat, the door shutting with a soft, echoing thud. Savannah climbs in behind the wheel without a word, and once again, she drives me home through a blur of tears I refuse to fight.

CHAPTER
TWENTY-SEVEN

NADIA

We walk into the house, and I drop my bag on the kitchen island. Savannah pulls out a chair and points at it. "Sit," she says, walking over to the cabinet. I comply and watch as she takes out two shot glasses and opens the bottle of Don Julio 1942. The amber-colored liquid flows into the small glasses, and she pushes one toward me. "Don't drink it yet, bitch," she says as she walks over to the refrigerator and pulls out a lime, carefully cutting it into small wedges. She grabs the salt shaker and places it there on the cutting board. "Ready? Because I want you to tell me what that woman said and what's wrong, but we also need this." Her hand extends toward the contents on the counter.

I nod. "Agreed." I lick the area between my thumb and index

finger and pour a small amount of salt there, and Savannah mimics my actions. We grab the shot glasses and look at each other. A small glint in her eye and a lifted corner of her lip is the only indication I get as we lick the salt and toss back the contents of the shot glass.

"Smooth," we say in unison, over the *clink* of the glass striking the stone counter. Then we both pick up a lime, sucking on it. Honestly, the liquor is top-shelf. We don't need the ritual that has followed us these past years, but we still do it out of habit. We plunk the limes down, and she refills the glasses swiftly. I watch the amber liquid swirl as its contents fill up the other glass in front of my best friend. She puts the bottle down, not bothering to cap it, and waits.

I lick my lips. "That woman is the bane of my existence. She has a" I lift my hand in the air, waving it casually, "thing for Manny and she is pissed about his lack of attention toward her many advances." I try to make it sound as clinical as possible. A transaction, but she's not buying it. Savannah lifts a brow, the questions she wants to ask is apparent, but she doesn't say a word, so I continue. "She described in great detail an occurrence between her and Manny that made me want to vomit." I stop speaking, feeling the bile rising already at the thought.

"Because you want him," she says casually, and I nod, not even bothering to bullshit her. Rubbing my hand across my face, I grimace, looking at her.

"Badly. Is it that obvious?" I ask her. She smiles knowingly before giving me a nod. "Well, that was one of the things. The other was that she mentioned Parker was there with a woman right before I got there, and he was making out with her right before the mystery woman left, and then he texted me." She cringes, her nose wrinkling in disgust like she smelled something bad, and that something is Parker's poor decision.

She stops me from going further. "So let me ask you something?" she says, and I wait patiently for her to ask. "Do you like Parker in that way?" Before I can answer, she continues. "Because I don't think you do. I think you like Manny. I think you want Manny so badly, and you have developed feelings for his daughter, too." She folds her arms over each other. "Let me ask you this. What made you so upset?" She tilts her chin at the tequila shots, and we do another before she fills the glasses again. I wonder if we will pass out before I can finish answering all her questions, and honestly, I'm not sure that's such a bad thing. When I confirm her suspicions, just as predicted, we both pass out shortly after.

I awake to the light streaming in through the windows. I glance over to Savannah, lying on the leather couch. A white cloth is draped across her forehead.

"Not the white rag of suffering," I moan as I try to stand up, but my vision blurs, and I flop down on the couch as cold perspiration beads upon my forehead.

She snorts. "Oh, yes," she says before plopping it off her forehead and walking to the sink to soak it. My eyes close. The light feels too painful, like little knives piercing my retinas. I hear her little socked feet pad over to me, placing the cool cloth compress over my brow now, and I sigh in contentment. "It looks like you need that more than I do." She chuckles, stepping away, and I hear the shower turn on. I lay there, stone-still, as the nausea subsides.

"I don't think I can get up yet," I say to no one. Maybe it's to myself, to encourage me not to try that again too soon.

So I lay there for another hour. Savannah comes waltzing in with a glass of water and some pain medication. "Here." She hands me a glass of hazy water, along with two pills.

"Thanks," I say as I pop them into my mouth, letting the cool electrolyte-infused water travel down my throat, chasing the pills down with it to my empty stomach.

"Go take a shower." She throws her hand toward the bedroom. "I'll make us some breakfast. Trust me," she says, walking to the kitchen. "A shower does wonders. You'll feel much better. I know

I do." I hear her taking things out of the cupboards, and I decide to heed her advice.

She leaves too soon with the promise to return before the summer ends. I hug her, holding on longer than I should as I watch her go. Alone with my thoughts, I plop myself into the hammock and sit there, my Kindle in hand and coffee along with water on the table beside me. A cool breeze blows off the lake, and I relax into it, slightly dozing off.

I hear a car door shutting, and I startle awake. I see Parker walking toward me, and I stiffen, embarrassed about my behavior and how I left. It wasn't all about him, but the combination of her recount of Manny and then how Parker lied to me made me freak out. I turn my legs around and sit there watching him stop before me. His hands rest in his shorts pocket as he finds the words he wants to say.

"I'm sorry, I should have told you." He looks at me sadly. I sit in my hammock, leaning forward to grab the water bottle and take a swig, to wet my dry, parched mouth, and also to give me something to do with this nervous anxiety I feel all the way down to my trembling hands. It's the third time I've refilled it, and I fought the urge to expel the contents of my stomach again after the plentiful confessions and the multiple tequila shots last night that were still making a reappearance in the porcelain bowl inside. Parker approaches the hammock and sits beside me, and my dizziness returns. I set both feet firmly on the ground to center myself. He watches me and places his hand in front of him.

"Right before I came on this trip, my girlfriend was supposed to come with me, but we got into a big fight and ended up calling things off." He runs his hand through his sandy blond hair. I take another drink from my water bottle.

"How long have you been together?" I ask curiously. He smiles as if recalling a memory only privy to him.

"Three years," he says sheepishly. "I was heartbroken and sad when she said we should see other people, and then I met you. That day at the park, I saw you there and I was so fucking sad. I looked at you eating your ice cream alone, carrying the weight of the world on your shoulders, and I thought you maybe needed a friend just as much as I did. I didn't know why you were here until you told me about your parents, but I knew that I enjoyed your company. After we met, I realized I might not feel that way for you, but I did care about you, and I still want you as my friend, Nadia." He looks down at his hands, twisting them together nervously. "I'm just really in love with Bethany. I have been for three years, and when she drove here to tell me she made a mistake…" He looks off into the distance. "I knew that I wasn't going to let her go without a fight ever again." I smile, looking at him and appreciating his honesty.

"You were going to tell me before I went to the bathroom, weren't you?" I ask, now remembering the conversation we never got to have.

"Yes," he says without reservation, "but I never got the chance."

We talk like that for an hour, and I tell him about Manny and the girl who cornered me in the bathroom, and how she told me all those mean things.

"What a bitch!" he says, snarling.

I agree wholeheartedly. "She must be so unhappy to have to say shit like that."

"You know, I thought he might have had a thing for you since that day at the town fields, when you went to interview with him." I look at him in surprise.

"What?" I mutter in disbelief. "No way." He only laughs.

"Yep. He looked like he wanted to strangle me or rip me away from you at the very least. Believe me when I say that that man is restraining himself and holding back his feelings for you." I sigh.

"Why does everything have to be so complicated?" I ask rhetorically.

"Does it, though?" he volleys. "Maybe you should just jump his bones?"

I smack him. "Parker, what the fuck is that kind of advice?" He laughs and I do the same, falling into him. We recover, and he nudges me.

"I say you go for it, though, if that makes you happy. Give it a chance. You'll never know unless you shoot your shot, right?" We stand there looking at each other, and his lip twitches. He pulls me into a hug.

"I'm going to miss you, Nadia. You know that? Please keep in touch with me, and I'd like for you to maybe get to know Beth." I hug him tighter.

"I'd really like that, Parker."

He releases me and stands. "Hey, I have to go. My family is all packed and just waiting for me to get back so we can leave. I've felt my phone vibrating in my pocket, and they are probably wondering where I am." He hikes his thumb behind him. "Well," he says, but he doesn't finish that thought. I stand from the hammock a little bit steadier on my feet. He opens the car door and closes it, starting the engine. The window goes down, and he pops his arm outside, hanging it out. "Bye, Nadia. See you soon." He waves and reverses out of the spot.

I stare after him long before the car disappears down the street, but I no longer see him. I'm envisioning Manny and what I'm going to do. Tomorrow I will see him, and maybe I will take Parker's advice. I mean, the worst that could happen is that he rejects me and I go back to being the nanny, or maybe even be dismissed, but after that moment at the park, underneath the blankets, I felt how much he wanted me in just one touch, one grasp of his hand with mine. I cringe inwardly at the thought of him denying me, but it's time to take chances. Starting tomorrow, I am going to live for myself.

CHAPTER
TWENTY-EIGHT

MANNY

She walks in, right on time, just like she always does. But now, after that night at the fireworks show, I feel it differently. It's like I have been rewired to notice everything about her. Even her promptness is a massive turn-on. It's in all the little things, you know? That shit means everything to me because I never had it before with my ex-wife. Something so domestic, so normal, like reliability or attention. Her scent slams into me when she steps through the door and passes me by. It's almost like a drug that's a mixture so pungent and intoxicating. I know it's only the floral scents of lavender and rose, but to me, it will always be associated with her.

She tosses her bag on the counter with this common act of familiarity, like she's right at home, as she then heads straight into the kitchen. I follow her slow, carefree movements, as she grabs a to-go mug from the cabinet and fills it with coffee, like she's already part of my damn morning routine. That's when I notice it's my to-go cup, with just black coffee in it. It's the way I usually take it. She opens the fridge next, humming a Taylor Swift song as she places her lunch bag inside. I just watch her, waiting for her to be done so that I can grab mine from the same spot, thank her for my coffee, and get out of here before I do something stupid like shove her up against the wall and kiss her like I've wanted to so many times. But she's already one step ahead of me, as she picks my lunch bag up, then turns and offers it to me with that damn smile playing at the edges of her mouth, like she was teasing me this whole time.

It's stupid, but her smile is what gets me the most. It's the same one she gives my daughter when she scores that base run or shows her a picture she colored. We never got that reaction from my ex-wife either, and it's not even close. All the years with her, and not once did she pack my lunch, or even care enough to see me off in the morning before work. No kiss goodbye, no "Have a good day, Manny." Hell, most days, I was lucky if she didn't just disappear back into the bedroom before I even walked out the door, or worse, not even be awake at this hour, not just for me, but for our daughter.

I step closer, my hand reaching for my bag. Her skin brushes mine for a second, and I feel it—that little jolt of electricity between us. She tries to hide her shiver as she pulls back, rubbing her arms, but I feel that, too. So I use this brief moment when her eyes close to advance closer toward her.

She can't be immune to this feeling between us, but maybe she's hoping for it just like I am. Her body's reaction to me tells me she feels something, too. I decide to take a chance. Instead of grabbing my lunch bag from her extended hand, I let it drop when she lets go, thinking I have a hold on it.

"I'm so sorry," she begins. She leans over in an attempt to pick it up, but I stop her.

"Leave it," I say. My voice sounds raspy even to my ears. I skim my hand down her arm. "Are you cold, Nadia?" I lower my gaze to look down at her chest, noticing that her nipples are hardened into little peaks poking through her tight, fitted sports tank top.

"No," she gasps. Her skin pebbles as my hand moves languidly down her arm and latches onto her small waist. I move her away from the refrigerator, knowing it isn't the cold that has her responding this way. Shuffling her over to close the refrigerator door, I effectively push us closer together.

"What's going on, Manny?" she asks, voice low, breath catching just a little. She looks up at me through those long lashes, and it fucks with me every single time, just like the first time I saw her. I should say something, but the words are all stuck in my throat, and I can't seem to focus. Her whiskey-colored eyes are burning with desire, and damn it, I feel an indescribable sense of possessiveness knowing it's me who lit that fire.

"I don't know," I mutter. The truth is, it doesn't even matter anymore. What matters is how I've been fighting this pull for what feels way too long. But right now I'm done fighting it, and I need her to know what she does to me.

I close the distance between us, pulling her into me without hesitation. Her body feels warm and soft, like everything I've been craving without even realizing it. "Tell me to stop," I murmur, my voice rougher than I expect, "and I will."

"You better not," she says, effectively cutting me off from whatever thoughts I had as she grabs hold of my shirt and smashes her lips against mine in a rough and hard kiss that has my knees almost buckling at the sensation. I feel like a teenager making out with my high school crush. She opens her mouth, and I seek entrance, officially taking over the kiss as our tongues dance around each other. She moans into my mouth, and I feel my cock twitch in delight at the thought of burying myself inside her.

As the heat between us rises, she pushes me up against the counter, fighting for dominance as she throws her arms around my neck, pulling me in and pushing those perky tits up against me. I lean forward, wanting more, but she stops it. Her hand tugs my hair back, snapping my head up and causing me to look into those eyes, pulling me under in a hypnotic trance. As I lock eyes with her, I can tell she's searching for something, feeling it at my very core until she speaks.

"Tell me something true, Manny," she breathes, her voice

ragged like she just sprinted a mile in under seven minutes. The amber color of her eyes swirls with a reddish hue flecked with specks of gold that hold me captive, compelling me to do as she asks. She waits, silent and still. Seconds stretch on into what feels like minutes, until I can't tell if I'm breathing anymore.

I don't look away, and I doubt I can even if I wanted to. Her breath ghosts over my lips, and my heart is still beating fast from the kiss I barely survived. She is still wrecking me without even touching me. I avoided this because I knew how this would feel if I had her. Just one kiss and I'm a goner.

So I give her what she wants. I tell her my first truth when I say, "I have wanted to do that since the day at the diner." I kiss the tip of her nose before pulling back, so she can see the sincerity in my words. "When you bent down to pick up that red crayon—" Now it's my turn to shudder at the memory. "I imagined a very different scenario of you on your knees, but it was of me thrusting my hard, weeping cock between those pretty heart-shaped lips of yours." She smiles at my choice of words, giving me the courage to continue. "I hated myself for wanting you," I readily admit, averting my gaze downward. "For being recently divorced and having those thoughts, so I tried to push you away," I finish, ashamed of my feelings.

She frowns at the recollection, and it guts me. I have to change the narrative to make her understand that maybe this was inevitable. It was written somewhere in the stars before we met. Kismet, if you will. Meant to fucking be. Because I've never wanted anything the way I want her.

Not just the way I want to sink into her, lose myself in her body. I want everything, and the possibility of something so much more. I lean closer, my voice rough, almost begging, as I continue to make her understand my predicament and my intentions.

"I don't want to fight it anymore. I don't want to be that asshole to you ever again. I swear it, Nadia. Never again. I won't lie to myself, and I won't lie to you. So believe me when I say that I do want you."

"I want you, too," she says, pulling me back down to plant a hard kiss on my lips. I ease up, skimming mine down her cheek in feather-light pecks as I place my lips back on her neck, lightly sucking on the spot where her earlobe rests against her soft skin. I lick my way down the hollow of her neck and back up in one long heated stroke of desire. I brush my lips back again one last time against her ear before tugging on her lobe with my teeth, eliciting the sound of her groan that will stay with me for the rest of the day. God, how I wanted to hear those same sounds with her writhing beneath me as I thrust into her over and over.

But I want to make her understand my meaning. "I don't just want you in my bed, Nadia," I say, pulling her to me and letting her feel the outline of my rigid cock against her. "I want you here in this house *and* in my bed."

I hear her gasp, obviously remembering the time I told her I don't take women to bed here. That's why I feel the need to get my point across. I want her to understand that this arrangement would be different and mean something to me because *she* is beginning to mean something to me. She is the exception, and I want to ensure I drive the point home. I need her to know that, but most of all, I need her to feel it.

Our lips brush against each other in a slow, hungry kiss, but then a noise startles us. We jolt apart like teenagers caught doing something we shouldn't. We are both breathing hard, forgetting why she's even at my house in the first place. I snatch the lunch box up with one hand and try to rearrange myself with the other, desperate to think of anything that might kill my throbbing cock still standing painfully erect between my legs. But it doesn't work. Not even close. I look over to Nadia, who spares me a sympathetic glance. My eyes narrow as she attempts to stifle her laugh.

"Papá," my little girl calls out to me. Yeah, that will do it. I go into dad mode.

"Yes, mijita?" I hide behind the counter, and Nadia is standing there shocked as I try to hide my cock that is deflating, albeit at a slower pace than I would like. Nadia must hear the strain in my voice as she looks downward while I rearrange myself again, so she takes that as her cue to shuffle my daughter out of eyesight and into her bedroom. She says something I can't hear, but it must make Catalina happy, because she squeals in delight, returning to her room easily. Nadia closes the door behind her and walks over to me.

"She's getting dressed now," she says, breathless, not from the words, but from how close we just came to being caught by my daughter.

"I was going to make us breakfast and take a little trip to the park before heading to my house." I watch her. Watch the way her tongue peeks out to wet her lips nervously. "Is that okay?" she asks, uncertainty in her words.

My voice comes out rougher than intended. "Yes, give me the address, and I'll meet you there to pick her up so you don't have to drive back here." A smile spreads across her face, her demeanor now light and relieved, and fuck, if it doesn't hit me straight in the chest, knowing that I'm the reason for it. I feel like the luckiest man on earth, just with the worst case of blue balls.

I notice her watching me, before I forget to tell her, "Oh, by the way, I have a meeting today after work. I'm meeting a client at the tavern to review a proposal. It won't be long, and I'm not eating there." I save dinner time for my family and eat with Catalina at home. I don't add that, but I realize how lonely it is. "Is that okay?" She searches my eyes, and I see that she relaxes.

"Yeah, sure," she answers, but I notice the hesitation flicker across her face before she lets it go. Then, a second later, and a little braver, as if she makes a decision, she offers, "I can make dinner if you want to come by." The way she says it, almost like she's scared I'll say no, makes me want to kiss her all over again to reassure her. She backtracks, misinterpreting my hesitation. "It will be late when you get her home, so I thought..." She trails off and looks away.

So I put her mind at ease. "I'd love that." Her smile broadens. I retrieve my lunch box, which is now on the counter, as I walk toward the door, getting ready to leave for my day.

"Bye, mija," I yell out, as I hear Catalina shout her goodbyes to me from behind closed doors. As I approach the front door of my house, a hand reaches out toward me, making me halt in my retreat. I turn my head to look down at the woman whom I had kissed so thoroughly just a minute ago. Her pink lips are still swollen, and her cheeks remain flushed. She must recall the same memory as she lifts onto her toes to press a simple kiss to my lips.

"Have a great day at work, Manny," she says, and my mouth drops open in disbelief, shutting it quickly before schooling my features. Did I say that shit out loud in the kitchen? I scan my memory of the events that transpired as I think back quickly, and when I see her face, I notice that she isn't smiling at me knowingly but meaningfully, like she is wholeheartedly wishing me a good day at work. And just like that, something in me cracks. I let out this shaky breath and manage a smile back, feeling like the dumbest, happiest fucker alive.

One sentence and I'm lit up inside, buzzing like a live wire. I release my breath and smile back, feeling like a lovestruck fool eager for affection, and maybe I am. I head out, still grinning like one. As I drive away from the house, I begin thinking that perhaps this could be it. This could be the thing I didn't even know I was looking for. Hearing those words was like a cure for an illness I've been fighting, giving me a lift I didn't realize I needed so badly. I've had my share of bad breaks with the worst possible partner. More so now, from being a single parent. I sometimes think God must have a sick sense of humor, but hell, maybe not this time. Maybe He finally threw me a fucking bone.

CHAPTER
TWENTY-NINE

NADIA

She bursts out of her bedroom, sparkling from head to toe, like she is caught in the aftermath of a glitter bomb explosion. She carries her tiny backpack, bouncing at her side, which speaks of adventures and map searching, reminding me of Dora the Explorer. Her hot pink t-shirt with butterflies shimmers with sparkles, echoing the vibe of her jeweled hair band, which tames her wild, ebony curls.

"I'm ready, Ms. Nadia!" she declares proudly, preening, as she shuts the door behind her and drifts into the open area.

I call out, turning from the stove. "Hey, place your backpack by the door, kiddo, and come sit up here so I can give you your breakfast." I pluck the English muffin from the toaster and plate it. I place the little spatula under the egg, which is cooked perfectly in the little egg pan I found discarded in one of the kitchen drawers. I top it off with a slice of cheese, and gently remove it from the pan, serving it into a golden, ooey-gooey sandwich.

"I love it when you make me these egg sandwiches, Ms. Nadia," Catalina says, her voice light and carefree. God, how I wish I was a child again. She licks her lips before taking a hearty bite, and the yellow egg yolk drips down her hand. Without hesitation, she lifts it to her mouth and licks the remaining egg, laughing. It's infectious and I can't help but join her. My heart swells as she eagerly asks me for another sandwich, thoroughly enjoying her breakfast.

Once, this simple meal had been a favorite of mine, but since my parents' passing, I haven't dared to make it again. The last time I tried this at the lake house, it stirred up such painful memories that I failed miserably, deciding to abandon the attempt halfway through. But this time feels different because I made it for Catalina. Somehow, spending time with her makes the ache in my chest begin to lessen. She reminds me of family, and I can't explain it. Maybe it's from how something begins to repair itself on its own. Each small act of kindness or laughter she graces me with when I take care of her stitches my broken heart back together. I miss my mom and dad fiercely, yet performing a role as her caregiver makes me feel good, and I enjoy it more than I thought I would.

I savor the last bites of my avocado toast as I gather up our plates, rinsing them off as Catalina, with a victorious grin, pops the final bite of her second sandwich into her mouth.

"Come on, pickles." I grab her hand in mine and lead us to the bathroom to brush our teeth before we go.

I hand her her bright pink toothbrush and begin to sense a pattern here. She carefully squeezes a neat line of toothpaste onto the soft bristles, her brows furrowing in concentration. As I start brushing my teeth, the monotonous sound fills the quiet space, and when I feel her gaze settle on me, I can tell there's a question she wants to ask. I can sense it in the way she hesitates, so I lift my chin in a silent invitation, letting her know to ask away.

She stares at me in the mirror. "Ms. Nadia, why do you call me pickles?" she asks, her toothbrush suspended mid-air as she awaits my reply. I spit the last of the minty foam, rinse thoroughly, and pat my face, smiling into the towel as I ponder her question. I meet her gaze in the mirror, and with a small motion of my hand for her to keep brushing, she complies, and I take a moment to slip my toothbrush back into the little cosmetic bag I carry everywhere.

Her little electric toothbrush swirls, the soft buzz filling the bathroom as she waits patiently, eyes wide with curiosity. I clear my throat, the words catching slightly before I find them. "Well, someone I loved very much used to call me that when I was your age, and I guess it just slipped out." I hesitate before adding. "It was my dad, and I guess you just remind me a lot of myself when I was little." She beams at me beneath a film of toothpaste froth dripping down her chin.

"Do you not love your dad anymore?" she asks, her voice so profoundly sincere that it takes me a heartbeat to answer.

"I do love him," I say softly, "but my parents aren't here anymore, Catalina. And I miss them so very much."

She spits out her toothpaste hurriedly, wiping her mouth, then flings her arms around me with as much comfort as her tiny body can muster.

"Oh, Ms. Nadia, I'm so sad for you," she whispers against me, her small hands patting my back. And something inside me, something I tried to bury deep beneath these couple of months, begins to shift. I realize that I haven't talked about my parents or thought about them in the way that I should. I haven't even touched their room at home. I just ran. The stages of grief are real. I know that somehow, I got trapped in the very first one—denial. If I ever want to truly heal, then I need to progress and let myself feel some of the things that go with loving and then losing someone.

Catalina pulls back just slightly, her head tilting to the side curiously. "Why did he call you pickles?" I smile, remembering the story and how the nickname came about.

"Well," I begin, my voice wrapped in the warmth of the memory, "I used to go to the movies with my parents all the time. My dad always asked me if I wanted any popcorn or candy, but I never did. I only wanted a pickle. A big, sour, mouth-puckering pickle from the concession stand." I laugh, and Catalina's eyes widen. "So that's how it stuck," I say, shrugging like it's no big deal. "Pickles." I glance at her, my heart softening as she hangs on my every word. "Now, it's your nickname."

"Ms. Nadia?" She looks up at me with those big blue eyes so much like her dad's, making my heart melt. I'm a sucker for this little girl, knowing that I'll give her whatever she asks for.

"Yes?" I begin to clean up the little puddles of water we left around the sink, trying to steady myself against the emotions swirling up from the depths of my heart. I thought I had forever closed the gates since my parents' passing.

She hesitates, then asks so sweetly that it nearly breaks me, "Do you think we could go to the movies and get pickles? Like you did with your dad?"

I blink against the sting of moisture in my eyes, the sharp ache suddenly swelling up in my chest. I want to ugly cry at the beautiful gesture she's offering without even knowing it. "Sure, kiddo." I tuck a stray curl behind her hair band. "I'd really like that." She beams at me and jumps down from the little stool by the sink, her whole body radiating with happiness, and I can't help but smile back.

We leave the library after a sweet little ceremony with light refreshments, held in honor of my mother's dedication as Volunteer of the Year. A plaque bearing her name now rests in the Friends of the Library Garden, nestled beside the flowers she helped plant a few years ago, her favorites. Hand in hand, Catalina and I walk out into the sunlight, her backpack bulging with so many adventures ready at her fingertips for us to read together. I cradle two books of my own against my chest—summer romance beach reads that take place on the island of Nantucket, written by one of my favorite authors. She lives on the same island as in her books, always weaving stories about fictional characters that live in grey-shingled cottages who ride their bikes through the salt-laced streets in the summer and who take leisurely Christmas strolls through the snow-covered cobbled stone walkways in the winter. She does it so seamlessly that I almost believe that it's real. I'm convinced that if I ever needed a police officer on Nantucket, it would be the very same chief of police from her stories, showing up with a kind smile and offering his help. I would already know his name, as does everyone else who lives there. That's how deep I've fallen into her world.

That's the feeling that envelops me whenever I am here at the lake house. It's the deep, familiar coziness, like reading your favorite book in the hammock and slipping into your comfiest pajamas that still smell like the woodsy scent of New Hampshire pine trees and the humid, sticky summer heat. It's the familiarity of the local shops on Main Street that I have frequented since I was a kid. I always envisioned coming here in the summers with my own kids and taking them to all the places my parents brought me, like the hidden gems that only the locals know about. My parents and I had plans for summer parties, endless lazy days in the dog days of summer by the water. And after they retired, they planned on moving here permanently, but they never got to see their dream unfold, and mine shattered in the process.

As I pull into the sloped driveway of the lake house, I hear Catalina gasp softly. "Ms. Nadia?" she asks in wonder as her gaze goes back and forth to take in the big house. "Do you live here?" I open the door and help her out of her car seat. The warm breeze from the lake welcomes me home, and I never tire of it.

"Yep, sure do, pickles." She smiles now at the name, understanding why I call her that. She shoulders her backpack securely and sprints up to the hammock I have on the covered porch that surrounds three-quarters of the house. Before she can launch herself into it, causing herself an injury, I tug her gently by the straps of her bag, effectively guiding her away from the hammock that would have guaranteed a bruise or bump at the very least. "Maybe later, kiddo, but first, I want to show you the inside. We can read some books while I make dinner, and then," I lower my voice to a whisper like I'm telling her a secret, "we'll watch a movie before your dad comes here to pick you up." She nods, looking up at me with a huge grin and practically vibrating with excitement about everything to come.

We walk through the door, and my steps echo on the tiled flooring in the entranceway. Catalina twirls in a slow circle, taking it all in and looking around with curiosity and excitement about being here. She darts toward the expansive windows at the back of the house, pressing her hands against the glass that overlooks the large patio leading to the lake.

"Wow," she says as her head turns from side to side, taking in the panoramic views of the lake that reflect sunlight streaming through large pine trees. My parents put a lot of care into the perfect view when they selected these floor-to-ceiling windows. It was the one thing they agreed on without argument, and even now, I'm glad they did because the view is truly stunning.

"Why don't I get us a snack? We can sit out on the swing on the deck and watch the boats zip by," I suggest, pulling out a chair at the table for Catalina. She slides into the seat and watches me grab a cutting board as I walk to the kitchen island. I don't see any apples in the bowl, so I open the fridge and grab a couple from the fruit bin that I core and slice. I add a generous helping of peanut butter and toss in some cubed cheese. She readily jumps up when I grab the plate and two water bottles. I have her pull a book from her backpack as we walk toward the backyard swing. She stands there momentarily, mesmerized by the lakeview, and I can't help but stand there alongside her, admiring it, too, despite having seen it countless times in my life, but it never gets old.

We settle onto the swing, the wooden beams creaking softly as we sway in a steady rhythm. We sit in comfortable silence as she takes a couple of apple slices and dips them into the peanut butter. After the snack, I place the plate on the grass and pick up the book. When I look at the title, I remember reading this book when I was her age. My parents stopped at a bookstore, and I quickly fell in love with the smells of the musty pages along with the cover of *Alice in Wonderland*. I clutched the book to my chest, refusing to let go, therefore forcing my parents to buy it. It was and continues to be my all-time favorite book. I open up the first page and begin to read. Catalina leans against me, her eyelids growing heavier with each page, until she finally begins to nod off.

"Come on, pickles," I whisper, gently brushing her hair from her face. "Let's get you inside so I can start dinner for us." Manny should be here in a few hours, and I know exactly what I want to make.

CHAPTER
THIRTY

MANNY

I leave the tavern a little later than planned. Before heading out, I call Nadia to tell her I'll be on my way soon and to ensure Catalina has eaten. While wrapping up the proposal, Mr. Tremblay asks if I want a drink. I could have stayed, but I just wanted to get home to my daughter and see that she was taken care of. Also, a big part of me wanted to see Nadia. After I left the house this morning with the worst case of blue balls, I found myself thinking about her the rest of the day. My employees even noticed my distraction at work, commenting on it, but I blew them off, making random excuses for my lack of attention to detail today.

Nadia had been at my house bright and early this morning and has already put in a twelve-hour day. She insists that she doesn't mind, but I do. I hate feeling like I'm taking advantage of her kindness, and that's what it feels like. I pay her, but still it's too much to ask. I punch the address into my phone and follow the voice prompts as it leads me down a winding dirt road onto the last mile to her lake house. As I take in the scenery around me, I notice the homes in this area are nice. Big, too. I wonder how she ended up with this house and if her parents are there with her. God, I hope not.

The robotic voice crackles through the speaker, announcing I've arrived, snapping me out of my racing thoughts as I park my truck alongside her car.

When I spare a glance at the digital clock, I notice that it's verging on close to 8 p.m. I already know Catalina's either fast asleep or fighting it like she always does, not wanting to miss a thing, especially if it's with Nadia. So why does that excite me to be here at this hour?

I can't say I blame Catalina for feeling this way because I wouldn't want to miss a moment away from her either. My pulse increases as a light turns on when I step onto the walkway, heading toward the front door. Before I even get the chance to knock, the door swings open. And there she is, holding it open in invitation as she casually rests her arm against the doorframe.

"Hey," she says, voice low. "She's asleep, so keep it down when you come in, yeah?" I arch an eyebrow at her bossy tone about my kid, but it doesn't piss me off. If anything, it crushes me, reminding me that those are the words a mom would say and the kind of thing Catalina deserves to hear, but never did.

I nod and step inside, toeing off my sneakers in the tiled entrance, careful to be quiet like she asked. The house is gorgeous and tidy, but what gets me are the smells drifting from the kitchen, which make my stomach growl loud enough to embarrass me.

Nadia giggles, attempting but failing miserably to stifle it. I shoot her a glare, but all it does is make her smile widen. She reaches for my hand, lacing her fingers with mine, leading me into her home. We move through the living room, and I catch a glimpse of blankets piled around the sofa, but no sign of Catalina. I'm just about to ask when Nadia tugs me into the kitchen and pulls out a chair for me to sit. That's when I notice that she is in her pajamas.

Her tiny sleep shorts leave nothing to the imagination, and a fitted tank top makes it impossible not to notice that she isn't wearing a bra. Nadia must see me attempting, but failing miserably, to avert my guilty gaze. She goes over to a chair by the window and pulls a cardigan from it, placing her arms through it and wrapping it around her. Part of me wants to tell her not to, that I wasn't bothered by it in the least, but instead I ask what I should be asking.

"Where's Catalina?" I glance around, but don't spot her anywhere. Nadia retrieves a plate from the open shelving and places it on the counter. She peels back the foil from a pan, and the rich smell of pasta sauce and melted cheese hits me so hard that it makes my stomach seize. She cuts a big piece of lasagna, slides it onto the plate, and pops it into the microwave without saying a word.

"I put her to bed in the spare bedroom," she says finally, and I look over at her, wondering why she just didn't leave her on the couch.

"Can I see her?" I ask, and her eyes soften.

"Of course, Manny. Let me take you to her." She crosses the room, and I rise from the chair, following her down the hallway. Her steps are light and soundless on the carpet as she stops, placing her finger against her mouth, signaling for me to be quiet.

I nod as she eases the door open, and I walk through. I look around, noticing the spacious room and the soft bedding of the queen-sized bed where Catalina is curled up under the thick covers, sleeping soundly. Her chest's steady rise and fall let me know she is in a deep slumber. What cuts me deep is when I see the long t-shirt that I assume is Nadia's, and how tightly she is hugging a long-eared stuffed animal, and by the looks of it, it is like the rabbit character from *Alice in Wonderland*. I walk over quietly, crouch beside the bed, and kiss her forehead lightly. I stand there for a second, lost in the moment, before slipping back out and closing the door behind me with a soft click.

When I return to the kitchen, Nadia places a plate before me. The steaming lasagna is piping hot, and the mouthwatering aroma wafting in the air makes my mouth water. I pick up the fork she placed by the plate and cut into the layered piece of heaven. Strings of melted cheese hang from the fork as I lift a heaping bite to my mouth. The flavor that bursts forth is indescribable. I didn't realize how much I missed home-cooked meals. You know, the kind that I don't have to actually make myself. My amá's food is excellent, but it's usually heavy dishes, whereas I prefer to grill more meat and vegetables. But Nadia's lasagna is to die for, and I can't help but wonder who taught her how to cook like this. And as I sit there, I wonder why it is that I want to know everything about this girl.

"What did you guys do today?" I ask in between bites of food.

She smiles and lifts her chin towards me, ignoring the question. "Did you want another piece?"

I nod. "Maybe not as big, though." She chuckles, cutting me another piece, and pops it into the microwave to heat it. I scrape the last bits off my plate before she takes it, rinses it, and grabs a clean one from the shelf. A moment later, she hands me a fresh plate with another steaming heap of lasagna. She sprinkles a little parmesan on top before sliding it across the kitchen island to me.

I pick it up eagerly, ready to devour another bite. Her eyes sparkle with amusement as she watches me eat.

"Do you like it?" she asks.

I shake my head, a playful grin tugging at my lips. "Nope," I answer matter-of-factly. "Hate it. Never had anything so terrible." She scoffs, and I lift my head at the sound of her laughter that follows. It makes me smile to see her like this. "I love it," I answer truthfully as I finish off the second piece in record time, since it wasn't that big and all. That's my excuse, and I'm sticking to it. I stand from the seat, take my plate over to the sink, and begin to clean off my plate. She steps to intercept it.

"Manny, you don't have to do that," she says, shaking her head and dropping her gaze. I gently guide her chin up, tilting her face toward mine. Then I lean down, placing a soft kiss on her pretty little mouth. She smiles against my lips, and when I finally pull away, I can't help but grin back at her.

"You cooked, so it's only fair I clean up," I counter. She grabs a couple of towels, handing me one as we fall into a steady rhythm of washing and drying the dishes side by side. She answers my earlier question, telling me about what she and Catalina did today, and it all feels so natural, like something we've done countless times before.

After it's all done, she looks at me, her stare lingering a little too long. "I was wondering," she pauses, biting her lower lip and choosing her following words before speaking. She seems to decide where she is going with this and asks, "Maybe you guys can just stay here for the night." I give her a look that I can only think is one of confusion, because that is not where I saw this going, but I am so down for it if it is. Whatever she sees in my expression must give her the confidence to continue. "I can bring Catalina back to your house in the morning after breakfast. That way, you can go home and get ready for your day without worrying about anyone else."

I smirk, trying to rile her up. "So you are trying to send me on my way already, Nadia."

She quickly shakes her head. Her hand reaches out, grabbing hold of my arm to stop me. "No, that's not exactly what I meant," she says shyly. I regard her curiously because now I am confused. Her eyes dart back and forth, avoiding mine, and then it hits me. She's not trying to get rid of me. She wants me to stay. I suck in a sudden breath, the realization hitting me. Her worried gaze finally lifts to meet mine.

"Let's be very clear, Nadia, and use all of our words, so I don't get confused, but from what I'm gathering, you are asking me to stay over, too?" If it's possible, the poor girl looks more nervous, wringing her hands together in circular motions, and I am a jackass for making her feel this way. I reach out to her, placing my hands on hers, and stilling her. Making her anxious wasn't my intention when all I asked for was clarity. So I continue to push her for answers, because I don't just want to know, I need to know.

"And where will I sleep, mi cariño?" I murmur, stepping closer and eating up the distance between us. I am really glad at this point that I went home to shower before meeting the client after work because I'm almost flush with her, and it's still not close enough. I wrap my arms around her, lifting her effortlessly as she instinctively hooks her legs around me. I set her down on the kitchen island, her body trembling slightly at the contact. I can't tell if it's from the chill of the stone countertops or the fact that I'm touching her.

THE CRUELEST TRUTH

Her skin feels like hot molten lava, and I want to burn in it even if it means being closer to her when I know I shouldn't. We are crossing all kinds of lines, and I feel more and more careless with each passing day because this woman makes me want to throw every rule I made about swearing off relationships out the door. I just want to grab on to her and never let go.

I step into her, spreading her legs wider as I move between them. My hands slide up her thick thighs, then move to her full ass, gripping tightly and pulling her closer against me. Her cardigan slips from her shoulders, and I push it the rest of the way off, letting it fall onto the countertop. I lean in, and her pupils dilate, her pink tongue flicking out to wet her lips. I track the movement, hunger curling low in my gut because I want a taste so badly. The scent of her minty toothpaste and coconut lip balm clings to her as I breathe it in, nuzzling my nose along her freshly cleaned face. Running my hands up her tanned legs, I stifle a groan. This woman has a body made for sin, and I want to defile it in more ways than I can count. "I'll ask you one more time, Nadia." My impatience comes through. "And I want you to tell me a truth."

She inhales sharply, her breath catching before she speaks. "A truth?" she asks, her voice barely above a whisper. I pull back just enough to meet her gaze and ensure she sees exactly what I'm asking.

"Yeah. A truth," I say lowly. "I need you to tell me what you want and, more importantly, where you want me to sleep, baby. If you want me on the couch, I'll sleep there. If you want me in your bed, I'll be there, too. I just need to know." I hold my stare, and I lean forward, trying to be patient as I wait for her response.

"I want you in my bed, Manny," she breathes out, finally putting me out of my misery. "And I want you to take me there now." I don't need to hear anything else. With her legs wrapped tight around my waist, I lift her easily.

"That one at the end," she points, and I carry her to her bedroom. I set her down gently on the bed, and for a second, I just stand there, taking her in. Then I step back, closing the door softly behind us. The moonlight spills through the windows, bathing her in an ethereal glow. She's sprawled out on the bed, looking up at me, and I swear, I've never seen anything more beautiful in my life.

"If you don't want this, tell me now," I say, my voice rough with need. I strip off my shirt, socks, then shove down my pants, stepping out of them until I'm left in nothing but my boxer briefs. She stares at me, wide-eyed, her gaze dropping lower.

My cock is already at full mast, straining against the fabric. I grip myself, trying to relieve the rapidly building ache. But then she reaches out, grabs my hand, and pulls me down on top of her. I brace myself over her, trying not to crush her with my larger frame. As I look into her eyes, I make a silent vow at this moment. One that I hope she can see written all over my face.

CHAPTER
THIRTY-ONE

NADIA

Manny stares at me, and I am at a loss for words. I can't believe we are here in my bedroom about to do this. The first time I saw him, he stared down at me with what I thought was disgust. I never could have imagined this moment between us would happen. But now, there is nothing in his gaze but adoration and the unspoken promise of tomorrow. After his recent confession, when I asked for a truth, he admitted that he had tried to fight off his initial reaction to me at the diner when I was on my knees in front of him. But now, all the fight has left him as he holds my stare.

"We don't have to do this tonight," he says in a hushed tone, almost as if it pains him to say those words. I can tell he wants me badly and feel it as his solid warmth invades my wet center.

His caring words thread around my heart like sutures, mending it in all the ripped places. I drag my tongue across my bottom lip, and his piercing blue eyes track the movement, holding me captive, darkening when my hand finds him through his briefs. He is thick, hot, and pulsing against my palm, and I shiver at the feel of him and what I envision it will be like when he finally pushes into me for the first time. There's no way I can wait any longer. I need all of him. I ache for the connection, the closeness, and the feeling of being totally his. I tighten my grip, and his breath hitches in response.

He squeezes his eyes shut briefly. "Fuck," he groans, lowering himself, and I readily move my legs apart so that his cock can rest at my clothed entrance. "Are you trying to torture me?" His voice strains as his cock pulses in my grip. He rests his forehead against my shoulder, his breath warm on my skin. I trail my tongue up the side of his neck, tasting the saltiness of his skin, before brushing a kiss against his ear.

"You're the one torturing me, Manny." My voice comes out shaky. "I'm the one still clothed."

He chuckles, the sound vibrating against me. Raising his face, he hovers closely so his lips graze mine without kissing. "Well," he murmurs playfully, "let's see what we can do about that, mi amor." His forearms cage me in, braced against either side of my head, as he brings his lips to mine in a slow, unhurried kiss. He kisses me deeply, like it's not enough, so I open for him. His tongue quickly sweeps into my mouth, claiming me as all other sounds fall away. Now, the only sounds I can hear are his moans along with the sound of my heartbeat, beating in sync with the pulsation between my legs. Moisture builds, and I'm dripping with desire, wanting more than anything to be filled by him.

He pulls away and stares at me, mere inches away, but the space between us seems endless. It's too far, but the heat in his darkened blue eyes is undeniable.

"God, you're beautiful." The words slip out before I can stop them. He freezes, stunned, like he has never received such a compliment, and I find that really hard to believe. Women throw themselves at him, and he must have a mirror, right? So why does this seem like such a surprise when I tell him another truth? Whatever emotion cracked through a moment ago, he schools it into something guarded. I know we will have to have a conversation at some point and unpack all our emotional baggage, but tonight, we don't have to say anything. We can just feel it and show it in the way our bodies mold into one another.

Some part of me aches to show him how beautiful I think he is. This feeling that has been brewing isn't just carnal attraction. To me, it means so much more, and I hope he feels it, too.

"You think I'm beautiful, baby?" His voice tries to downplay the emotion he lets show. "I can't even describe what I see when I look at you. You are the most perfect thing I've ever set eyes upon." He kisses me softly and pulls back to sit on his knees, looking down at me. I wonder what he sees when he looks at me that way? He lifts my arms above my head, tugging my tank top up and over, tossing it somewhere onto the bedroom floor. His gaze drops instantly, raking over my chest, and his breathing quickens. One hand cups my breast with a gentleness that almost undoes me because he touches me like I mean something to him. God, do I want to mean something to him?

The other hand toys with my nipple in slow, teasing circles. I arch off the bed in an unspoken invitation for him to take more because I want whatever he offers. He trails his hands lower, following the path of his gaze, and hooks his fingers into the waistband of my sleep shorts. In one fluid motion, he slides them down over my hips and legs, peeling them away from my wet center. I close my eyes, relishing this moment of pure bliss. It's finally happening—but then nothing. I open my eyes to find him completely still and staring at the wetness that is undoubtedly visible to him. His breathing turns ragged. My cheeks flush with embarrassment. God, can he smell my arousal? How much I want him?

He rests back on his feet, tugging the sleep shorts off one leg at a time before tossing them aside. He pushes my legs apart. "Baby, I want to taste you so bad," he says, lifting my legs and planting my heels firmly on the bed. He pushes my knees out, spreading me wider and exposing me completely to his unyielding stare.

THE CRUELEST TRUTH

"Please," I cry out, but I don't even know what I am begging for now. I just want it all—his mouth, his hands, his cock. All I do know is that I am desperate for him to rip me apart, just so he can put me back together.

I don't even register his mouth is there until I almost buck off the bed at the foreign sensation.

"Damn, it's been so long." My arm flies over my face because, fuck me, did I say that shit out loud? If I did, he doesn't comment, and I'm too lost in the sensation to care as he picks one leg up and throws it over his shoulder. His head tilts to plunge his tongue into me over and over again. He licks me from my entrance until he reaches my clit. He thrusts two fingers into me and flicks his tongue over where I need him the most. It's like he can read my body. And the sounds his fingers make as he fucks me with them, that sound of how wet I am should be embarrassing, but the look of satisfaction on Manny's face is such a turn-on. He's ecstatic that he made me this way, and I know I am because I feel it dripping down my leg along with the repeated licks from his tongue. He puts his mouth on my clit, and when he sucks me there, I'm done for. I cry out, my body bucking from the blissful orgasm that has me shaking as it rips through my body. I tug his hair as he tries to still go at my oversensitive area. I feel his loss of body heat immediately, but when I open my eyes, I see him staring down at me, a smirk playing at his lips as I pant.

I'm mesmerized, watching as Manny seductively crawls up my body until he reaches my mouth, kissing me thoroughly until I can taste myself on him.

"Can you taste how sweet your pussy is, baby?" I can, but I'm unable to speak. He has tongue-fucked me speechless, so I give him an incoherent reply that has him stifling a laugh. He rests himself at my opening and places the tip at my entrance. He looks at me, waiting, silently asking for permission.

"When did you put that condom on?" I blurt out in disbelief, and this time I can feel him laugh. "Did I totally miss that?" I place my forearm across my eyes, groaning, but I quickly drop it. Instead, I grasp his shoulder as he pushes into me in the most delicious way. I feel the stretch of his thick, hard cock as he seats himself fully inside me. He rests some of his weight on me this time, and I love how his body feels against mine. He is all hard muscle, contrasting with the softness of his curly chest hair that tickles against my bare chest. I love it all, and I never want this feeling to end. He picks up his pace, thrusting into me harder each time, and I lift my legs around him. He places one forearm by me, and the other he uses to lift my ass so he can get even deeper, if that's possible.

"Fuck baby," he says in a strained voice. Like it is taking everything in him to keep fucking me this way.

"Please, Manny. Don't stop," I beg him. "I'm so close." He picks up his pace, fucking into me harder, hitting that one spot over and over until I scream out. "Oh, God, Manny, right there!" I shut my eyes, but he's in my face, and I'm so afraid because he may already be in my heart, too.

"Look at me, mi amor." His voice is raw with emotion and unspoken truths. It sounds like he's already there, ready to find his release. I force my eyes open, just like he wants, finding his gaze locked on mine. "I want to see you come." His words are strained, like the effort he is using to drag them out takes every bit of strength he possesses. I want to close my eyes from the overwhelming sense of pleasure that washes over me, as my body convulses with such an intense orgasm. But, I fight that urge, as I hold onto this connection as my hand clasps around his neck. His eyes never leave mine, and I feel more seen than ever. As we share this intimacy, it feels much more than the first time, and I try not to get my hopes up. With one final thrust, he lets go, burying himself deep as he spills into the latex barrier. I can feel him still pulsing inside me, and I lock my legs tighter around his waist, wanting to feel every desperate inch of him, and keeping him here forever in this moment. I'm afraid once this is over, we won't have another. One thing I've had the hard lesson of learning is that there might not be another time to treasure something so beautiful.

"So beautiful," he murmurs, just as the same words form in my mind. But he isn't talking about the moment, he's talking about me. My eyes sting with sudden warmth as he cups my cheeks and kisses me like I belong to him. When he pulls back, he leaves a soft kiss lingering on my lips before slipping off the bed and disappearing into the bathroom. A moment later, he reemerges, retrieves his briefs from where they lay crumpled on the floor, and slides them on. I reach for my clothes, tugging on my shorts and pulling my tank top over my head. Manny crosses the room, pulls back the covers, and sinks into the bed beside me. His hand finds mine as he gently tugs me down with him.

His chin rests on my shoulder as his body molds to mine under the warm weight of the blankets. "This bed is fucking fantastic," he says, breaking the comfortable silence.

I snort, unable to help it. "Yeah," I say, grinning. "It's pretty great. Especially with you in it." He tugs me closer, nuzzling into the curve of my neck and pressing soft kisses there that make me giggle. My whole body relaxes as his fingers trace lazy circles on my thigh. I sigh, sinking deeper into his warm embrace.

"Baby," he murmurs, his voice already rough with sleep.

"Mhm?" I mumble, barely hanging on to a coherent thought.

"Are your parents coming home?" he asks hesitantly. I stiffen at the word "parents" before the rest of his question even registers. He must sense the change, because he tightens his arms around me, like I might bolt out of here. And he may be right.

"No," I answer. That one word, saying enough, yet nothing at all. I know he wants more than that. His head drops down. I can barely hear him, but his question is still there.

His voice drops lower, his breath brushing my neck. "Not tonight?" he asks, even softer now, almost afraid of the answer. I gulp down the emotions that threaten their way up, but I've suppressed them for a while now. But how he's made love to me and then how he holds me this way just makes me feel so raw and exposed.

"Never," I say, my voice breaking softly. I hear him take in a sharp, pained breath as he places the most gentle kiss on the nape of my neck. I shiver in response. "But that's a truth for another day." No more questions follow. All I can feel is the anchoring strength of his muscular arms wrapping tightly around me, keeping me grounded. And for the first time in what feels like forever, I fall asleep in a dreamless and safe slumber.

CHAPTER
THIRTY-TWO

MANNY

I wake up early before the sun, much like I do every day, without the use of an alarm. My body is trained with the routine of waking up for work and getting Catalina ready for school, except this morning is different. I pad lightly across the carpet, peeling my clothes off that lay discarded on the bedroom floor from mere hours ago. I pull on my jeans, and I can't help but drink in her form, lying peacefully on the bed that I just had her on multiple times. It makes me wish I had more time with her. So many more mornings to wake up together, but even if there's not another night, at least I had that one night with her. I shake my head at the thought, because who am I kidding? One night is hardly enough. Wanting her is no longer a question.

I hover at the edge of the bed, every fiber of my being aching to crawl back in, to feel her skin against mine and hold her in my arms again. Her hair fans out across her pillow in a long, wavy mess that surrounds her head like a halo, as the morning light streams through her bedroom window, bathing her in golden light that glows against her tanned skin. The sheets slipped off her torso, revealing her softness that I want to worship once more. She's all woman with ample breasts, a soft belly, and thick thighs, along with an ass that I appreciated grabbing onto as I thrust into her over and over again. Without thinking, I move closer, gently pulling the covers over her, in a protective embrace. I lean in, brushing my lips against her forehead.

Her lashes flutter until her eyes open, sleepily. "Manny?" She yawns, stretching like a cat basking in the sun.

"Yes, mi amor," I say, brushing a loose curl from her face. "I am going to grab us some breakfast before Catalina wakes up. I'll be back before you miss me."

She smiles lazily. "I already miss you," she answers. "I'm getting right up…" She trails off, her body contradicting her words as she turns around, slowly melting deeper into the pillow. A grin spreads as I watch her for one heartbeat longer. Then I leave her there and exit her bedroom door as quietly as possible, trying my damnedest not to make a sound in the hallway, as I go to grab us that breakfast I promised.

I already placed the order at the Bagel Café, so it's a quick trip, and before I know it, I'm back in her kitchen, brewing the coffee along with my churning wayward thoughts. As I think back to the night we shared, I can't help but remember her reaction to the question about her parents. She said "Never," and to me, that sounds like they died, or something bad happened where they aren't returning. Not like, I'm disowned or I don't talk to them. The finality with which she said that word caused her pain, and I'm willing to bet that it wasn't that long ago. It seems fresh, and I can understand that. I have yet to unpack all the trauma with my ex.

I grab a couple of mugs from the shelf and laugh at the one I'm holding. It's teal green and says, *Pretending to Listen*. I scoff and place it back, grabbing the matching set that says, *I'm weird*, and *I love weird*.

"Perfect." I think this fits us. I place them on the counter and pour each cup full of piping hot coffee. The steam curls up from the mugs as I grab her flavored oat milk and put it in the frother. I have seen her do this, and she even has the same one at my house. I almost spit my coffee out when she took out her portable frother from her purse and whisked her non-dairy milk before me.

What I first thought was presumptuous, I find endearing, or maybe my feelings are changing for this woman in a way I didn't expect. She has managed to break through my high defenses and penetrate through the tiniest crack in my exterior, cracking it wide open. As if my soul calls to hers, she appears there in the doorway, her hip leaning against the wooden beam of her craftsman-style home. She watches me, biting her bottom lip, and I want to do nothing more than bend her over that sofa in the living area and take her from behind. As if reading my mind, her eyes widen and she laughs.

She shakes with the effort it takes to suppress a laugh, but fails miserably. "Maybe later," she teases, her voice laced with promise, before pushing off the wooden beam and sauntering my way. Her hips sway, knowing that I'm watching her seductive act as she goes to the kitchen island to see what I brought. When she spots the bagels I got us, her steps hurry, seduction gone in favor of hunger.

"Bagel Café?" Her eyes light up as she picks one out of the bag, steam still wafting from the freshness of the recently baked sourdough. "I love this place." She pulls it apart and places a small piece in her mouth. "Reminds me of a Jersey-style bagel." She stuffs a larger piece into her mouth this time as she continues to speak. "They are the best." Her voice is muffled. I pick up her mug with froth on top and hand it to her. She smiles. "Aw, you remembered." When she looks at me like this, I feel like I have won a prize.

"Of course, mi cariño." She fucking beams at my Spanish term of endearment. "I remember everything when it comes to you." I mean it more than I should at this point, but it's true. Her brows scrunch, and I can tell there is a question coming.

"Manny?" And there it is.

"Yeah, baby?" She takes a slow sip of her coffee, and when her tongue slips out to catch the froth from her lip, I nearly choke on my drink. I curse under my breath. Her brows rise in question. "Nothing, continue what you were saying." I need to control myself. My daughter could come walking in at any moment and I haven't had the talk with her yet about what this thing with Nadia is starting to mean. If it progresses, then we can have a chat with Catalina, but maybe—

"Why did you call me mi cariño that time at the bar?" She bites her bottom lip, like she already regrets asking, but I can tell that she already wants to ask me more.

My mind stops reeling when she asks me about that. It was an accident, a mere slip, but one that I felt deep in my bones. I was wondering when she was going to bring that up. Mi cariño, mi amor, mi vida. They are all words that feel too big for this stage of whatever we're in, yet all of those things I associate with her are just a different way to express how I feel about her. My sweetheart, my love, my life. They are all hers because when I envision us together, it isn't just a possibility, it's a promise. I sensed it, and it's why I had to fight it, because I knew that even though my ex gutted me at her leaving us, maybe even cheating on me, this woman has the potential to rip my life apart. Not just me, but also my daughter. And that is the part that I fear the most, because my daughter is already falling for her, too.

"Are you ready for another truth, baby?" She pulls up a chair at the island, slides into it, and makes herself comfortable.

"Yes," she says reluctantly. "Tell me." Her eyes show vulnerability that I readily want to push away.

I nod, ready to get it all out and anything else she wants to know. I blow out a breath. Okay, here it goes. "That time at the bar when I saw you for the second or maybe third time..." I pause, averting my eyes from hers. "I...I thought you might be stalking me." There, I said it. I hang my head in shame. But I swing it back up at the snort that comes out of Nadia.

"Oh, my God, you did not!" she says, laughing. Bagel particles fly out of her mouth as I watch in horror. Why does she still look cute, even now? Oh, damn, I have it bad. I stifle a moan, my hand covering my face as I place it down, shaking with my own stupidity.

"I know. I know," I say. "I get it, but you don't understand. I had that woman, Sylvie, stalking me, and I just thought…" I see her stiffen, and I need to know what's wrong. It's the same type of posture she made yesterday. Is there a connection? Oh, fuck no. I walk over to her, bending at her side. I place my hands on her cheeks, pulling her face to look up at me. "Baby, what's wrong?" I ask with concern etched on every muscle, and I need to know how to make her smile again.

"It's nothing," she says softly, and I know she's lying. She won't even look at me.

"Nope, you need to tell me what it is. When I mentioned that she-devil's name, you got upset. I saw it. What happened? Did she tell you something?" She looks up at me and I know that bitch said something to her. "Tell me now. What did she say?"

She sighs like the thought of telling me pains her. I can't even imagine. She runs her hand over her face before she meets my gaze once again. "She told me about your hookup." She braces herself for whatever it is I am going to say, but rage consumes me.

"The fuck I did." Her eyes shoot back up to me, hope blooming in her eyes.

"You didn't do anything with her?" she asks, hopeful, and I can't lie. Although I didn't sleep with her, I might have. I'll never be happy that Catalina was sick that night, but I'm grateful that I had to leave before I made a mistake. Drowning in my grief made me lack good judgment. She must see the guilt on my face, because her shoulders drop and she pulls into herself.

"I never slept with that woman. I did kiss her and maybe a little more, but nothing like I did with you." While she doesn't seem to like it, she is happy that I didn't fuck that woman, and I am, too.

"That was a bad night," she says, looking at me. "She told me some terrible things about Parker, too."

"What things?" I ask, because I had forgotten all about that guy. I try not to show my jealousy, but I must do a piss-poor job at it because she immediately sets my mind at ease.

"First of all, Parker is just a friend. We did not have a romantic relationship. He was pining for his ex, and while I didn't know it until that horrific woman told me they were making out, I left upset, not because I was mad that Parker was back with his ex, but because of what she did with you." I move closer to her.

I realize I never told her my truth. "You wanted to know why I called you that at the bar?" She nods, so I continue. "It was because I see myself when I look into your eyes. The same sadness and loneliness I felt. It was like looking at the same side of a coin—my mirror image. I was drawn to you. Maybe like a moth to a flame. You know that it could burn you, but you are just drawn to it, so damn close, and think fuck the consequences."

We stand there, looking into each other's eyes, and all that we don't say is conveyed in the briefest of kisses before I force myself to back away. I groan at the time. "I have to get to work, as much as I don't want to, mi amor. But let's get Catalina up, huh? I'd like to say goodbye before I leave."

I hold my hand out to her, and she stands, smiling up at me. As I walk to wake up my daughter hand in hand with this woman at my side, I can't help but wonder what it would be like to do this every day. I refuse to get my hopes up because this is only for the summer, and good things don't last. At least, not for me.

CHAPTER THIRTY-THREE

NADIA

As soon as we woke Catalina up that morning, walking in together hand in hand, something shifted between us. Manny left for work, but when he came home late that afternoon, he asked me to stay for dinner. One day turned into another, and before we knew it, we fit into each other's lives seamlessly. We took turns going to my house and then his. We made s'mores over the fire pit in his backyard, under a blanket of stars, laughing together and stealing kisses like lovestruck teenagers. We took walks after dinner together with Catalina swinging between us, much to the disappointment of the women in his neighborhood, who were obvious fans. But Manny wasn't too upset. In fact, when they looked his way with hopeful smiles through ridiculously bright red lipstick, he slid his hand possessively over my ass, leaving it there for his admirers to see and dislike me a little bit more.

I caught one of the women making snide comments, but he smirked, unaffected and uncaring of their attention. I couldn't help but bite back a grin about his public display of affection, especially regarding his female groupies. They could look all they wanted to, but he was mine. We had dinners together on the deck overlooking the lake, wine after Catalina went to sleep, and a sleepover at my house, which led to lots more of us exploring each other on every piece of furniture in my room and the shower, before falling asleep tangled in one another. We were never together this way at his house. Yet.

Tonight is the first time I will be staying over. No more lingering looks, or long-winded goodbyes, wishing I didn't have to leave. Catalina asked Manny if we could all go to a movie on Friday. I work most Saturdays, so that's out of the question. Nothing gets by that girl. If you tell her something, she won't forget, so here I am, waiting for Manny to get home after work on a Friday so that we can make the 6:30 feature.

Every day, Catalina asked if it was Friday yet, and every day this week, I told her, "Not yet, pickles." So when I told her, "It's Friday!" her face lit up, and we broke into a bit of dance right there in the kitchen, spinning and laughing, both of us too excited to keep still. Catalina was happy to go to the movies with me after that story about my father. I'm just happy to be able to share that with her, and in turn, remember a good time in my life with my parents.

I try not to think too much about the end of August lurking around the corner. I am trying to enjoy the moment, but I see it slipping away, knowing that this is a temporary situation and I'll soon be leaving for college. I've spent every waking day with them, holding hands and cuddling around campfires. Caring for Catalina during the day when Manny is at work, then dinner together, and now going out like a family tonight seems more than a temporary situation. It feels like another step forward, just to have it all end? Maybe I should have a conversation about what happens at the end of August.

I hear Catalina jump off the couch with a *thud* as she spins around, running to me. She grabs my arm, shaking it. "He's here!"

she shrieks, peering through the window as she whips the curtain back in place at the sound of Manny's truck door closing. She's been staring out the window intermittently for the last fifteen minutes, waiting for her father to pull into the driveway. Manny bounds up the front steps, and I barely have time to calm her down before he opens the door to find Catalina jumping around and ushering him in.

"Hurry, Papá!" she cries, grabbing his lunch box from him and pushing him toward the shower. She hands it to me, and I can't help but stifle a laugh at her bossiness. "Go change, or we are going to be late!" He casts me an amused look as I blow him a kiss behind Catalina's back. As I unpack the lunch box, I freeze. There's only two items inside. I pull out two pre-packaged pickles, taking them out and placing them on the counter. Catalina scampers over, grabbing them with a squeal. "He got them!" She dances, clutching the pickles to her chest like they're the most precious gift in the world.

I swallow hard against the lump rising in my throat, knowing that I shouldn't be emotional over a fucking snack, but it's not the snack, it's what it means. It's the fact that Catalina told him about the story with my dad and how, even though he worked all day, he still stopped to get us this for our first movie together, just like I planned to do when we got there. It's more about the fact that he remembered and cared enough to do so.

I try to fight the urge to ugly cry at the kind gesture. I blink away the moisture blurring my vision. "Did you tell your dad the story?" I ask, humbled by the action.

She nods, her smile infectious. "I did, and he said he was going to get them for us so we could share a happy memory of our own, Ms. Nadia." I drop to her eye level and pull her into a hug.

"Thank you, pickles." I rub my nose in her face, and she giggles. "That was a very nice thing to do."

"You're welcome, Ms. Nadia." She pulls back and runs toward Manny's bedroom. She is about to throw herself into the door, but Manny opens it, catching her mid-push.

"Woah there, mijita." He picks her up and twirls her around. Her chuckles erupt into a fit of laughter, and I can't help the smile that spreads across my face, too.

Manny grabs his keys from the counter, his gaze landing on me, still standing there holding the pickles. He watches me carefully, like he's searching for something in my face, a reaction of whether it was a good idea or not to do it. I grab a Ziploc and a few napkins, throwing them into my purse. "Thank you for these," I say softly. He doesn't speak, just nods and extends his hand out, taking mine.

"Are you finally ready to go to the movies?" Catalina asks, as Manny and I shout "Yes!" in unison. We look at each other smiling, as he squeezes my hand, locking the door behind us.

We walk to the truck and after strapping Catalina into her booster seat, he hops in and starts the vehicle. "So..." he begins, hesitating with his hand on the steering wheel, looking guilty as sin. He pulls out of the driveway, still thinking. Catalina and I exchange looks, both of us wondering what's happening. "Okay, ladies, hear me out," he says, glancing over at me as he takes my hand in his, and his thumb traces lazy circles across my skin.

Catalina groans from the back seat. At the stop sign, instead of turning right toward the cinema, he turns left, heading in the opposite direction. "I thought maybe we would try something a little different tonight," he begins, but it is cut off by the whines that escape from the little girl in the back seat.

"Papá, you promised we were going to the movies." She crosses her arms over her chest, ready to fight it out with that irresistible pout of hers that has her daddy melting and giving in. I look back and witness what I can only imagine her teenage years will look like in about ten years, inwardly groaning at the thought.

"Yes, mijita, I did, but I thought we would do something much better." Her eyebrows lift, just like her father's do, and I can't help but laugh at the similarity. Manny glances over at me, and I shrug. "*Not helping,*" he mouths. I clear my throat.

"So that sounds interesting. What did you have planned for us instead? Is it a surprise, Manny?" I look at him expectantly, flicking my attention to Catalina, who is now somewhat intrigued, and so am I.

I bite my lip, unsure if I overstepped. I hope I was giving him exactly what he wanted by helping, stepping in when he needed backup. When he looks over at me, his eyes catch on my mouth, lingering there a second longer than necessary, and when his eyes lift to meet mine, I brace myself for his reaction, expecting frustration, but what I see instead makes me pause. His eyes soften, and he mouths, *"Thank you."* His gratitude shows in his eyes, as if he truly appreciates my help with Catalina. Honestly, I don't know how to unpack that, so instead I avert my gaze, focusing out the window as he starts explaining to Catalina where we're headed.

Twenty minutes later, we pull into the Harbour Playhouse. The building looks like a red barn, surrounded by twinkling lights that reflect off the lake's edge. He shuts the truck off and comes my way to open my door and help Catalina out of the truck. Our footsteps crunch on the gravel as we walk up to a poster with the words *'Now Showing.'* A little girl with a broad, toothy smile and a red bow in her hair is front and center, along with the title of the show. "Matilda?" I look at him, surprised. He smiles and takes our hands.

"Come on, girls." He tugs on our hands, leading us in. "Let's enjoy the show."

When we return to Manny's house, it is well past Catalina's bedtime. She fell asleep in the back seat of Manny's truck, her little cheek resting on her hand, mouth parted. Manny opens the door quietly, lifting her out of the truck with ease, and cradling her against his chest as he carries her into the house. I walk ahead of him, opening the front door and guiding them into her bedroom. Pulling back the covers, I help peel off her little sneakers and slip her into soft pajamas. Manny places a kiss on her forehead and walks toward the door as I bend down to kiss her, too, in a similar fashion. When I look up, Manny's standing just outside her room, watching me with an unreadable expression. He holds his hand out without a word, and I slip mine into his, tugging me gently toward the kitchen.

I stifle a yawn and move to get my bag ready to sling it over my arm when he stops me, removing it and placing it back on the counter. "Where are you going, mi cariño?" He pulls me closer, his hands sliding up to cup my face, as his thumb traces my cheek. "I thought you were staying over tonight?" he asks, concern in his eyes, searching mine for an answer he's afraid to hear. The truth is that I never want to leave. But the words won't come, so I say nothing.

As I look up at him, there is more showing in his eyes than a simple good time, and I know that before I leave for school soon, maybe even tonight, it might be the moment to broach the subject with him. The "what happens next" conversation that I hate to have, but I want to know where we stand. "I wasn't sure and didn't want to assume," I tell him honestly.

He brings his lips to mine and pulls away just enough to whisper, "Let's go to my room."

He picks up my bag, flinging it over his shoulder, and I fight the giddiness and nervousness I feel as we walk hand in hand to his bedroom. The one that, not so long ago, he told me he never brought women to. As I look around, I notice that his room is simple, but comfortable, and the lighting is warm and inviting. He places my bag on the chair in the corner, as I take in the surroundings. Despite taking care of his daughter, I always respected his privacy. I was told to never come into his room or his office, and I have kept his requests, respecting the boundaries he has set.

He walks over to me and pulls me into his arms, running his hand along my sides. He grabs my shirt and lifts it off in one swift tug, tossing it onto the floor behind him. He lowers me onto the bed, as I sit back on my forearms, hoping to admire the view above me. He strips his clothes off without even looking away and it is the most provocative striptease I've ever encountered as he leans forward, fully naked with his cock bobbing in invitation. He pushes me back and pulls off my pants, tugging them off along with my thong and dropping them from his hands. He crawls forward, as I scamper upward, hoping to give him more room, but he halts my movements, straddling me. His cock hits my stomach as a bead of precum leaves a sticky trail on my chest. I lick my lips, needing to taste him as I run my finger over the tip, feeling the wetness coat my fingers. He watches my movements with a heated stare as I bring it up to my mouth and lick the saltiness from my fingers. His eyes burn with the intensity of my actions, causing him to push my legs aside.

I grab his arm, halting his movement. "Manny, please," I say, and he looks at me.

"What do you want, baby?" he asks huskily. Pained at taking this slow.

"I want to taste more of you," I plead, placing my hands on his legs, beckoning him to move forward. He straddles me as his cock is mere inches from my mouth. He is thick and hard, and so very mine. I lean forward, sticking my tongue out to lick his tip, and he groans, moving forward. I take this opportunity to grab his ass, angling him closer.

I can't take it. I'm desperate for him. "Fuck my mouth, Manny," I beg. "Please." He moves over, cradling his hand under my head as he holds me in place with one hand, using the other to feed me his cock. I open for him, and his taste floods me. The feel of him as I explore his soft, velvety cock with my tongue has me squirming, trying to stop the building ache between my legs that is begging to be filled by only him. He pushes his length in and out in a rhythm that has me gasping for breath in between thrusts, but I don't complain even when he picks up his pace. I open my throat, taking more of him in.

He moans and stops mid-thrust. "I am going to come like this if I continue, and I want to fuck you first, then paint you in my cum." I nod, so ready for it, as he pulls out of my mouth in one stroke, and a band of saliva trails down my chin. He scoots down the bed, leaning into me, and kisses me so deeply. His tongue is everywhere and not nearly enough. He breaks the kiss, steps off the bed, and pulls me until my legs hang off. He lifts my legs, throwing them over his shoulder. As his cock rests at my entrance, he looks at us, and I can only imagine what he is thinking as his breathing becomes more ragged. I can tell he is about to lose control, and I am so lucky to be the one making him do so.

"I need to fuck you bare, baby," he groans. "Please tell me you are on birth control." I nod eagerly, and that's all it takes for him to thrust to the hilt. I gasp at the sensation of being filled wholly by him. He begins to move at a fast pace. The way he takes me is carnal and rough, and I love every moment of it. He holds me to him, grabbing onto my ass to pull me into him as he repeatedly hits that spot that drives me wild. It's like he already knows my body so well, playing it like an instrument. As he leans forward a little, changing the angle just slightly, the movement has me gasping as my orgasm rapidly builds. He must know that is where I need him, because he picks up the pace, hitting it repeatedly until I see stars and scream his name. He finds his own release a few thrusts later, as he pulls out and shoots strings of cum over my bare chest.

As we both come down from our endorphin high, he stares at me and the mess we've made before he leaves me reluctantly, in the direction of the bathroom. I lay there, breathing hard, coming back to reality from the mind-blowing orgasm that overtook me. He walks over to me with a warm cloth as he cleans me up and dries me off with another. He takes them to the bathroom, and when he returns, he falls down beside me, naked and uncaring about us being here like this. He rolls over to me and looks into my eyes, cupping my cheek so lovingly as he kisses me, conveying all the things in that act we don't dare speak of, not wanting to acknowledge the truth. That's okay, for now. I have to believe we still have a little time to work it out.

CHAPTER
THIRTY-FOUR

MANNY

The weeks are passing by quickly, and this one is no exception. I sit outside the tavern as Nadia finishes up. She chose to have an earlier shift so that she wouldn't get out so late and would have more time to spend with us instead. I hated seeing her leave in the morning, but she has to work at the tavern, and I never hated a place more in my life. This is her last shift there, and it makes me realize that she is also slowly wrapping things up here at her lake home. I know that a conversation needs to be had, but I also know that we are both ignoring what's to come, pretending that if we don't acknowledge it, it won't happen. I plan on having the much-needed discussion tonight after Catalina goes to bed. I got a bottle of her favorite wine, and I plan on sitting outside with a blanket on the patio, discussing how we can make this work between us, long distance.

She walks out with the owner's niece, Mandy, because everyone in town knows her, as well as Gage, whom I know from coming here occasionally with the guys. She hugs them both, and they walk away, chatting with one another. Nadia picks up her pace when she sees me waving. She opens the truck door, and as she hops in, I can't help but imagine what my life would be like with her in it permanently, instead of the alternative.

Nadia reaches for my hand, squeezing it. "Thanks for picking me up, guys." She always includes my daughter in everything. She turns around, and Catalina beams at her.

"Ms. Nadia, are you going to be able to see my t-ball game now that you aren't working any more Saturdays?" she asks innocently. Nadia looks to me for guidance, and I nod, encouraging her to say what I hope is a yes.

"I'd love that, pickles. I'll be there. Maybe I can get a picture of you with your team, too?" I look over to her watching Catalina. It looks like she is trying to memorize her in case she doesn't get another chance to see her, and that won't do. More than ever, this conversation is happening tonight. We pull up to the house, and I order a pizza for us to share. After bathtime, Nadia continues to read Catalina her cherished bedtime stories. She comes out holding her copy of *Alice in Wonderland* to her chest. She looks so sad, and I want to wipe that look off her face. "She's asleep," is all she says as she places the book in her bag, walking my way. I stare at her, and she explains, "We finished the story tonight." Her eyes convey more than that statement, and I know what she means. Everything is coming to an end.

"Let's go outside and have some wine." I extend my hand out to her, a blanket thrown over my arm and a wine bottle with two glasses in hand. We walk out onto the patio into the still, humid night. I bring my speaker out with me so that our conversation remains private, just in case anyone is nearby. As I hit play, Pink's "Just Give Me a Reason" begins. Even though I live in a more residential area, the stars are still visible, peeking under their own blanket of night. Nadia pulls her legs up on the swinging bench. I pour a glass of wine for both of us and hand her one, placing the bottle on the table beside it. I sit beside her, putting my body as close to hers as possible. She leans into me, and I drape a blanket over us as she tugs one side of it, covering her sun-kissed legs. Even though it is warm outside, I feel a chill, as does she, judging by the goose bumps on her arms. "Are you cold, baby?" I ask, and she shrugs.

"Not really," she says sadly. I take a big sip of my wine, wondering how to say what I need to say. I don't have to because she beats me to it.

"Manny, what happens in two weeks?" She looks over at me, biting her lip before she turns away. I stare at her before answering, but she doesn't meet my eyes.

I gently touch her face, lifting my hand to glide her chin toward me. Her eyes are closed, as if it pains her to hear whatever I am going to say.

"Open your eyes, mi amor." She stares at me with worry, her amber-colored eyes swirling with every emotion. They are watery at the moment, as if, in any second, they will spill tears onto her rosy cheeks. "Tell me a truth, Nadia," I beg her to say the words I want to hear. A tear falls, streaking her face with salty wetness. I kiss her cheek where the tear landed and lick my way up, kissing her eye softly. She shudders, and I can feel it—those unspoken words, being so close to her. "Tell me, baby. Please, I need to know."

She searches my eyes and must find the answer she is looking for because she nods. She touches my hand, and I immediately intertwine my fingers with hers. "I'm afraid," she whispers.

"What are you afraid of, mi amor?" She inhales deeply, finding her courage.

"I am afraid to leave the lake house and return to a life that no longer exists." I stare at her, wondering what she means by that. She bites her lip hesitantly before she looks up at me and tells me how her parents died in a car accident, leaving her all alone to figure out her life. She tells me about the lake house and how she came here to seek clarity and find herself. How she left her home without cleaning the mess she found when she walked into her parents' room before she ran away. That she buried them, without headstones, unable to even think of what she was going to have inscribed on them, because she was so angry at all the lies they told her. She doesn't go into detail, saying that it's too long a story and for another day, and I don't push her.

"And did you, mi amor?" I ask, squeezing her hand. "Did you find what you needed? Did you find what you were looking for?" I ask, hoping she found the support and clarity to go on living a life without her family.

"I did." She pauses, looking up at the night sky as a falling star shoots across the sky. She smiles as another tear falls from her eyes.

I pick up her hand and bring it to my lips in a soft kiss. "Make a wish, baby?" I nudge her with my shoulder, causing her to move forward. She looks over at me and then back up at the sky.

"I don't need to, Manny, because I wished to find myself, and I did. I wanted to feel loved again, and you and Catalina gave me that. And most of all, I wanted to feel like I was a part of a family again, and I do." She meets my eyes and I'm at a loss for words because how can I tell her how much she has helped me, how much she means to me, and how I never want to let her go.

So, it's my turn to share my truth. I don't know how to begin, but I start with the show last week. "The truth about changing the movie last week to that show, Matilda, was because when I came into the house after work one day, I saw you with Catalina, and that song from Matilda came on." Her eyes crinkle in confusion. "'On My Way' by Rusted Roots?" She nods in understanding, a smile spreading across her face at the recollection of that day. "I saw you with my daughter doing things a mother would do, and it helped to fill the cracks in my heart. I once thought it was shattered beyond repair." I hang my head in shame. "I vowed not to let anyone in again, closed myself off to any relationship, because my priority was Catalina. I failed her once with her mother, and I didn't want to bring another woman into my life who might have the ability not just to hurt me, but her, too. I don't think I could go through something like that again."

She squeezes my hand and turns toward me, placing her legs on the ground. "Manny, I am falling in love with you and it scares me," she says. "I already love your little girl, and I don't want to leave you both." I take her into my arms, lifting her into my lap as I stroke her hair. She drops her face into me, throwing her arms around my neck, the wine glasses long forgotten on the table.

"The truth is that I love you, too, Nadia, and I don't know how we are going to keep this going between us, but we will find a way."

"I want that, too, Manny."

I kiss her, throwing every emotion into that kiss, hoping she can feel how I love her and want her in our lives. I hope my ex gets the help she needs in rehab, so that we can all move on from this and find the happiness we all deserve.

The week flies by as we plan how to make this relationship work. Nadia has to return to school at the end of the month, but she plans to leave in two weeks to prepare for the semester. It is her last year. That's doable. After that, we can find out where we want to live, because I know I cannot be separated from this woman again. One year seems like such a long time, but it isn't too much between breaks and holidays. Besides, it is within driving distance. Catalina has similar holiday breaks. By the time we know it, a year will have passed, and then we can move forward with our lives. I will have to tell my ex about the new development, but since she isn't out of rehab yet, I have some time to broach that subject with her. I don't want to throw it in her face, and it seems like she is really trying to get the help she needs after this last incident, where she hit rock bottom.

Nadia is sitting on the kitchen island, talking to her best friend Savannah, telling her everything that has happened between us, and she must be supportive because I hear her squealing on the other end of the line. I smile, deciding to give them some privacy. I check on Catalina, who is happily coloring in her room. After ensuring she's settled, I head upstairs to my office to finish some proposals that must be sent out by tomorrow morning. It's just a relaxed Sunday morning, and I can't wait to have more of these quiet moments and more of the laughter we've shared these past weeks. To enjoy this simple happiness I feel with the woman who has helped me in more ways than one, not just with my feelings, but with Catalina's, too.

CHAPTER
THIRTY-FIVE

NADIA

Catalina invited me to see her last t-ball game, and how could I not after that sweet little thing looked up at me with so much love in her eyes? I almost melted on the spot at my sweet girl asking me to come to her game, as if there was any doubt that I wouldn't. So here I am, standing next to my man, watching Catalina get up to bat. She glances over to us before she straightens out her little form and focuses all her attention on hitting the ball off the tee, her brow furrows in concentration. She swings with all her might, launching the ball upward toward third base. She doesn't even hesitate when she makes her first lunge forward.

I scream "Run!" while fist pumping the air as Manny whistles loudly, his fingers in his mouth, as she rounds first, running to second. "Dang, that girl is going to get a scholarship. I can feel it." I smack him on the arm, and he chuckles.

"Let's hope she continues. She might like something else."

I shake my head. "Nope, she's amazing." The look he gives me makes me want to hug him, but we focus on Catalina. I can't help but stifle a laugh at the second baseman who has his hands over his head to protect himself from the ball, not noticing it lands right behind him. Catalina comes running straight for him and he sees her, his eyes widening as he runs away frantically, looking for the ball. When he sees it, it's too late, and Catalina is safe. She waves her little hand in the air, and I dance around in a circle.

When I stop, Sylvie is there, much like the first day I was here to meet Manny for the nanny interview, but so much has changed. She gives me a look that makes her look like she just sucked on lemons. I fight the urge to roll my eyes. Instead, this time, I school my features in indifference because I know that Manny loves me and he won't let this slide. So, I stand there, watching her try her best to hit on my man, trusting him to take care of it.

"Manny," she purrs. "Victoria was hoping that Catalina could come over to our house for a little party afterward with the team, and of course, you are invited to stay as long as you want." She looks over at me, flicking her highlighted hair over her shoulder, then she looks at her nails. "You could bring the nanny over if you need to. That's not a problem." She gives me a once-over before focusing her attention on him once again.

I stand there, watching this train wreck happen, feeling sorry for him as she tries once again to throw herself at him. I almost feel sorry for her if she wasn't such a jerk to me that day at the tavern. I am also silently hoping she over-dyes her hair and it falls out after her next coloring, but I'm not petty. I didn't say it out loud, so it's not the same thing if you only think it, right? I'm snapped out of my daydreaming as Manny removes her hand from his chest.

"Look, Sylvie, I didn't want to hurt your feelings, but you are not getting the hint that I'm not interested. And Nadia isn't the nanny anymore. She is my girlfriend." She whips her head toward me and then back to Manny.

She points her finger at me. "You're with her? You know she

was dating that other guy behind your back, right?" I look at her like *what the fuck*, then turn toward Manny, shaking my head. He kisses it, reassuring me that he knows it's not true.

"I know all about Parker, her *friend.* I also know what you told her that night at the tavern, Sylvie. I want you to leave Nadia alone and respect that we are together." He turns away from her while she stands there looking at me with so much hatred, and I have no idea why. "Also," Manny continues, "we have plans to do something already, so tell Victoria that we are sorry we can't make it." He doesn't look her way again, dismissing her, and I do the same. Damn, that was hard to watch, but I love this man even more, if that's possible. We watch Catalina make it home, and her team wins the game.

"Let's go out for some ice cream," I suggest as we close the doors, ready to drive off to my house for the night. Catalina has a little bag packed, and she loves to say the word "sleepover" all the time, but I hate the word so much because it just reminds me that Manny and I have lived separate lives, and soon, I will be away from them both.

Manny glances in the rearview mirror. "What do you say, Catalina? Want to grab some ice cream?" She vibrates in her booster seat with uncontrolled energy, and I am seriously second-guessing my choice. *How about hamburgers or something less sugary? A salad? Oh, boy.*

"Yes, I want ice cream!" she exclaims from the back seat. "I want three big scoops of chocolate ice cream, Papá." She kicks the back of my seat, and I look over to Manny, who is clearly enjoying this. I look over at him, shrugging inward in an attempt to make myself look more invisible and mouth a "*Sorry,*" his way, but he shrugs and drives in the direction of the seasonal ice cream stand that Parker and I met at the first week I arrived here. Gosh, it seems like so long ago instead of only a couple of months. I am glad to hear that he is back home and things are going well with his girlfriend. During our last phone call, he mentioned that he is considering proposing to her at the end of this term. I couldn't be happier for him, and before we hung up, I promised to visit and hang out with them soon.

We pull up, and Catalina is already trying to unbuckle herself from the seat, much to Manny's dismay. I look at her wiggling downward into the seat and almost sliding out as Manny opens the door with her half stuck. "¡Dios mío!" He grabs her hand and maneuvers it from the tangled strap she got stuck in as he unbuckles the rest of it, carrying her out of the truck sideways, before placing her on the grass. She looks angry at him, but Manny ignores her little fit, so I grab her hand, leading her to the stand.

"Okay, let's go pick out our flavors," I announce as she immediately forgets about the car seat fiasco and follows me hand in hand, talking about the different flavors of chocolate ice cream. Manny orders a butter pecan and one scoop of rocky road for Catalina, much to her multiple protests, and I still look at the menu, trying to decide. "Oh, I think I'll get the cookie dough scoop with sprinkles, please."

Immediately, Catalina speaks up, "Me, too! Sprinkles, please!"

I look down at her, laughing. "Okay, make that two with sprinkles."

Manny moves to the counter to pay as the young teenage girl coats the cup in sprinkles. Catalina is talking to a woman who has the cutest little Pomeranian dog. She has been asking about a puppy, but we thought it would be a difficult time to get one now. Maybe we could pick one up together at the shelter when I finish school. The young girl hands me my cup.

"Let me get your daughter's, too." I freeze, not wanting to look at Manny, but also not wanting to bring his attention to it, if he didn't hear. She dips it into the sprinkles and hands it to me. "She looks so much like you," the young girl comments. Manny turns to look for Catalina, his eyes crinkling as he looks over at her and then back at the girl. She looks at Manny and laughs. "Well, she obviously has your eyes," misinterpreting his shock to be one of annoyance. His hands rise up. "Okay, but she does have your wife's mouth and smile." We both look back to see her smile, and I notice that same dimple popping out. I never noticed, but it makes me happy for some weird reason. "She's so pretty," the young girl says, clearly oblivious to the awkward situation, although she was trying to be nice. I thank her for the compliment as we walk silently to Catalina. Manny doesn't say anything about the exchange, and neither do I.

Manny's mother picked up Catalina shortly after, and I almost feel bad about handing her over after all that ice cream, but instead, Catalina is in a post-sugar coma as Manny moves the booster seat out of his truck and puts it into his mom's car. "See, I told you not to worry too much. She'll sleep all the way back to Massachusetts." She laughs, and Manny nods, agreeing with her.

"It was so nice to meet you, Mrs. Torres." She looks me over and I feel a little self-conscious. I wonder what she sees when she looks at me that way. It's almost like she is looking for something, searching my face, but I have no idea why.

"It was nice to meet you, too, Nadia. I do hope to see you at the house sometime soon." Her smile is genuine and kind. I give her a quick hug as Manny and I wave as they drive off. Manny made a reservation for dinner, and we are going out on a date. I can't be more excited. We have early dinner reservations, so I am getting ready in front of the mirror, waiting for Manny to get out of the shower. We have a night to ourselves, but really, all I want to do is selfishly stay home with him, wrapped up in his arms when we don't have to be quiet or worry about anyone walking in if he bends me over the table and takes me from behind. Just the thought of it has me clenching my thighs, trying to think of something else.

"Hey." He pops into the bathroom, and I jump, my face red from the dirty thought I was having. It's almost like he can tell as he arches his brow and looks at my flushed cheeks. I look away as he comes up from behind me in his towel, placing himself behind me as he grabs me by the inner thighs and brings me into his hard length. I gasp at the feel of him. I see a drop of water running down his bare torso, and I track its movement. Manny kisses up my neck, sucking on the skin there, where I am sure it will leave a mark.

"I plan on taking advantage of our time together tonight, where I can worship you without interruption, and I want you to scream my name so loud that the neighbors hear, baby, okay?" he asks, and I nod eagerly.

"Yes, please." He chuckles and walks away, swatting my ass and leaving me wet from not only his body, but from the heat building at my center.

THE CRUELEST TRUTH

"Now, hurry up and get ready. I want to take my girlfriend out on a proper date. We can fuck all night when we get back," he says with a smirk. I am liquid putty as I struggle to finish my makeup and curl my hair. I shudder at the thought of what's to come and wish we could stay in.

My phone rings, flashing with an unknown caller, and I send it to voicemail. I just want to have a nice rest of my weekend, and any call can wait until Monday. With that, I leave my phone on the counter, and every thought that isn't about Manny goes silent right along with it.

CHAPTER
THIRTY-SIX

NADIA

I pick up the call on the fourth ring. "Hello, handsome. To what do I owe the pleasure?" He laughs on the other end of the line. I love our playful banter. It's been heaven these last few weeks, since we gave in to this thing between us, and it's just effortless. We have been avoiding the issue of my finishing college and returning this fall, saying that we'll find a way to make it work, but I'm eager to tell him that I'm considering doing it remotely. I am just waiting for the perfect time to surprise him. The thought of leaving him and Catalina guts me, and I don't want to go. My home is here now, and I couldn't be happier. Even Savannah had a great time when she was here last and approves, which in itself is a significant accomplishment because that girl doesn't like anyone, but she does like Manny and, of course, Catalina.

"Babe, focus," he snaps into the phone, causing me to wake from my daydreams of family bliss.

"Yeah, got it. What's up?"

"I was hoping you could go into my office and look for a proposal for a job that I wrote up. I printed it out, and it's in the file labeled Sullivan."

I walk up the stairs to the area that has Manny's extra-large office, which was originally a bedroom. The top floor was converted into his office space, making the house only two bedrooms, but it works because the space is large enough for a Murphy bed placed against the wall, disguised as shelving.

I open the door and step inside. "Okay," I report, "I'm in the office." I huff and blow a piece of hair that has fallen out of my messy bun. I had been cleaning up and then doing some yoga outside. "Now where?"

"Go to the desk, and it's in one of the top drawers on the right side." I sit in the chair and drop the phone onto the desk, putting it on speaker. "Are you there?' he asks quickly.

I glare at the phone like it personally affronted me. "So impatient," I mutter under my breath.

"Babe?"

"Yes, I'm here. Just put the phone on speaker so I can have my hands free to do your bidding."

He laughs seductively. "Well, if you find the papers for me, I'll use these hands to do your bidding when I get home."

I pause mid-reach. "I'll hold you to that." I huff. "Not fair, Manny. You can't turn me on like that, making promises when you're not even around to fulfill them, now are you?" I counter, now feeling the need in his heated words.

"Well, Catalina isn't home, and we have the house all to ourselves. I'll be sure to take full advantage of the situation later."

"Promises. Promises," I sing as I continue my search. I pull open the drawer and rifle through some papers until I hit glass. "Hm. A picture?" I say aloud, and Manny comes through the phone.

"Baby, that's the wrong drawer. I said the top drawer on the right," he reiterates as I ignore him, shifting through the items to remove the picture from the drawer. I pick it up, seeing Manny and a woman holding a baby. This must be Manny's ex-wife, so obviously I want to get a better look. I pull it closer, and shock pulls at me because I've seen that face. It's the same one Officer Stanley showed me a mere few months ago, which turned my life upside down. I drop the picture, and the frame shatters.

"Oh, God. I'm going to be sick." I hold onto the desk with a death grip as I throw up violently in the trash can beside his desk. The sobs start immediately after, as a distant voice calls out to me. I feel like I'm underwater, and all the thoughts I tried to suppress after my parents' death come up to the surface.

Manny screams at me, his concern evident as he freaks the fuck out on the other end of the line, but I don't care. My whole world has been turned upside down. I pick up the picture once more, as the shards of glass pierce my fingertips, causing a crimson trail of blood to coat the image of my sister. Maybe it's an omen, a sign of what's to come, or a sacrifice for a sin committed.

I drop to the floor as a soul-wrenching cry releases out of me, and I don't even recognize the sounds coming out of my mouth. I pick up the phone, in a hurry to call Savannah. Instead, I hear his voice coming through. I forgot he was even there on the line, so wrapped up in my own despair.

"Baby, talk to me! Are you okay? I'm on my way." I don't want to talk to him. I want to leave. To run and never look back. So I end the call and phone the only person I can count on.

"Savannah," I hiccup into the phone.

"Nadia, what the fuck? Are you okay?" I hear her talking to someone as the door closes, and she returns to the phone. "What's wrong?" I can't say anything. Words get lodged in my throat. All I can feel is pain. She doesn't hesitate.

"I'm on my way. Fuck," she mutters as I hear her car start. "I'm on my way. I'll meet you at the lake house, Nadia. I'll come to you." I hear the screeching of tires, and the call disconnects. I go to the bathroom and pack all my things, ready to leave and never come back. He lied to me. He knew, and he lied to me. That's all I can think of as I stop short when I reach Catalina's room. I sit on her bed and cry until there's nothing left. I walk over to her dresser, reaching for the picture of us from the day at her t-ball game. God, how things can change in the blink of an eye, and don't I know it.

I don't know how long I've been sitting there, but I still hold onto Catalina's little rabbit that I gave her. I glance at the clock and notice that it's almost time for Manny's mom to bring over Catalina. I clean up the mess in Manny's office and walk to the bathroom on autopilot. I feel like I'm having an out-of-body experience. As I brush my teeth and touch up the last of my makeup, there is a knock at the door, and I glance at the time. It must be them. I promised Manny that I would be here for his mom, since he was away today, and then when he gets here, I'm out. I don't care what he has to say, and this is just too much.

"I'm coming," I announce when the ringing turns to knocking. I pick up the pace as I take the last couple of steps toward the door and open it widely. A woman with long blonde hair cascading in waves down her back stands there. She is rail-thin, and when she turns my way, her cheeks appear sunken, like she is slightly malnourished. But she almost loses her footing when she sees me standing there, stumbling back. I notice brown eyes that used to look at me with love—a reminder of when my father would hold me tight and call me his love bug. I think of movie nights and pickles. The same nickname I call Catalina, her daughter. Her lips frown when she sees me, bringing my attention to it.

"Oh, God, the mouth." My encounter with the girl at the ice cream place. She said Catalina and I have the same mouth and smile. We do, because I see it clear as day. I look at her, eyes narrowing, and I've never hated anyone more in my entire life. She threw her family away, and then she destroyed mine.

"Nadia," she says, surprised yet hopeful. "I'm Layla, your—"

I cut her off. My finger is pointed in her direction, telling her to stop. "Do not finish that sentence. You are nothing to me. Definitely not my sister." I stare at her, hating her very presence. "You killed my parents, and now you are out after you caused their death!" I scream at her as a couple of neighbors walk by, and they're not even trying to pretend not to listen.

She looks affronted by my words but calms her features, pulling her hair around in front of her. "I came to see my daughter." She looks around as if her daughter will magically appear. I scoff at the audacity of this woman. "Where's Manny?" She tries to get past me, but I narrow the view of the house by closing the door.

"You have supervised visitation, from what I was told." I cross my arms over my chest.

As if she can see the pieces finally clicking together, she turns to me. "Why are you here, Nadia, with my family?"

Just then, Manny pulls into the driveway and runs up to the house. Layla stands there with her arms crossed over her chest in a confrontational stance similar to the one I mimic.

I place my hand over my head. "Fuck, he has a type." Of course he does. He looks at me, trying to figure out what I'm saying. The confusion on his face makes me think he doesn't know either.

She raises her hand up. "Finally. Manny, I came to see my daughter, and she—" She doesn't finish that sentence as Manny approaches me, cradling my head in his hands.

"What happened, mi amor?" He looks into my eyes, and I close them. I can't even look at him or fathom how fucked up this situation truly is.

I hear a loud gasp and sobs coming from behind him, to see Layla losing it. "Manny, please, no." She sobs louder, and I stop whatever I was feeling to look at this woman. "Why," she begins, "of all the women in the world, did you fall in love with my sister?" Manny whips his head around and looks at her wide-eyed and panicked, confirming my suspicions. He didn't know. Why does that make me feel slightly relieved? I don't know, but it sure as hell does.

He turns back to me as if seeing me for the first time, searching my eyes and looking over my mouth as he runs his hands over his face. "Fuck!" He shuts his eyes, and when he opens them, I see so much sadness. He pulls me to him. "Nadia, baby." He holds onto me like I am something precious he is afraid will disappear in a moment if he lets go, and he may be right. He forces my chin upward. "Look at me." His low voice slowly tries to calm my fight-or-flight response. Everything in my mind tells me to run, but as my eyes find his, I want to stay and fight for him. For us. "Baby, I swear I didn't know," he pleads. I believe him, but I just can't be here anymore.

THE CRUELEST TRUTH

He turns quickly, enraged, facing his ex-wife. "Catalina isn't here," he tells her. "You can't show up here unannounced anymore. You have supervised visitation, Layla, and today isn't one of those days." He runs his hand through his hair. "I didn't even know when you were getting out."

She looks at Manny, and something like remorse shows in her expression. "I know. I just got out of rehab, and I wanted to come by. You're right, I should have called." I stiffen in Manny's arms, and he holds me tight. She watches us and shakes her head, looking at us together, before speaking. "You know, I tried to talk to him several times and he refused to see me." I know who she's talking about, but I don't want to listen, but I can't stop either. Something in me wants to know the truth. Maybe it's because I haven't learned any of it; this is the only person who can give it to me, and I don't know whether to believe her, but I stay there, unmoving in Manny's arms.

"When I discovered he was my father, I got his address and sent him letters. I assumed he got them because he never sent them back, but he also never replied to them. I sent him school pictures of me yearly, hoping he would send me one of himself. One day, I even saw him at the movies, where I used to sneak in. One of the teenagers who worked there let me in every weekend, and I would stay there watching all the movies. You were there with your mom, too, and I watched you, wondering what it would be like to go with you. But when he saw me there, he pretended not to know me, and I knew. I knew he chose not to respond to my letters, and my Christmas gift didn't get lost in the mail or sent to another house, but I didn't get one because he didn't even want to know me."

I listen to her story and almost cry, thinking of the little girl who was crushed by someone who was supposed to love her, but instead made her feel unworthy. In turn, she did the same things to Catalina, except Manny was there, and he made her life so much better. "It was an accident. I'm—"

"Leave Layla," Manny says, his stare hard and jaw clenched. "It's not just about you. This is my home. Nadia also lost both of her parents because of what you did. You were hurt, sure, but you need to stop." He shakes his head. "Can you, for once, stop being so selfish?" If the look on her face is any indication, she looks verbally slapped. She nods once and walks off. Her shoulders slumped over. Before she opens her car door, she gives me one last look.

"For what it's worth, Nadia, I'm sorry." With that, she gets into her car and drives off. I fall to the ground, but Manny catches me, lifting me into his arms and taking me inside. He pulls me into his lap on the couch.

"I'm so sorry, baby. I had no idea. I love you. Please stay with me. I can't lose you."

I lift myself off his lap and stand looking at him. He reluctantly lets me go, hanging his head in his hands. "I just don't know if I can do it. The cruelest truths keep surfacing, Manny. The wave of emotions I feel upon learning all these things is breaking me apart. I'm battered and broken, trying to piece my life back together, and just when I thought I had found it—" I trail off, trying to explain how I thought of them as my new family, but I don't need to explain because he knows.

"You are my family, mi amor. You and Catalina." When I don't look up at him, he stands from the couch, pacing back and forth. Manny walks toward me and takes my hand in his. "I've given you all my truths, baby. Tell me. What cruelest truths, mi amor? Make me understand," he pleads. The desperation in his voice is hard to accept.

I shake my head. Anger rises in my voice as I lose control of my emotions. "Oh, let's see. How about finding out that my parents' marriage was a lie? My dad cheated on my mom with Layla's mother. That's why they were distracted that night. The fighting—" I laugh, but I almost don't register that it is coming from me. The cruelty in it as I try to slice him with the pain I feel. "It all makes sense now. My parents leaving me behind. All alone without having the chance to explain. How could love be so cruel, Manny?" I look at him as tears are rolling down his cheeks, much like mine. I step back. "But the cruelest truth?" I run my hand over my mouth to wipe the tears pooling there. "The cruelest truth is finding the love of my life and falling in love with his daughter, just to find out that your ex-wife, her mother," I break down at the next words, "was the one who killed my parents because she was so fucking selfish, or worse, broken."

I grab my purse and walk to the door. He stands trying to prevent me from leaving, to see reason. I put my hand out to stop him. "No!" I open the door, looking back at the man who, only a few hours ago, was my future, making the sweetest plans that will never come to pass. So I muster up enough energy to let him know. "And yet the cruelest truth of them all is learning that maybe, just maybe, love isn't enough." I slam the door and jog down the steps, throwing my bag and purse into the car, taking the last of my heart and leaving it there on his doorstep with everything I had left to give.

CHAPTER THIRTY-SEVEN

MANNY

I hadn't expected that when Nadia opened the drawer to my desk, she would find the picture of my ex-wife. I also didn't think it would matter if she did. Little did I know that my past and my future would collide. How did I not see it? The similarities. The day the girl at the ice cream counter commented on how much my daughter looked like Nadia. She never talked about how her parents died, just that it was an accident. The picture that Layla and Nadia portrayed of their father is entirely different. One was a devoted father, and the other absent, and worse, he refused to acknowledge his other daughter.

I saw Layla struggle through our marriage, but I never once thought that she would lose her shit and stalk the guy. The older man that I believed she was having an affair with turned out to be her father. I was such a fool. The resentment I carried around for her emotional distance, especially toward Catalina, had festered so long that I was blinded by it. I was sick and tired of her self-absorbed attitude. And instead of breaking the cycle, she became everything she hated about her absent father and her mother's cold indifference. That's more fucked up than anything I could have ever predicted. Layla will always be Catalina's mother, and she'll be in her life as much as Catalina wants her to be. Though Nadia was starting to become a permanent fixture, I'm not so sure that's still an option. How do you reconcile loving someone who, just by existing, reminds you of everything you are trying to escape?

I watched Nadia leave, and I know that she isn't coming back. An hour later, Amá comes over with Catalina, and she knows something is wrong from the look on my face. I don't dare mention anything in front of my daughter, and when she asks where Nadia is, I can't even talk about it. I manage to get out a "She had to leave," and when she asked when she was going to come back, I almost broke down right there. Amá took that as a cue to take Catalina to her room and set her up with her new LEGO set. When she came out of her room, she approached me and hugged me tightly. I suppress the tears that threaten to fall, catching her up to date on what happened before she got here.

"Ay, mijo. I am so sorry." She sits there with a cup of coffee, watching for signs of my imminent breakdown, and I am almost there. "I've never seen you this worked up, even after your divorce." She takes a sip of her coffee, studying my features. "You really love this girl?" Her eyes soften when she sees the answer written all over my face.

"I do, Amá. She's the one. I was attracted to Layla, but I never had that connection to her. With Nadia, I do. I hate that the only woman I finally fall in love with is Layla's sister." I am ashamed, especially when Nadia said I had a type. I don't know if she realized she said that aloud, but I heard it loud and clear. I didn't fall in love with the better version of her sister. I fell in love with someone who shared a similar pain to the one I felt. A woman who saw past my assholeness and took a chance on loving me, breaking down my barriers about no relationships, and then loving my daughter despite how I made her feel sometimes. When I chose to accept us and let her into my life, it was beautiful for the short time it lasted, and I wish I could have that back just for a day. "What do I do?" I ask desperately.

She looks at me like I'm an idiot. "Pfft. No seas estúpido," she says. She shakes her head, like she can't believe I'd be so stupid. "You fight for her, mijo. You find her and make her see how much you love her. Whatever it takes."

I stand with conviction and a sense of determination anew. "Amá, can you—" She cuts me off mid-sentence.

"Si, mijo. Ándale." She shoos me away with her hand. "I'll stay here until you don't need me. Go get her. Don't worry about Catalina."

I nod. Running out the door. I jump into the truck and start pulling out, but I forget that I don't know where she went. I remember we had each other on Life 360 when she was watching Catalina, so I pull up the app and see her at the town center. I drive with purpose and later pull into the spot near her car. I close the truck door, scanning the area for where she could be. That's when I notice her sitting on the park bench, once again looking so sad and lost. My heart shatters even more. I hate how this happened, and I wish I could have told her about Layla, but I don't know if it would have ended any other way than us breaking apart. Why does life have to be so unfair?

Walking toward her, I hear a screech of tires and then a loud crash. A woman screams, and a crowd gathers on the street, where a mother holds onto her little boy, crying, touching his face, and kissing him. Nadia spots me and runs over to me as we investigate the commotion. My knees almost buckle at the sight of Layla spread out on the pavement under a pool of blood. Nadia gasps and holds onto my arm for support. I don't know if it is for her or me, but we cling to each other like each other's lifeline.

Sirens approach. I run over to her with Nadia on my heels. I crouch down to see her eyes flutter. She's still alive. "Layla!" I scream. "It's going to be okay. The ambulance is almost here. Just hang on, please. Let's get you to the hospital. It will all be okay." The paramedics arrive and push everyone out of the way, including us.

THE CRUELEST TRUTH

"What happened?" I hear the paramedics ask the crowd.

"She saved my son's life." A woman steps forward, sobbing as she holds onto her toddler. "He ran out into the road when I was trying to tie my daughter's shoe. I only looked away for a second, and when I looked up, he was in the middle of the road." She clutches her little boy tighter. "That woman pushed him out of the way and saved his life." Her son cries, his knees and elbows scraped, but thanks to Layla, he is alive.

"Where are you taking her?" Manny asks the paramedics, who have now put Layla onto a gurney and are lifting her into an ambulance.

The paramedics give us a once-over. "Are you family?" he asks, and we nod. He tells us, and then we are both getting into Manny's truck on our way to the hospital together. We walk into the emergency department and ask the woman at the front desk about Layla. She lets us know that she is being cared for now, and a doctor will come out and speak to us soon. We cannot see her because the staff is busy with her, so we find a couple of seats, plop into them, and wait.

We sit side by side in the waiting room. Nadia is only inches away, but it feels miles apart. I look at her, but she doesn't acknowledge me. She stares ahead in an almost trance-like state. I don't reach for her either, and somehow I feel that someone I envisioned a future with just hours ago, is nothing but a stranger to me now.

I recall the terrible things I told Layla. So many ugly things. Hurtful things. I even said she was selfish. Oh, God. I place my head in my hands, sorry for what I said. The actions of that woman fighting for her life were anything but. The cruel truth was that I was angry. I took my frustration out on her. Someone who was once my wife, Catalina's mother. She might not have been the best wife and mother, but truth be told, I gave up on her a long time ago, too. And now, as I sit here in this waiting room, with her on the other side of this door, fighting for her life, I wonder if I could have been kinder to her or maybe helped her more. We don't have to be the product of the person who raised us. We can be better. She just never had anyone who believed in her, myself included.

That is something I will have to live with every day.

A man in scrubs comes our way, and I can tell from the expression in his tired eyes that things are rough in there. I brace myself for the words he has to say and steel my expression to the one I wore mere months ago. Nadia rises from the chair, tears in her eyes, and I don't know what she is thinking. Is she sad for her sister? Does she still think of Layla as the villain in her story?

"Hello," he says, clearing his throat, extending his hand to us. "I'm Dr. Fitzpatrick."

"I'm Manny Torres." I take his hand firmly.

"Oh, Mr. Torres." He raises his brow. "Yes, your wife is in critical condition. She is being prepped for surgery now. She had a lot of bleeding, and we had to resuscitate her and replace the blood she lost at the accident." I stand there and listen, and not once do I correct him when he calls her my wife. I look over to Nadia, and her face is blank as well. She didn't even flinch. "Because she has a rare blood type, we are calling the local blood banks to have some sent over."

Nadia's head shoots up. "What is her blood type?" I hear her ask, but I look at her face, watching as her eyes are focused on the doctor. He looks over at her. He looks at me and I nod, letting him know he can answer her question.

"B negative," he says. Nadia shuts her eyes. When she opens them, she looks at the doctor, extending her hand to him.

"Hi, sorry," she says. "I'm Nadia Kennedy, Layla's sister, and I can donate blood if you need it."

The doctor's eyes widen. "That's great news. Let's take you to the lab and fast-track the process." He starts walking briskly, gesturing for us to follow. "Have you been to this hospital before? he questions, swiping his badge to unlock doors as we move through the hallways. His questions come quickly, one after another, as we keep up with his fast pace.

"Yes," she replies. "I have been here multiple times for different visits because I grew up here. My mom was from here, actually. They should be able to access my record and see my blood type on file, too."

After donating blood, we sit in the lab area awaiting more news on Layla. I watch her sip juice and nibble on a snack. She remains silent, and I don't want to bring up anything for fear of saying the wrong thing and her leaving. Even in silence, I'd rather have her here with me than not at all. After Nadia says she feels okay to leave, we walk to another waiting area, located on the second floor, where the surgical services and operating rooms are situated.

I'm nodding off when a door opens and a man with a blue hat and matching scrubs comes out to greet us. Another woman with a clipboard follows, and by the look on their faces, I know that whatever they are here to tell us isn't good. I hear a few words in between sentences. "We tried everything we could. We couldn't save her. I'm so sorry for your loss." They leave us there, and I can't process anything other than the fact that Catalina's mother is dead. What am I going to tell my little girl? I stand up, and before I can talk to her, a familiar voice shouts, "Nadia!" as a woman comes running down the hall.

"Savannah!" Nadia cries out, meeting her friend mid-stride. They hug each other closely, and she leads her away, before sparing me a glance. She looks at me sadly, and I stand there, unable to move. I want to scream. To run after her and tell her she can't go. I hear ma's words, "Do everything you can to keep her," but I can't. How can I after all that's happened? So I let Savannah take her away, knowing that a piece of my heart goes with her and knowing that Nadia may be right. Maybe love just isn't enough.

CHAPTER
THIRTY-EIGHT

NADIA

Savannah has stayed with me at the lake house, helping me close everything up. I finally listened to the voice message from Officer Stanley, letting me know that Layla had been discharged from rehab. He asked me to call him, so here I am, returning his phone call a little late. He picks up on the second ring, announcing his name just as he did every time I called requesting an update about the case, except now it's me giving him the update.

If only I had wanted to know the truth, to hear everything he had to say about Layla, even to know her name, but I refused to hear anything that had to do with my dad's other daughter. So many things could have been different if I had just listened that day with Savannah in his office at the police station.

"I'm so sorry, Nadia. What happened to your parents was an

accident. As much as I disapprove of how she went about trying to talk to your father and get his attention, I wish things had been different." He sighs. "Maybe there would have been a different outcome or maybe not, but she did try to reach out, and the way that she saved that little boy," he pauses, choosing his following words, "that wasn't such a selfish thing to do."

I slump in my chair by the window overlooking the lake. "Thank you, Officer Stanley—"

He interrupts. "Please, call me Mitch. Anytime you need anything, please don't hesitate to call Nadia. You take care of yourself." With that, I disconnect the call, feeling more lost than ever. I have so many unanswered questions, and I wish I could have more closure, but maybe I'll never know, and that's okay, too.

I didn't want to attend the funeral and have to witness Catalina and Manny with their family, and not be able to be with them. After knowing that she is my sister, it just didn't sit right with me. I thought I'd be more of a distraction than a help, especially with Layla's mother going. I don't know what I would do if I saw that woman. I don't want to cause any problems, so I stand there with Savannah, under a tree, paying my respects to a sister I never knew existed until recently. I wonder what it would have been like to have a sibling. She was an only child, too. I guess we will never know.

I see Manny holding Catalina as they leave the gravesite. She rests her head on Manny's shoulder as tears stain her cheeks. She carries her rabbit tightly in her grip as its floppy ears bounce off Manny's shoulder. They drive away, and I can't help but want to run after them. I felt the same way the day they drove off from the fireworks at the lake. Except this time it is so different. I knew that I would see them again, that there would be a tomorrow, yet my heart still ached. Now, my heart feels like it's ripped in two, because I know there will not be another morning, caring for Catalina and wishing Manny a good day at work. I won't see them again, and they aren't coming back.

I walk over to Layla's grave. As I stand there, over the casket that has been lowered into the ground, I turn back to see Savannah waiting for me. She lifts her chin, urging me to do what I came here to do, and that is to get the closure I need with my sister. I take the silver-looking symbol from my pocket, attached to a leather cord. I flip the Celtic Sister Knot Heart over in my hand, feeling the cool metal on my skin. I kneel on one knee, peering into the casket that houses my sister's eternal resting place.

"Layla," I begin, then pause to gather the strength to say the rest. "I know that I never had the chance to really know you. I wish I had more time because I think we could have gotten along under different circumstances. I'm sorry for how my father treated you. I didn't know." I wipe away my tears, thinking about everything she went through and how blind I'd been to the truth. "I'm sorry that I fell in love with Manny, that he'd been the one to help me heal. Maybe we healed each other and were exactly what the other needed. What I'm not sorry for is that I fell in love with your daughter." The tears fall faster now, as I rush to finish before I lose my nerve, so I can get out of this cemetery and this town that will never be the same for me anymore. "I promise to always be there for her and ensure she has a good role model. Not being with Manny may be hard, but I will be there for my niece." I flip the medallion onto the casket, which lands with a *thud* onto the wooden casket below.

"I want you to keep this, to remember that you are not alone, that even in death our bond as sisters is still intact, and rest in knowing that you are missed and loved. I have a lot of regrets, Layla, but meeting you for just a brief time will never be one of them." I stand, brushing the dirt from my knee, and walk away from the gravesite toward my friend, who isn't bound to me by blood, but by love and is the only sister I have ever known.

I fight the urge to leave town without driving by Manny's house or stopping to say goodbye. What will that do but cause more heartache? He never came to my house, and I can't blame him. I pushed him away, and we both need time to grieve in our own ways. He had to bury his ex-wife and the mother of his child. Catalina needs him more than I do. I take another trip around the house, pausing on the mantel where a new picture of Manny, Catalina, and me rests. Our faces smiling, not knowing the devastation that would come so soon. I pick it up and place it in my bag. As I lock up the rest of the lake house and load the last of my belongings, I stand, looking at the place in front of me that brought me so much joy growing up and so much pain these past months. This place will forever remind me of the happy times with my parents and the happiness, although brief, that I found with Manny and Catalina. I lower the window down in the car, letting the wind whip my hair around. Keane's "Somewhere Only We Go" plays and I sing along with the chorus, letting myself feel the bittersweet lyrics of a love that ended before it began.

As I drive through Main Street, I look at Planet Pancakes and see Odette in the window, smiling at a customer. It makes me think of Manny and Catalina, as does the ice cream place, and the town fields where she ran those bases, her hair flowing behind as she scored a run. I smile at the memory, taking it with me, hoping that I may see them again soon. I need to stay focused and finish my degree, and then maybe there will be another chance for me to be happy.

I arrive at home late in the evening, and Savannah meets me there, having left after the funeral. She helps me get all my stuff into the house. I first walk to my parents' bedroom, expecting to see the shattered mirror and reek of stale perfume permeating the air, but nothing. The room smells like my lavender and rose shampoo and body wash. The mirror has also been replaced. I close the door, and when I return, I walk up to Savannah and hug her. "I never tell you how much I love and appreciate having you in my life." Savannah stiffens and then relaxes at my words.

"Nadia, you never have to tell me. I know, and I do it because you are my family." Tears streak down my cheeks.

"I feel the same, Savannah," I tell her as she squeezes my hand.

"What are you going to do now that you are back here?" she asks innocently, and I shrug.

"I think I'm going to let myself grieve for one. Maybe box up more of my parents' things like I did at the lake house." I laugh, although there wasn't anything funny about what I'm saying. "The possibilities are endless."

She sighs dramatically. "Well, if you need anything at all—"

I cut her off. "I'll call, and thanks for being the best sister-friend I could have asked for." I close the door behind her, and although she eventually leaves me, she tries to stay, despite me shooing her out the door. She's done enough for me, and I need to start taking care of myself, so I throw my suitcase into my room and fall asleep quickly, embracing the possibility of a better day tomorrow.

When I awake in the morning, I unpack and sort the mail. Most is junk or bills I need to deal with, but one envelope with familiar handwriting catches my eye. When I open it, I see it's from Layla. I take it with me and walk to my father's office. I remember her saying how she wrote to him every year, but he didn't answer her back, so I decide to go through each file in search of the missing letters and the key to understanding what happened all those years ago. I pull open another file cabinet that contains a file folder labeled as miscellaneous. "That's weird," I mutter. But when I open it, my heart cracks at seeing all those letters. The bastard saved them all. I upend the box and spread them out on the floor, organizing them by date and adding the new one to the end of the stack. Surrounded by her words, I decide to uncover their past, so that I may navigate my future.

I barely slept last night, haunted by dreams of Manny and Catalina, and my mind replaying the things that Layla said. One thing that made me almost bolt upright in bed, is remembering Layla saying that she had written my father so many notes that were never returned. So today, I am on a mission to read them and learn more about what happened all those years ago. I get dressed and brew some coffee. Walking into my father's office, I place the steaming mug of coffee on the desk, sitting in his chair that I helped pick out. I used to sit in his lap as he worked. I can almost smell his cologne, embedded in the upholstery. It smells like leather, furniture polish, and sandalwood. I inhale deeply, almost hearing him laugh when I told him I wanted to be just like him. I only knew one side of him, and it kills me that he could have been so different with his other daughter. Despite the circumstances, she didn't deserve it. The one who hurt the worst was my mother. God, how she must have felt at his betrayal. After she tried so hard to get pregnant with me, I guess I'll never know everything that happened.

I once again retrieve the miscellaneous file, containing the now-organized stack of letters I found yesterday. I open it, picking up the one dated fifteen years back. It is of a young Layla, so hopeful to meet her father. I can feel the excitement, and then I notice a picture of her in the envelope with her grade, which reads, 'To my dad.' My tears fall on the scattered stationery as I pull another sheet of paper out, and I sob louder, seeing it is a letter from my dad that he never sent. "Why, Dad? Why did you not send it? You fucking coward!" I scream into the office void. He tells her how pretty she looks in her picture and asks about her grades. He tells her about me and hopes we can meet someday.

I decide that I can only read one more before I am emotionally drained. He answered every one of her letters. It appears they stopped when she entered high school. I'm honestly surprised that she continued that long. The next day, I get up and do the same thing, and then each day goes the same until I have read them all and I understand a little more about my sister, I can sense her anger at the end for not having received a response and in her last letter, she talks about finding someone who loves her. She tells him about his grandchild and how beautiful she is. Layla talks about her family and how she is trying to be the person they need. It all ended so tragically. I suppose that's where her story ends and mine begins.

CHAPTER
THIRTY-NINE

MANNY

School starts on Monday, and Nadia will return to the city. I haven't been the same since she left. She took a piece of my heart that I can't get back. It was the hardest thing I have ever had to go through in my life. My divorce from Layla was nothing in comparison to caring for Catalina, who not only lost her mother but also lost Nadia, who did more for her in that short time than her biological mother had. She instantly became a part of our lives these past few months, and then vanished without so much as a goodbye. So, of course, the impact was devastating, not only for Catalina but for me. I had let myself be open to the idea of someone who would be there for me and my daughter, to have my fear confirmed when it all went to shit, and I had to nurse my broken heart along with a little girl who didn't ask for any of this.

THE CRUELEST TRUTH

My mother stayed to help care for us both, but Catalina has struggled, holding onto the rabbit that Nadia gave her. When I asked her if I could read her a bedtime story, she just curled up around herself, shaking her head. So today, I was happy that she decided to go out with my mother to buy school supplies. She starts school this week, and our town is fortunate to have an all-day kindergarten. I appreciate having such supportive parents who pick up and leave to help me whenever I ask. Catalina has been adding sparkle stickers to all her folders and notebooks to ensure everyone knows they are hers. I bring the last of her bags into her room, and she squeals in delight. I walk out, and my stomach growls at the delicious smells permeating from the kitchen.

"Amá, what are you making for dinner? It smells amazing." I pick up the cover from the casserole dish, inhaling the aromatic meat stew. "Calabacita con puerco," she says proudly, coming over to turn the pork and squash stew. My mouth waters, and I realize it's the first time since everything happened that I have had an appetite. As if noticing the same thing, she grabs a bowl and serves me a hearty portion with some fresh rosemary olive oil bread.

"Look, Papá." Catalina comes in with her new school backpack, loaded up to the top with her brand-new school supplies. She puts the backpack on her shoulder, and I see my little girl growing up so fast right before my eyes, and there is nothing I can do about it. I wish I could slow it down, because before I know it, she will be graduating from college. She runs back into her room to place her stuff away. Another smaller version of my meal is placed by my chair, and Amá grabs herself some food sitting in the chair beside me. I can tell she wants to ask me more, but is afraid to pry. I don't know why, it's never stopped her before.

"Spit it out, Amá," I tell her, and she chuckles.

"Mira?" She laughs. "I was going to ask you if you plan on doing something about getting your girlfriend back, mijo." My spoon stops midway to my mouth. I give her a look that would scare most men away, but she laughs at me instead. "No me mires así." She chuckles, clearly unimpressed if she's telling me not to look at her that way and laughing at me. I smirk as I take another mouthful of her stew.

I sigh, knowing that she is relentless, so I might as well get it over with. "Okay." I put my fork down in the bowl. "I'm listening if you have any suggestions."

"I thought you'd never ask." She leans in, and that's how I'm trying to find Nadia at the university home to over thirty thousand students. She's a business major, so she's probably somewhere around the business school. I've been walking around campus for over four hours, and still nothing. I decide to pick through my lunch bag and sit on a park bench in the commons. It is getting cooler, but not cold enough to make me want to sit inside.

I grab a handful of nuts and drink my seltzer water. I'm glad that I decided to bring the lunch I usually take to work with me. I feel like I blend in this way. I laugh to myself, remembering my college years. God knows that was so different. For one, I had Catalina at the end of my senior year. In fact, I was about the same age as Nadia, juggling so many things.

Although I love my daughter, I wish that I was able to finish my last year without a newborn and Layla, who was unable to care for our daughter as she struggled with her own issues and postpartum depression, or at least that is what they diagnosed her with then. God, Layla. I hang my head, taking another bite of my sandwich. I feel a buzz across my skin, and when I lift my head, as if she could sense my presence, Nadia turns around, catching my stare, and I stop mid-chew, standing and dropping my lunch on the leaf-covered grass. Her mouth opens to tell her friend something, who nods and walks away.

She stands there, deciding whether she wants to approach, but I don't give her the chance. I run over to her and stop right before I get to her. There are tears in her eyes. "Manny," she whispers, and I close the distance, scooping her in my arms.

"Mi cariño." I hold her tightly like I never want to let her go, breathing in her scent of lavender and roses. God, how I want to bottle that scent and bring it home with me. She looks around, and I set her mind at ease. "She didn't come. She's at home with my mom. I wanted to see and talk to you. Is that okay?" She nods, and I take her hand in mine as we walk over to the park bench where my discarded lunch lies on the ground.

THE CRUELEST TRUTH

Snow falls outside my front windows that overlook the yard, and there is a knock at the door. I see the postal service dropping off a package at my door, so I walk over to it, and when I open it, I see a box addressed to me from Nadia. As I pick it up and bring it to the counter, I search for some scissors to cut the clear tape away, allowing me to open the flaps of the parcel. When I peer inside, I see a present for me and one for Catalina. I pull the black fabric apart to see the white writing across it. *BET TOGE?* I look at it, wondering if it has a hidden meaning, but nope, that's just what it says. I put it on anyway, not understanding the meaning.

I pick up the other box, and it is a beautiful hardback of *Alice in Wonderland.* Inside, there is an inscription.

> Catalina,
> Women are stronger when they arm
> themselves with a few simple
> truths, so read lots, love more, and
> be happy, Pickles.
> Love, Nadia

I call out to Catalina so that she can see her gift. She comes running over, clutching the book to her chest. "Do you think she's coming back someday soon, Papá?" Catalina asks, her eyes hopeful.

I shrug. "I sure hope so, mijita," I tell her. I'm staring at my apron when there is another knock at the door.

"Another present, Papá?" Catalina asks, her hand clasped together in a prayer sign.

"Ha. Let's see, Mijita." I shake my head at her cuteness. When I turn to open the door, pulling it open, I almost stagger backward because there is an apron similar to mine, and Nadia is wearing it, smiling up at me. I look at her apron, wondering where the hell she got them, because I would ask for a refund.

"*TER THER*," I read aloud. Her smile widens, and I can't help but notice the mischievous gleam in her eye.

"Aren't you going to let me in, Manny?" she asks, and Catalina, hearing her voice, throws herself at her.

"Nadia, you came back!" she screams.

"I sure did, pickles. Sorry it took so long." She holds onto Nadia, who steps through the door with Catalina wrapped around her torso.

Amá comes through Catalina's door and stops, seeing Nadia standing in the living room. Nadia skips over to her and gives her a big hug. "I'm so glad you made it," Amá says. I look at both of them, wondering how they planned this without me knowing, but I couldn't care less at this point. All I know is that I am happy to have her back with us. I pull her into my side, and my mom reads our aprons, her eyes tracking over the words, as a tear slips from her eye that she quickly tries to wipe away. Nadia picking up the meaning finally puts me out of my misery. "Look, Manny." She points to the words.

When you put the aprons side by side, they read *BETTER TOGETHER*. I peer down and see that it does, and I chuckle. "Cute. It might be my favorite apron yet, but only if you are staying here to wear it beside me."

She looks in my eyes, grabbing my hands in hers. "Always, Manny," and that is all it takes for me to pick her up and kiss her, twirling her around. Catalina comes up to us and joins in. Amá has given up trying to hide her tears, which fall freely down her face.

CHAPTER
FORTY

NADIA

"Are you sure you want to do this now?" Savannah asks hesitantly.

"Absolutely," I say with my voice steady and my purpose focused. As we walk across the yard to where my parents' headstone lies atop their gravesite, the design is exactly how I envisioned it when I had the piece customized. I decided to place *In Loving Memory* in arcing, elegant script letters across the top above our last name, Kennedy, in a bold font. Then, my parents' individual information is on each side, along with their dates, and a vase separates the two plots. It says *Until we meet again* underneath. I wish I had the chance to speak to them one last time, to hear their voices and feel their hugs, but I know they loved me and that will have to be enough. I have no doubts about that. I place the flowers in their vase, spread them out, and step back to look at the place that houses my parents' bodies, but at least their souls are free.

"I'm proud of you, Nadia." Savannah turns to me with a soft, approving smile.

I nod. My eyes linger on the headstone. Sometimes I can't believe they are gone. "I hope they found the peace they deserve, Savannah." I place a kiss on my hand and gently touch each side of their headstones. Then, with my best friend beside me, I walk away. "I know I have," I mutter more to myself than to Savannah. I just needed this closure and to allow myself to truly grieve. I feel like a weight has lifted, and now that I have put this part of my life behind me and allowed myself this chance, I feel like I can fully open myself up to love again.

I send the "it's official" text to Boss Daddy. Seeing that name makes me chuckle, as I recall when I first gave Manny that title in my phone contacts. A second later, the phone rings. I know I don't even have to explain further because he already knows what I am talking about.

"Of course you did, mi amor." He exudes confidence through the line. He never had a doubt. I got the job offer I was hoping for after I finished my senior year internship, pending graduation. I texted Manny to let him know, and he was just as excited as I was, but not surprised. We decided to keep my parents' home in the city since I'll still need to visit the office occasionally. But the best thing about this job? I can work remotely, which means I can stay at the lake house full-time, be there for Catalina, and pick her up from school when needed.

Manny and Catalina have moved in with me, and his house is currently on the market. Today is my graduation, and we are at my house, ready to end this chapter in my life so we can begin the next one together. Manny drives us and I kiss him goodbye when I see Savannah. We start lining up to enter the building for the final ceremonies. Manny's parents have adopted me into their family and are in the stands, waiting for me to pass by so they can snap pictures.

As the university's dean and faculty stand on stage, they read each name of the graduating class one by one, until I hear them call my name. I pause as I look at my family. Manny, Catalina, his sister, and parents are out in the stands with other graduates' family members today, and of course, Savannah, who is a couple of rows in front of me, is cheering me on. My parents may not be around physically, but I know they are here in spirit, and they would be proud of my accomplishments.

As I walk onto the stage, accepting my piece of paper, which isn't a diploma at all but represents my hard work, I notice Catalina running toward me as I make my way back to my seat. Manny isn't quick enough to catch her, but I do before she leaps into my arms. I carry her back to my seat with me as she grabs the piece of paper from me, swinging it proudly at her father. Manny starts moving toward us to walk Catalina back to their seats, but I wave him off, letting him know it's okay.

He mouths an *"Are you sure?"* and I blow him a kiss in reply. As he returns to his seat, he still watches me with worry etched on his brow. I place Catalina in my lap as they call out the rest of the names, and we chat and cheer for others who come after me. When it's time to change our tassels over, she takes my hat and places it on her head.

"Hey, pickles, what are you doing?" I ask as she holds it onto her head.

"I'm going to be just like you, Ms. Nadia, when I grow up," she says. I stare at her, prouder than ever at her resilience. I kiss her forehead, snuggling her to me.

"No, pickles, you are going to be so much more," I tell her as tears well in my eyes. I find Manny right after we exit, as he grabs a very reluctant Catalina from my arms. "See you in a few minutes, guys." I wave to them as I take the final walk with my peers.

THE CRUELEST TRUTH

We sit outside the house, quiet now that Catalina has gone to bed. The sound of peepers is the only noise echoing through the woods. A gentle breeze blows across the lake as we sit, sharing a glass of wine and gazing up at the clear, starry night sky. It's unreal to think things were so different last year. Manny sips his wine, while mine rests empty, discarded on the table along with an empty wine bottle.

We made a promise not to keep secrets from each other anymore, so what started as a game of learning about one another continues, except we use it to explore things we still don't know.

"Tell me a truth, Manny," I say, watching as he sips his wine and then rests his glass firmly near his knee. He looks at me, amusement flickers in his eyes because we sat here learning the basics about each other a year ago. Now we sit here in a very committed relationship, wanting to know everything about one another. In fact, I am fairly certain Manny asked Savannah what type of ring I would like if he were to propose, but I definitely didn't hear that from her.

"Hey!" I nudge him playfully.

He laughs, full and unrestrained, so different from when we first met, and I swear, it might be my favorite sound in the world. "Okay, okay," he says, holding his hands up in surrender. "You first," he says, watching me intently.

I grab his glass and finish his wine, placing it beside mine on the table. "Okay. Here we go. It took a while for me to finally come around that day, when you went to my school to look for me."

His eyebrows shoot up to his hairline. "Um. Yeah, mi amor." He chuckles. "I was the one waiting, remember?" he says mockingly with no malice in his tone.

I nod and continue. "When I heard you had been searching for me for hours, waiting on a park bench as you ate your lunch, I realized how much I missed you. When I asked you how long you were going to wait there until you found me, do you remember what you said?" I ask, searching his eyes for the truth.

His eyes soften as he nods. "As long as it takes."

"Yeah," I say softly. "As long as it takes. You would have shown up the next day and the next until you found me, and I believed it when you said that." I look out over the lake, where the moon is reflected on the water, making it seem much brighter than it is.

Manny swallows. "The truth was that I didn't want to leave you. It was so hard to walk away, but I had to trust you and give you the time you needed to miss me or find the answers you needed to make the right decision. I had to trust you to believe enough in us. Otherwise, we would be destined to fail." I hear him exhale, getting every word he wants to say out in the air between us—no more secrets.

I reach out, take his rough and warm hand in mine. "So when you left reluctantly that day, I told you I needed some time to think things through, but the one thing I didn't need to think about, Manny, was if I love you, because the answer would be yes. Always. With my whole heart."

He leans in and kisses me, pulling back slowly with his eyes locked on mine, as he searches for the truth. He must see it there reflecting back at him with clarity as he whispers, "Always, mi cariño."

THE END

ACKNOWLEDGMENTS

To my readers — Thank you for taking a chance on my book. With so many stories out there, the fact that you choose to spend your time with mine means the world to me. I am deeply grateful for your time, trust, and interest.

To my family— Thank you for giving me the time and space to write, even when it meant cheering at your games while wearing a headset and looking completely ridiculous. Your pride in me never wavers— even if my books never make it into a brick-and-mortar store. Because of you, I feel like a best-selling author every single day. You believe in me when I lose faith in myself, and for that, I am so grateful for your love and support.

To my PA—Morgan Evans, you are without a doubt the best, and I'd be completely lost without you. Your feedback, thoughtful comments, and help with all things author-related are invaluable. I am so grateful that I found you— your steady support, reassuring words, and problem-solving skills make all the difference. I appreciate you more than words can say.

To my alpha/beta reader— Jena Morrill, thank you for your thoughtful feedback, insightful recommendations, and sharp eye for detail. I'm incredibly grateful for all the hours you've spent reading my rough drafts, which is no simple task. I am so lucky to have you by my side during this process.

To my besties—You know who you are. My circle is small, but close. Thank you for being there when I need you. Your constant love and support never go unnoticed, and I'm beyond grateful to have you in my life.

ABOUT THE AUTHOR

L. Renee Richard is a Hispanic author who lives in rural New England with her family. She's a born and raised South Texan girl who implements BIPOC characters into her books, imbued with her cherished Hispanic culture. She is an avid reader, complete with her never-ending TBR, and a romantic at heart who appreciates strong female main characters and good book boyfriends in the books she reads or writes. She loves summers in New England, sitting on the beach with a book, driving with the windows down through rural roads on cool autumn nights, and iced matcha lattes. Her books promise angsty romance where the journey to a happily ever after isn't always easy, but it's worth the trip.

KEEP IN TOUCH WITH
L. RENEE RICHARD

Author page:
www.authorlreneerichard.com
Amazon:
http://www.amazon.com/author/lreneerichard
Facebook page:
https://www.facebook.com/Author-L-Renee-
Richard-105887815914160
Instagram:
https://instagram.com/l.renee.
richard?igshid=OGQ5ZDc2ODk2ZA==
TikTok:
TikTok @l.renee.richard
Join my hype team:
https://forms.gle/9cnsA4gSfbezY7a17
Sign up for my newsletter:
https://mailchi.mp/authorlreneerichard/signup